IRON MARSHAL

— A Western Duo —

Lauran Paine

CENTER POINT LARGE PRINT
THORNDIKE, MAINE

This Center Point Large Print edition is published
in the year 2016 by arrangement with
Golden West Literary Agency.

The text of this Large Print edition is unabridged.
In other aspects, this book may vary
from the original edition.

Set in 16-point Times New Roman type.

ISBN: 978-1-68324-048-8 (hardcover)
ISBN: 978-1-68324-052-5 (paperback)

Library of Congress Cataloging-in-Publication Data

Names: Paine, Lauran, author. | Paine, Lauran. Lost valley. | Paine,
Lauran. Iron marshal.
Title: Iron marshal : a western duo / Lauran Paine.
Description: Center Point Large Print edition. | Thorndike, Maine :
Center Point Large Print, 2016. | ©2011
Identifiers: LCCN 2016014674| ISBN 9781683240488 (hardcover :
   alk. paper) | ISBN 9781683240525 (pbk. : alk. paper)
Subjects: LCSH: Large type books. | GSAFD: Western stories.
5 2016 | DDC 813/.54—dc23
:.gov/2016014674

ain
v, Cornwall

MIX
Paper from
responsible sources
FSC® C013056

IRON
MARSHAL

Center Point
Large Print

Also by Lauran Paine and available from
Center Point Large Print:

Man from Durango
Prairie Empire
Sheriff of Hangtown
Rough Justice
Kansas Kid
Trail of Shadows
Night of the Rustler's Moon
Wagon Train West

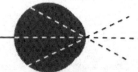

**This Large Print Book carries the
Seal of Approval of N.A.V.H.**

Table of Contents

LOST VALLEY

I

The Pawnees called it Larahipu, which was their word for traders, but while they meant it as a designation of the people who lived in Lost Valley, the mountain men who first saw Lost Valley thought the Pawnees had given that name to the valley, not the Arapahoes who lived there. Then the mountain men corrupted Larahipu into Arapaho, and down the years Larahipu Valley became Lost Valley. The Arapahoes disappeared, but James Hyland, who had first reached Lost Valley with Ashley's buckskin buccaneers when the entire territory belonged to Mexico, built a log post on Arapaho land, settled down, and prospered. James was a canny trader, but more than that he had arrived in the New World from stony Scotland where rich, good land was as scarce as new money, and James's feeling for land drove him to acquire as much of Lost Valley as he could.

James died in his bed at eighty-eight leaving to his only son Angus his settlement, which had grown out of the log trading post, and forty thousand acres of open range land. Angus created Lost Valley Ranch, added more thousands of acres to it, sold the post and most of the town of Hyland, built a great stone house on Lost Valley

Ranch, brought in pure-bred bulls to upgrade his thousands of razor-backed Texas cattle, and went to his reward at sixty-eight leaving to his only son Douglas not only Lost Valley Ranch, more than a hundred thousand acres, but a legacy of complete solvency.

The ranch was still growing when Douglas stepped past his grandfather's moccasins and into his father's cowman's boots. Lost Valley Ranch was all Douglas knew. It was also all he cared to know. He was a powerfully built man of average height and smoky blue eyes. He had come to manhood astride horses, knew more about hard work in all kinds of weather than he knew about almost anything else, although Angus had forced him to spend four years in the East at school. In the town named for his grandfather, people knew Douglas Hyland as a rich, unsmiling, taciturn individual as honest as the day was long, strictly fair in all his dealings, and uncompromising in what he expected of life, and people. He employed nine range men. His foreman, Joe Lamont, did all the hiring, and Joe was the blindly loyal vassal of the lord of Lost Valley. He hired only top hands, men who would serve Hyland interests as though they were their own. Joe ran Lost Valley Ranch as though it were a kingdom, and in many respects it was, and always had been. Lost Valley Ranch had a two-acre cemetery a mile southwest of the main ranch yard where

Hyland riders had gone into the ground after shoot-outs with Indians, renegades, rustlers, and anyone else whose temper was aroused at being ordered off Hyland land.

In town, people respected Douglas Hyland, avoided disputes with his nine range men, and viewed Joe Lamont as a shadow of his employer. It had been said often in town that no one had to like the men of Lost Valley Ranch, but the best way to get along, and to profit from getting along, was to give them plenty of respect. Fear certainly was part of that respect, but the main reason people respected Douglas Hyland and his men was because, according to Douglas Hyland's strict rules, his men did not become troublesome in town—or, if they did, they were fired the very next day—and the ranch had always been one of the largest contributors to the town's economy. It still was, but less so now than during the previous two generations.

The town had grown inevitably since it was located near good water and bisecting roads. There was timber one day's wagon ride northeastward in the mountains, and the next closest town to Hyland in Lost Valley was sixty miles due south, down where the Army had had a post and fort in the early days. Down there at Bridgeport a spur of the railroad tracks made a sashay past a solid two acres of corrals and loading chutes. Bridgeport was larger than

Hyland, primarily because of the spur tracks. Cattle came from hundreds of miles to be shipped out of Bridgeport, and this could have obtained at Hyland instead of Bridgeport except that the earlier Hylands had absolutely refused to permit tracks across even the remote parts of Lost Valley Ranch. They had always guarded their privacy, their cow domain, with fierce resolution, and they still did. Douglas was a fair, occasionally susceptible man in many ways, but any mention of trespassing and he became something altogether different. As Joe Lamont had once summarized it for Sheriff Hatfield: "Treat Mister Hyland fair and there's no better friend on earth. Double-cross him or edge over onto Lost Valley land, and a man'll have trouble every Monday morning for the rest of his life."

Hatfield knew it was the truth because he'd rescued more than one incensed pot-hunter, wolfer, or squatter who had in mind fighting back. Evan Hatfield had always said the same thing to them: "You go on over to the saloon, look for the toughest-looking, orneriest-faced, worn-down leather-hided son-of-a-bitch in there, and he'll be a Hyland rider. Then you multiply him by nine and that'll give you an idea of what you'll be up against if you get troublesome with Lost Valley Ranch."

Once, seven years earlier, a free-graze cowman out of New Mexico had trailed four hundred cows and long yearlings over Lost Valley Ranch on a northward course to Montana. That time, when Joe Lamont ordered them off before sundown, they had shot the horse from beneath Joe and gone into camp five miles farther along in the willow breaks of Arapaho Creek, and, before dawn, when they were rolling out and reaching for their boots, they had looked up into the closed-down faces of eleven men on horseback, sitting like stones, with their carbines pointed and cocked.

Douglas Hyland, wrapped in a blanket coat, had asked which of those men had fired on his range boss. When the leathery free-grazers had come up to their feet to fight, what followed, according to the free-grazer who had hired those cowboys, was a near massacre. By the time Sheriff Hatfield got out there to make a formal investigation, then rode back to town, Lost Valley Ranch was loafing around town in full force, and the free-grazers flatly refused to sign a complaint, and denied ever saying there had been a fight.

Evan and Douglas Hyland crossed to the saloon, got a bottle, took it to a table. When Evan Hatfield sat down to remonstrate, hard-eyed, square-jawed Douglas Hyland had said: "There wouldn't have been a fight if they hadn't wanted one. I don't make trouble and I don't allow my men to do it. I run a cow outfit, Evan, and they work it for me. We mind our business. If someone comes onto my land like those men did, they get run off. That's all there is to it. I'm the law on Lost Valley Ranch and you're the law everywhere else."

Evan had had two drinks with Douglas Hyland without saying a word about the free-graze fracas. Without a signed formal complaint all he could have done in any case was grumble and growl, and with a man like Douglas Hyland that was pointless. They were friends, had been for quite a few years, but Hyland rarely socialized in town and Evan Hatfield only rode to the home place when he had business out there. It was an easy, comfortable arrangement. And, too, Sheriff Hatfield had over the years almost no trouble with Hyland riders, and that was worth something because most of the other cow outfits on the periphery of Lost Valley Ranch, that hired seasonal range men, could not control their riders when they arrived in town of a Saturday night with a pent-up week-long thirst and urge to hooraw the place.

The last time Evan Hatfield had been summoned to Lost Valley Ranch it had not been by Lamont or Hyland, but by some local people who saw a straggling, ragged band of Indians establishing one of their rag-tag camps along Arapaho Creek, and had hastened to town to tell Evan so that he could get up there and chase them off before Hyland's men found them. Evan had ridden hard to reach the *rancheria* first and failed. Douglas and Joe with five of their riders were already over there, sitting their saddles, silently watching from a rolling land swell, and down along the creek Indians were noisily going about their unkempt camp, with eight or ten strong hearts also sitting their horses out a couple of hundred yards, between the Hyland men and the creek.

Everything was there, armed, defiant Indians, better-armed and rawhide-tough cattlemen. One spark would have started the fight when Sheriff Hatfield rode between the groups, snarled at the Indians to go back to their camp and put down those guns, then walked his horse toward the cowmen on the land swell. He did not look back but he knew without doing so that those strong hearts had not moved, had not obeyed him.

Douglas Hyland nodded at Evan without speaking. Joe Lamont and the other range men took their cue from Hyland; they, too, nodded without speaking. Back a mile or two, westerly, two riders were driving a recalcitrant old wicked-horn cow toward the creek. Evan watched this, then turned toward Hyland.

"The Indians go after that old cow?"

Hyland, gloved hands atop the saddle horn, shook his head. "No. I sent the men to find an old gummer and drive her down there." At the sheriff's stare, Hyland gestured. "Did you ever see anything like that? I remember them with good horses, healthy kids, good buckskin instead of those calico rags."

His horsemen drove the old cow to the camp. When the Arapahoes gathered uneasily to stand like statues and watch, one of the riders shot the old cow. The other one gestured with his hands, then they turned and loped toward the waiting men on the land swell. The Indians called back and forth; old squaws ran for their fleshing knives. They were already drawing the blood and rolling back the hide before Hyland's herders reached the land swell, and those strong hearts, looking back, then forward, finally came close to talk. All but one of them turned back. That lone Arapaho cradled his worn-out Winchester, drew himself very erect, rode toward the land swell, and, when he was about five hundred feet distant, he raised one arm high, palm forward.

Douglas Hyland did the same. Not a word was spoken. Then the strong heart turned back, and Sheriff Hatfield rummaged in a vest pocket for his makings and went to work rolling a smoke.

Douglas Hyland said: "We couldn't wipe them out, Evan. We tried for fifty years and couldn't do it. But we took everything they had." Then he turned, finally, toward the sheriff. "How'd you happen to be out here?"

Hatfield trickled smoke, looking down where Indians were swarming over what remained of

16

the old gummer cow. "Some passers-by saw them trailing over your land and hurried down to tell me before you found 'em." Hatfield turned and smiled. "You're right, we took everything they had. . . . Well, I got to get back."

II

Evan Hatfield was a large, big-boned man who carried his better than two hundred pounds handily. He was powerful enough to break a jaw with either fist, and even-tempered. He had come out of Missouri thirteen years earlier, had buried his wife along with a lot of other emigrants down along the Missouri River bottoms, and had never remarried. He had gone from freighting to law enforcement by accident, and had been a lawman ever since.

Hatfield knew the law. Every snowbound winter for ten years he'd read law books. But in summary all that he'd read led toward a conviction he'd had before he'd ever seen a law book. People knew right from wrong. All a ton of law books did was try to define each instance, which lawyers loved to do, and which worthwhile people did not need a definition of because they inherently knew what they should not do. That was how Evan Hatfield administered the law in his territory, and in a way he was not very different from Douglas Hyland. He would not argue with lawbreakers; he would simply enforce the law against them.

But the Thursday morning it rained and the dawn stage came in an hour late because the creeks were all above their banks, Evan Hatfield met a gangling, straw-haired man with button shoes, a curly-brimmed derby hat, and a raw-boned, rangy build packed down inside a gray two-button coat. His name was Enos Orcutt, and, as they sat talking in Hatfield's office, one of the fundamental differences of right and wrong came more and more to Evan's attention. It was not a case of someone doing wrong when they knew what was right. Enos Orcutt unfolded a map, placed it in front of Hatfield atop the desk, and pointed to a small square almost in the center of the map, which had been traced out in blue pencil.

"One hundred and sixty acres, Sheriff, bordering on that unnamed creek, properly filed on at the Land Office over in Denver. What I want to know is how exactly to find it."

Evan silently rolled and lit a smoke. Then he said: "You got the homestead papers, Mister Orcutt?" When Orcutt brought forth the thick envelope and emptied it, Sheriff Hatfield said: "That's not an unnamed creek."

"It's shown that way on the plans at the Land Office in Denver."

"Then they'd ought to send some map-drawers down here," muttered Evan, reading the papers of homestead compliance. "That's Arapaho Creek." He smoked, read, killed the cigarette finally, solemnly folded the papers, re-inserted them into the envelope, and held it forth. "Mister Orcutt, before you go out there, I think you'd ought to stay in town and rest up for a spell."

The raw-boned, fair-complexioned man pocketed his map and envelope, eyed Sheriff Hatfield steadily for a moment. "Someone else is squatting on my land, is that it?"

"No. But someone else is using that land, and has been using it for over fifty years. Three generations of them."

The raw-boned tall man was not indignant. "It happens. They told me at the Land Office it happens very often."

Evan leaned back with a silent sigh. "Yeah, I suppose it does. You hang around town, Mister Orcutt, and I'll ride out there."

"I'll hire a horse and go with you. I want to see my . . ."

"No. You stay here!"

Orcutt's steady gaze hardened slightly. "You don't believe they'll give up the land, Sheriff?"

"I want to explain things first, Mister Orcutt. . . . Loan me the map, will you?" The folded rough paper changed hands. As Sheriff Hatfield held it, he said: "What in the hell did

19

you file on land down here for? It's cold in winter, blazing hot in summer, and a hundred and sixty acres isn't a drop in the bucket to what a man needs to make a living in Lost Valley."

"It'll be a start, Sheriff. I've been through Lost Valley before. I traveled for a gun company as a peddler for six years. I always liked Lost Valley."

Evan Hatfield nodded a little. "It's nice to travel through, for a fact, Mister Orcutt, but . . . a gun salesman? You aim to open a store here in town?"

"No, I aim to work my land and put up a house."

"Are you married?"

"No." The younger man smiled. "I don't need a family. I just want to settle down and get my hands dirty, Sheriff. I've always wanted my own piece of land, and with emigrants coming out of the East in droves now, I figured I'd better start building my place before all the good land was taken up."

Sheriff Hatfield knew emigrants. There were quite a few of them passing through nowadays, and some were even taking up foothill land on the outer boundaries of Lost Valley. But this was not the same at all. That one hundred and sixty acres was approximately where he had sat watching Douglas Hyland give those starving Indians an old gummer cow. It was not a matter of right or wrong. Orcutt's homestead application was in order, his map was correctly drawn down to the

20

exact scale, along the township corners and proper metes and bounds. But that happened to be Lost Valley Ranch land, and from what Evan Hatfield knew of the Hylands, they did not surround free-graze in order to control it, the way most of the large cow outfits did, the Hylands held deeds. That was how James, then Angus, and now Douglas operated. They bought title. It wasn't right versus wrong; it was clearly someone's mistake.

He told Enos Orcutt where the rooming house was, saw him pointed in that direction, then Evan went down to the livery barn. The rain had stopped, but the heavens were gray, and the ground under his horse's hoofs was soggy, in some places sticky and clinging. Also, there was a raw little north-to-south wind blowing about belly-high to a tall man.

He made fair time and fortunately his encounter with the stranger named Orcutt had occurred early in the morning, otherwise he would not have reached the great stone house before mid-afternoon, which meant he would not have been able to return to town until well after dark, and in raw weather that was not something a man accustomed to ordering his life so that he could avoid being out in raw weather did not cherish. Most of the riders were gone when he rode into the yard, past the buildings and up the slight incline to the big stone house with its elegant horse-head tie posts set at intervals beyond the broad sweep of verandah. One rider was leaving by the carved oaken front door when Sheriff Hatfield tied up. He and the rider nodded, then Douglas Hyland stepped forth to watch and wait, and, as Hatfield approached, Hyland said— "Coffee's hot in the study, Evan."—and led the way.

Why a single man required such a magnificent house was an unanswered question through Lost Valley. Inside, no expense had been spared; the furniture was from the East, the oil paintings were massively framed and obviously of considerable value, even in the eyes of someone like Sheriff Hatfield who knew nothing about art. The study had a great stone fireplace and rich-toned leather chairs. It also had a large old carved desk. That was where Douglas Hyland filled two cups with black coffee and handed one to the sheriff as he gestured Hatfield to one of the big chairs. Then Hyland stood gazing at his guest, the formalities over with, as far as he was concerned. But he followed range custom. Instead of asking point-blank why Hatfield had ridden to the ranch on such a raw day, he said: "The rain was welcome, eh?"

Evan swallowed hot coffee before replying. "To range men it was. To me, well, I'd prefer it to rain only at night, and to dry out before morning." He smiled.

Hyland nodded without returning the smile and went to the edge of the massive desk to lean. "Trouble?"

Evan sighed. He would have preferred to just sit in the warmth of the room and sip his coffee. Now, he set the cup aside, dug out Orcutt's map, strode to the desk, and spread it out. Hyland looked, leaned for a closer look, and pointed with a blunt finger at the blue-penciled square. "What is that?"

"It's a hundred and sixty acres a man named Orcutt filed on up in Denver."

Hyland slowly looked around and upward. Then he straightened up and drank some coffee before speaking in a level, almost amused, tone of voice. "He's mistaken, Evan."

Hatfield, too, stared at the little blue square in the expanse of the big unfolded map. It was small indeed. "Mister Hyland, he's got a patent to that land."

"You saw it?"

"Yes."

Douglas Hyland finished the coffee and put the cup down, hard. "Someone has made a mistake, maybe not Orcutt, maybe some land clerk or an agent. That's Hyland land, Evan." He stepped behind the desk, looking directly at Hatfield. "Where is this man . . . he's not over there on that land, is he?"

"No. He's back in town."

Hyland sank down, the fire crackled at his back,

little fingers of raw wind scratched along the windows in the east wall, and Evan turned to resume his seat while he waited for Douglas Hyland to speak again. It was not a very long wait.

"I'll have to go through all the deeds. It'll take a day or so, but I'll find it. That's part of the original ranch my grandfather put together. That's the old part, Evan, but I've seen the deeds. Some of them are in Spanish. He traded for thousands of what they called *varas* and we call acres, not very long after he came out here." Douglas did not look angry or upset, which was a relief to the sheriff. "It's a mistake, but, until I find the deed, I don't think that man had ought to go out there."

Hatfield nodded to that; he did not think Enos Orcutt had better go out there, either. He had not thought so since Orcutt had first unfolded the map back in town. "I'll talk to him. He seems like a reasonable man."

Douglas Hyland leaned to study the map again, then he picked up a pencil and wrote what Evan assumed were descriptions of the land. When he tossed down the pencil, Hyland said: "That's impossible."

Evan agreed. "Like you said, someone made a mistake."

The cowman arose to poke a split log into the fireplace and turned back with a wag of his head. "Damned government clerks."

Evan nodded, finished his coffee, and loosened in the chair, enjoying the heat.

Douglas Hyland went to a glass-fronted upright cabinet and brought back a bottle of whiskey. He refilled Hatfield's cup, then his own, and laced the coffee. As he went to return the bottle to the cupboard, he said: "I remember my father saying that someday there would be settlers out here. So far, though, we've seen very few."

"Back along the far foothills they've been taking up land for the past couple of years," stated the lawman. "Maybe you haven't got over there as much as I have. But they're here, all right. I'd guess we'll get a lot more. The railroads are offering reduced fares to get the business, and they dump those people out at this end of the tracks. Your pa was dead right. I think most of the cowmen own land around the free graze, though . . . the ones like yourself that have deeds . . . and that ought to keep settlers out of the valley."

Douglas Hyland returned to his desk and sat down, looked at the big map, then meticulously folded it, and tossed it aside. "I don't like to see it happen, Evan."

"Neither do I. I don't suppose anyone really likes something like this." Hatfield paused, then said: "It's caused trouble other places. I'd hate to see it start up like that around here."

Hyland nodded. "Yes. Well, this stranger, is he a range man?"

Evan, thinking of the curly-brim derby hat and button shoes, wagged his head. "Used to be a gun peddler. I don't know anything else about him except that he sure doesn't look to me like he was ever a range man."

Hyland arose, handed the sheriff the map, and said: "You'll be hungry. Let's go see what the cook's got."

As they passed through the large, elegant rooms, Evan Hatfield took a moment to envy anyone who had two generations of canny planners behind them. Then the wind rattled some windows as they passed through, and Hatfield began thinking about the long, uncomfortable ride ahead of him.

III

Sheriff Hatfield arose late and had breakfast, as he commonly did, at the café diagonally across from his jailhouse office. Because it was later than usual, he was almost the only patron of the café man. It had been a raw ride back to town last night, but this morning the sun was brilliant, the ground was firming up underfoot, and there was no vestige of that chilly wind that had prevailed last night. The café man was a former freighter whose rough existence had finally brought him to staying indoors most of the time as age and old aches caught up with him. His name was Barlow Smith. Around town they called him Barley. He was a heavy-set individual who thirty years earlier had been as powerful as oak, and good-natured. He was still good-natured. He and Sheriff Hatfield had been Saturday night poker players along with several other men around town for five or six years. Now, Barley brought along a mug of java and leaned behind the counter as Hatfield ate. He said: "Damned weather in this country, a man never knows whether to put on his woolen long johns in the morning or not, and, if he don't, it'll come a cold wind sure as hell."

Evan nodded, and held forth his cup.

As Barley Smith refilled it with black coffee, he said: "Had a gunman in here this morning early who drank five cups of coffee with his steak and potatoes. Five cups. That's enough to float a flat-boat."

Hatfield sipped and set the cup aside. "Raw-boned young feller with light hair and button shoes?"

"That's him. You know him?"

"No, but I met him yesterday morning."

"He had me roll up some meat in a paper to take out with him."

Evan stopped chewing and raised his eyes. "Take out where?"

"I don't know. He just said he'd need something to eat before he come back to town."

Sheriff Hatfield finished eating, downed the coffee in a pair of swallows, arose, dumped some silver on the counter top, and turned away, leaving Barley Smith looking after him in a puzzled way.

At the livery barn they confirmed Hatfield's suspicions. A day man said: "Yeah, he hired a horse and rode out . . . hell, it must-been two hours back."

"Which way?"

The day man did not know; he'd been busy dunging out and forking feed. Hatfield said: "Fetch my horse."

As the day man went to obey, the sheriff crossed to the harness room for his outfit. After all the horsebacking he'd done yesterday, he had not anticipated repeating the experience for a while, but, hell, it was a very knowledgeable individual in this life who knew at breakfast time what he might have done by evening. Still, the horse was rested, fed, and frisky, the weather was nearly perfect, and there were advantages to being out of Hyland for a few hours.

He headed for Arapaho Creek by the most direct overland route he knew. As he rode, the irritation subsided to be replaced by uneasiness. He could not forbid Orcutt from going out there. In fact, if the man's title to that hundred and sixty acres was valid, not even Douglas Hyland could keep him off it. And, for a fact, since Lost Valley

28

Ranch cattle were kept off this lowland range during summer so that it would be available to winter them on, there was not much chance any Hyland riders would be over there.

Evan relaxed as his horse loped over the gently undulating grassland. He had left town in a tense, troubled frame of mind, but by the time he had the willow tops in view out where the creek wandered, he was no longer tense at all, and he was only mildly troubled. The land was empty. He could see for miles in all directions, without sighting any movement, any livestock or horsemen. When he came up over the last swale with the meandering creek in front a mile or so, he saw Orcutt's livery animal standing hipshot in willow shade over where that Indian camp had been, and reined off in that direction. He did not see Orcutt until he was dismounting to tie his own horse, then the rangy man in his incongruous curly-brim derby hat and button shoes strolled out of some thickets farther along, watched Hatfield for a while, and finally ambled up to greet him with a smile.

"Good morning, Sheriff. There's no one squatting here."

Hatfield fished forth the folded map and handed it over as he said: "I didn't say anyone was, Mister Orcutt. I said folks had been using the land, meaning they'd been grazing cattle over it." As Orcutt took the map, Hatfield added: "How did you find it without the map?"

"I have another map, Sheriff." Orcutt raised his face. "Hyland claims it, doesn't he? I talked to some men at the saloon last night. This is all Hyland land, they told me, thousands and thousands of acres of it."

Evan Hatfield went to work making his first smoke of the day. "Douglas Hyland told me he has a deed to this hundred and sixty, Mister Orcutt."

"Did he show it to you?"

"No. He's going to hunt it up today." When Evan saw the rueful expression of skepticism, he added: "Mister Hyland doesn't have to lie to anyone, and he doesn't have to claim a hundred and sixty acres. He uses more land than that just for his marking ground. The reason I followed you out here is because Lost Valley Ranch has a rule about strangers wandering over Hyland land. To save all of us some headaches, it'd be better if you stayed away from here until it's settled about whose land this is."

"It's my land, Sheriff. You saw the patents they gave me in Denver."

"Uhn-huh, and Mister Hyland'll have patents, too. You see my point, Mister Orcutt?"

The raw-boned younger man stood a moment without replying, then he smiled at Evan Hatfield. "All right. Hell, a week or so isn't going to make that much difference, I guess. Not after all the years I've waited, saving up the money to do this . . . but it's my land, Sheriff."

Dryly Evan said: "Yeah. It's someone's land. One time I sat my horse right over yonder and watched some hungry Indians carve up an old cow about where we're standing. They thought it was their land, too." He dropped the cigarette and stamped on it. "Mister Orcutt, look around you. In Lost Valley it takes a hundred acres to maintain one cow. This here hundred and sixty would support one and a half cows." He wagged his head.

Orcutt smiled back. "Do you know how much potatoes sell for in town, Sheriff?"

Evan stood gazing at the younger man. "You mean . . . farm this land?"

"What's so strange about that, Mister Hatfield? Iowa and Kansas and Nebraska and Illinois . . . that's all they do. They don't turn cattle loose to wander all over just eating the grass."

"This isn't farm land, Mister Orcutt. Look at it."

"I have looked at it. Every time I'd pass through on the stage, I'd look at it. This morning I scuffed around, dug some little holes. It's good earth, Sheriff, no rocks, and there's the creek for irrigation. Have you ever been out to California? They make ditches and carry water to their fields out there. You should see the crops they raise."

Sheriff Hatfield lifted his hat, scratched, reset

the hat, and said nothing. He had seen emigrants up along the distant foothills scratching in the flinty soil up there, planting corn and beans and squash. Back in Missouri he had seen farmed land by the uninterrupted mile, but this was not farming country. This country was for cattle. Then he caught sight of far movement and turned slightly to watch a solitary horseman loping toward them.

But the rider turned northward before he saw them and went out of sight beyond the westward stretch of creek willows several miles away. It could only have been one of Douglas Hyland's men; Evan was sure of that. He turned to untie his horse as he said: "If you've seen enough, suppose we head back to town, Mister Orcutt."

Enos Orcutt watched Sheriff Hatfield untie his horse without making a move to do the same, but when Evan turned, the younger man shrugged and went toward his livery animal. He was quiet until they were riding leisurely side-by-side through the golden-lighted pleasant morning, their animals perfectly content to be heading back, then he said: "Sheriff, I'm satisfied my title to that land back yonder is valid."

Evan's retort was rueful. "And suppose it isn't?"

"It is. I'm as certain of that as I am that night will fall after supper this evening. What I wanted to say was . . . I've heard about Douglas Hyland and his riders. What I'd like you to tell me is . . . if my title is good, where will you stand?"

Evan felt annoyance stirring deep down. "Why do you think a man wears this badge? To uphold the law."

"Then you'll take my side against Mister Hyland?"

Evan leaned, expectorated, straightened up, and looked dead ahead. "I don't take sides with anyone or against anyone. My job is to maintain order and keep the peace. I'm here to make sure the law is obeyed."

"And if my title is good . . . ?"

"We'll have to wait and see, Mister Orcutt. Now let's lope these horses or we're going to miss supper."

They said very little to each other all the way back. Evan's impression was that Enos Orcutt was beginning to cool toward him. It did not bother Evan at all. He had rarely performed his duties without having someone turn sullen toward him afterward. When people were at odds and a third person came along to lay down the law, one or the other of the argumentative people ended up mad at the law. Sometimes both of them.

They reached town in midafternoon, went down a back alley to the livery barn. Evan Hatfield left his horse in the hands of the day man, nodded to Orcutt, and strolled in the direction of his jailhouse office. He did not notice the pair of lounging cattlemen over in the shade of the saloon overhang, but they noticed him and watched as he entered his building.

Evan pulled off his hat. He was thirsty and a little bit hungry. Sitting on a wall bench, legs crossed and relaxed, as motionless as a stone, Douglas Hyland said: "Good afternoon, Evan."

Hatfield turned, considered the craggy features, let his breath out in a sweep, and spoke. "Good afternoon." Then he went to the dipper for a drink, and after that stepped to his desk chair, flung his hat atop the litter of papers and dodgers, and said: "I didn't expect you in town."

Hyland's blue eyes showed irony. "I didn't expect to be in town today." He paused, looking steadily across the room. "Where is this feller who has the land title?"

"I just left him at the livery barn. He rode out along the creek this morning and I went after him and brought him back."

"Is he staying at the rooming house?"

"As far as I know he is." Hatfield had a strange feeling. "Something wrong?"

Hyland faintly nodded. "You're a good man at keeping your mouth closed, Evan. I noticed that years back. I guess I have to explain something to you."

Hatfield leaned his elbows on the desk, staring. "Orcutt's title is good?"

"I want you to tell me you will not say a word about any of this."

The sheriff leaned and stared. In his mind something was sending out a tiny warning.

"Well, Evan . . . ?"

Hatfield answered slowly. "You know my position. I represent the law. I operate on the notion that there's right and wrong. The law punishes folks who kick over the traces. I can't take sides, Douglas. Don't tell me anything that's going to play hell with my job."

Hyland waited a moment before speaking, and now his voice was less rough than usual. "It's going to play hell with your job whether I tell you or not. But on the ride to town this morning I could see only one way to handle this. You have to know, otherwise it's going to be a hell of a lot harder for all of us. All I'm asking is that you keep it to yourself for a while."

Evan felt the warning more strongly than ever, but he had faith in Douglas Hyland's judgment, so he nodded. "I'll say nothing . . . but, if that has to change, I'll tell you first."

Hyland arose, crossed to the desk, and spread several very old pieces of paper on the desk top. Then he placed an equally old, yellowish, bone-dry map beside the papers. In a toneless voice he said: "Those are the Mexican deeds. That is the old Mexican map my grandfather got from the Mex officials down at Albuquerque. They had never been north of New Mexico."

Evan frowned. He did not know fifty words of

Spanish and both the map and old papers were filled with it in spidery handwriting. "Can you read this stuff?" he asked.

Hyland shook his head. "Not good enough to make it all out. That's why I need time, that's why I want you to know what I'm going to do."

"You're going to find someone who can decipher it? But if those are the deeds . . . ?"

"Evan, my grandfather was not a surveyor. In his day a man swung his arm to include fifty thousand acres of land, and they signed their papers accordingly."

Evan was beginning to understand. "You mean these deeds don't take in the land along the creek Orcutt is claiming?"

Hyland leaned back. "Evan, these deeds probably do not take in twenty thousand acres, not just along the creek but north and west, too. I'd never read them before. Not until late last night after you left. I studied them all night. Evan, if they don't convey title to the Hylands for all the land between town and my home place, it won't just be the hundred and sixty acres Orcutt is claiming. Do you see what I'm faced with?"

Evan saw perfectly, and it stunned him. For three generations, since long before anyone in Lost Valley could remember, or their parents could remember, that land had been Hyland range.

Hyland quietly said: "Orcutt will only be the

first." He stood looking down at Hatfield. "They'll come in here by the dozens. By the hundreds. Divide twenty thousand by a hundred and sixty, and that's how many emigrants we'll have arriving in Hyland. It's not just Lost Valley Ranch. If they come here like that, they'll outnumber us all to hell. That means they'll be after the free-graze land the other cow outfits don't have title to, but which they surround with deeded land."

Hyland began carefully to fold his papers. He pocketed them and returned to the wall bench. "No cowman I know, Evan, is going to sit on his butt and watch something like that happen." Hyland waited until Sheriff Hatfield had digested all this and was leaning back off the desk, then Hyland also said: "That's why I need you to keep this in strict confidence until I can get back from Albuquerque, then go up to Denver as well."

Evan groped for his makings and lowered his head to roll the cigarette he felt no need for. When he'd lighted up, he looked at Douglas Hyland. "How in the hell didn't someone in your family figure this out before?"

"My grandfather spoke Spanish. Neither my father nor I had any reason to learn it. But in school back East I had a little of it. In my grandfather's day there were lots of Mex traders and stockmen in Colorado, and even Wyoming and Montana. My father evidently did as I've done . . . assumed the Mexican deeds were correct."

"How long is it going to take you to get this figured out?"

Hyland arose tiredly. "I don't know. But I'll leave for Albuquerque in the morning. Maybe a couple of weeks, maybe a month."

IV

The following morning Evan Hatfield sat at the café counter thoughtfully drinking coffee, while around him the other single men who lived in town noisily talked and ate. Hatfield was in a troubled world of his own and the roof could have fallen in without his noticing it.

Later, he was in the office across the road when Steve Clampitt, the general store proprietor, walked in with the morning mail, placed it atop the desk, and said: "Beautiful day, Evan."

Hatfield looked up. He hadn't noticed. "Got time for a cup of coffee?"

Clampitt had the time and sat down as the sheriff filled two cups over by the wood stove and turned with them as he said: "How's business?"

"Good," stated the wiry, graying storekeeper, and grinned. "How's business with you?"

Evan grinned back. "Not so good, and that's the way I like it."

Clampitt tasted the coffee. "I'm getting calls for things I never stocked much before. Plows and harrows and such like. Those settlers up along the far hills are taking hold. Like everyone else around town, I thought they'd starve out the first winter."

Evan returned to the desk chair. "A lot of them do, Steve. The last time I was up through there I saw abandoned hovels one after another."

Clampitt had an observation to offer about that. "They tell me as fast as one leaves the country, another one comes along to take his place. And there's some good comes of it. I been offered bushels of beans and corn, even fresh vegetables. It expands my trade, handling stuff like that." Clampitt leaned back to get comfortable in the chair. "I don't give 'em credit, and that slows them down a lot. Mostly they got no money. But we trade a lot." He finished the coffee but did not stir from the chair. "I've heard talk that they're going to come down closer to town." Clampitt looked steadily at the sheriff. "I don't see how, with all the land already taken up down here, but I keep hearing that talk."

"Who from, the settlers?"

"Not so much from them. From freighters mostly. They pass through those shanty town settlements up there and pick up all the gossip." Clampitt smiled again. "The best source of information is a freighter. He knows more'n most newspapers. I tell you, Evan, we're in a period of change."

Hatfield's coffee tasted bitter to him. "I hope not, Steve. I don't see too much wrong with things as they are."

Clampitt finally arose. "Well, one thing about change . . . it usually means growth, and stores like mine do a lot better." He thanked Evan for the coffee and departed, leaving the sheriff gazing at the door for a moment, before turning his attention to the mail.

It was not very interesting. It rarely was. Among the letters were four envelopes with Wanted posters enclosed, which he studied, then filed in a cardboard box in a corner he kept for that purpose. Otherwise, there was a letter from a wife back in Kansas whose man had deserted her and she thought he might be in Colorado. Along with this letter was a description of the wayward husband. It could have fitted two-thirds of the men Evan Hatfield saw every day.

The final letter was from the Southern Pacific Railroad Company with an enclosed map showing railroad land in alternating sections so that Sheriff Hatfield would be knowledgeable when settlers came around to enquire where specific parcels of land were. None of those square miles of land—six hundred and forty acres—was within fifty miles of Hyland and most of them were more than a hundred miles distant.

The letter was obviously one of thousands printed for transmittal to town authorities throughout the entire territory up as far as the Canadian line. Hatfield sat studying it until Enos Orcutt walked in, then he shoved the map aside and leaned back to say: "Good morning."

Orcutt was no longer wearing his two-button coat, little curly-brimmed hat, and button shoes. He looked quite different in a range man's butternut shirt, cowhide boots, and broad-brimmed hat. He laughed at Sheriff Hatfield's expression and sounded a little self-conscious as he said—"The only thing that doesn't feel right is the gun."—and took the chair Steve Clampitt had relinquished an hour back.

Hatfield gazed at the ivory-butted Colt. It was nickel-plated; rarely did anyone show up in town with a gun like that, and in fact it was a matter of scornful amusement among range riders when they encountered someone wearing such a weapon.

"Fancy," he told Orcutt.

The lanky man agreed. "Not exactly ordinary, for a fact, Sheriff, but it's one of the demonstrators I used when I was peddling them. I have two more, one silver-inlaid, and the other gold-plated."

Hatfield winced. "Don't wear 'em on Saturday night at the saloon," he said good-naturedly, and they both laughed. Then Orcutt settled back in the chair, his smile gone.

"I heard around town that Mister Hyland was here last evening."

Hatfield nodded. "Yeah."

"You talked with him?"

"Yes, we talked."

"Is that all, Sheriff?"

Evan shifted slightly in the chair. "No, that's not all. He asked about you and I told him as much as I knew."

"What did he say about my land?"

"Well, Mister Orcutt, he brought me his deeds, if that's what you're here about. They seemed all right to me, but I'm no land agent."

"Sheriff, I can't believe the people over in Denver don't know their jobs. I keep thinking about this, and I keep coming back to that. They had big maps and legal descriptions. They deal in land all day long."

"There never was a man born, Mister Orcutt, who couldn't be mistaken. That goes for government people as well as anyone else. But one way or the other, my situation is pretty obvious to me . . . keep you from antagonizing Lost Valley Ranch, and keep them from burying you."

"What am I supposed to do, then . . . sit here in Hyland twiddling my thumbs?"

"You said it yourself . . . another week or so isn't going to make all that much difference."

Orcutt slumped in the chair. "Yes, I said it. But

summer's moving right along. I'd like to get a cabin up before winter."

Evan Hatfield gazed pensively at the younger man. "You got a team and wagon?"

"No."

"Mister Orcutt, the nearest timber of house logs is sixty miles northeast, to the mountains. That's three days going out, empty, and five days coming back with a load. And you got to make maybe six, eight trips just to get four walls up for a small house. Then comes the roof, and, if you'd begun last spring, you just maybe could have got it done. This late in the season all you'll be able to do is stockpile the logs and wait until next spring to draw-knife the bark off 'em and start putting them up. And you don't even have a team and wagon."

Orcutt said: "How about a soddy?"

Hatfield sighed. "Next to a creek, Mister Orcutt? I know they build them up in the foothills. I've seen settler soddies up there, but that's high ground. Even so there's nothing less healthful than wintering in a house dug out of the ground. Even in high country they drip water after the first big snow and don't dry out until midsummer. But you dig a soddy hole over in the breaks along Arapaho Creek, Mister Orcutt, and you'll be up to your ankles in water all winter long."

The younger man sat gazing across the room at

Hatfield. "You're for the Hyland interests, aren't you, Sheriff?"

Hatfield waited a moment before speaking. "I'll let that pass. I told you on the ride back to town I'm for the law."

"Everything I say you scuttle for me."

"Mister Orcutt, maybe that's because I've been out here a long time. I've seen it all happen many times. If you don't want to hear it from me, hire a horse, ride up to the foothills, and visit those shanty towns up there. Ask those folks."

Orcutt was momentarily silent before saying: "Last night I walked out east of town to a wagon camp and had supper with some folks from Pennsylvania."

Hatfield nodded. There were always wagoners passing through. Ever since he'd been in Hyland they'd come straggling along, and had continued to straggle along, usually bound for Oregon.

"They got some maps in Denver, too."

Hatfield's gaze narrowed almost imperceptibly. "Of this country?"

"Yes, there are four adults. They're filed on four hundred-and-sixty-acre parcels. They've got deeds to a full section of Arapaho Creek land."

Hatfield waited a moment, then went digging for his makings. As he worked up a smoke, he said—"One square mile."—and the younger man nodded. As the sheriff lit up, he shook his head. "Hell."

44

Orcutt, watching Hatfield, repeated what he'd said earlier. "You don't like to see the cattle interests challenged, do you?"

This time, Evan Hatfield's temper slipped a notch. "I don't like to see people buried. I don't like to see them get burned out and shot up."

Orcutt had evidently arrived at the jailhouse office with this kind of confrontation in mind, because now he said: "We discussed that last night at the wagon camp. I told them about my experience. They're going to stand up for their rights."

Evan growled back. "Rights, my butt. Even if they've got 'em, Mister Orcutt, I've yet to see a piece of land I'd want to get shot over."

"That's your job, Sheriff . . . to make sure folks who got rights are protected."

Now Evan's anger was simmering very close to the surface. "You've traveled the country, Mister Orcutt. You know there are cattlemen grazing over every mile of it. Do you think one lawman can be everywhere?"

"Lawmen can raise posses, Sheriff."

"You're greener'n I thought. Sure I can raise posses. I do it every now and then to chase down rustlers and horse thieves. Every cow outfit gives me men when I need 'em, and every house here in Hyland has guns in it, men who know how to use them, and folks who are willing to help when I need it against outlaws." Evan leaned across the desk. "I couldn't raise five men to protect squatters from cattlemen. Not five, Mister Orcutt."

"Last night around the fire one of those Pennsylvanians said they'd called in the Army over east of here in the Nebraska hills country when this sort of thing came up."

Evan arose, got himself a cup of coffee, refilled another cup, and handed it to Enos Orcutt, then went back to his chair. "The nearest Army post, Mister Orcutt, is up at Fort Laramie in Wyoming. Do you know how far that is from Hyland?"

Orcutt knew. "I've been through there many times, Sheriff. I know how far it is. We can wait."

Evan sighed. "Then do it. Wait right here in town, but don't go setting up any camps along Arapaho Creek."

"You don't have the authority to forbid us from . . ."

"God damn it, Mister Orcutt, I'm not forbidding you from doing anything. I'm just trying to keep the peace. By now you've talked to enough folks around town to know that Lost Valley Ranch is death on trespassers. I'm trying to keep you and them apart. I thought I made that plain to you." Evan gulped coffee and shoved the cup aside. "What's a week or two? You said that yourself. What's the name of those folks you visited with last night?"

"Schmidt and Langer. Why, are you going out there?"

Evan nodded. "I'll go talk to them."

Orcutt looked doubtful and Hatfield saw the look. "Sheriff, I doubt that you'll have much luck."

Evan shrugged thick shoulders.

"Do you want me to ride along with you?"

Evan thought about that, and almost decided against it. "Seems to me you got them stirred up last night. I don't need that kind of help when I'm talking to them."

"I didn't stir them up. Well, I didn't do it on purpose. I told them what's happened to me around here, and what I think the trouble is."

"Sure you did. Me. I'm the trouble."

Enos Orcutt drained his cup before speaking again. "The trouble is, Sheriff, three generations of a family named Hyland have been riding roughshod over free-graze land. Hyland, and the other cowmen in Lost Valley."

"And that's not stirring them up?" said Evan, arising from behind his desk. "You stay here in town." He went to the wall rack, took down a booted carbine, slung it carelessly over a shoulder, and went back to get his hat at the desk. "Mister Orcutt, we've talked about this until hell's half froze over. What it boils down to is simply this . . . stay off Hyland range for a couple more weeks. It may inconvenience you, but that's a hell of a lot better than getting shot or whipped

47

raw. It'd be better to have to put off building your cabin until next spring, than not to be around to build it at all."

Hatfield opened the door, held it open until his guest walked out ahead of him, then closed it. He nodded and turned southward in the direction of the livery barn, mad all the way through.

Behind him, Orcutt stood as though he were undecided, watching the larger, older man's progress, then Orcutt crossed toward the general store.

It was not quite midday. There was a pleasant layer of heat over the world, not a breath of wind from any direction, and at the livery barn, when Sheriff Hatfield growled for his horse, the liveryman looked startled, not just at Hatfield's flinty look and growl, but because Hatfield had that booted Winchester slung over his shoulder.

V

East of Hyland, where the creek ran diagonally across miles of grazed-over grassland, there were about a dozen places where emigrants passing through, and freighters, set up camps. Most of those places had been used so much they had permanent stone rings for cooking and limbless trees for tethering livestock. Sheriff Hatfield had no difficulty finding the camp he was looking for. It consisted of two battered, sturdy old wagons, a dozen horses hobbled nearby down along the creek where the grass was best, and smoke still rising from breakfast fires.

There were four children hunting bird nests along the lower creek who saw Hatfield approaching, and fled like quail back to the camp, and by the time Hatfield got up there two men were waiting, and behind them, hovering over near the wagons, two women and the children were motionlessly watching.

Evan rode up, halted, and soberly nodded. The men nodded back just as soberly, then one, a bull-necked, nearly square man with unshorn sun-bleached hair motioned toward the fire ring. "Get down, Sheriff. We got hot coffee."

Evan dismounted, hobbled his animal, and went to the stone ring. The other man was taller, but he, too, was powerfully put together. He offered a big hand and said: "Otto Langer. This is Henry Schmidt, Sheriff." Then Langer went for the tin cups to pour coffee.

Evan considered the wagons, the peering women, then turned farther to look at the livestock. Mostly, settlers had poor, overworked horses. These people had good big strong young animals in fair flesh. Their camp was orderly, the way camps commonly were among people who had been living on the ground for a long time. He faced the men, who were waiting, watching him closely. Neither man was armed. They wore the thick, flat-heeled boots of drovers, and wore suspenders instead of belts. Their hats, too, were different, but their faces showed the sun squint, the bronze shadings, of all people who faced into the sun most of every day, and that included range men.

Evan tasted the coffee. It was strong enough to float a horseshoe, but he smiled a little and said: "Thanks. It's fine coffee."

Neither of the men spoke.

Evan shifted his stance a little, then spoke bluntly. "You folks got maps of the land around here, and you got deeds to some land over on Arapaho Creek. A young feller named Orcutt told me that this morning. What I rode out to tell you is that the title to that land lies with a man named Douglas Hyland."

The shorter, bull-necked man said bleakly: "We know who he is."

The man's tone made Sheriff Hatfield gaze steadily at him as he resumed speaking. "Mister Schmidt, my position is to keep the peace. I'll ask you folks the same thing I asked Mister Orcutt . . . stay off Hyland's range for a couple of weeks. Until it can be figured out whether the men at the Land Office in Denver made a mistake about that land, or not."

The taller man, Otto Langer, said: "Sheriff, we got families. It's hard enough in summertime but in winter . . ." He wagged his head. "We got to get shelters built before snow flies."

Evan leaned gently to put the tin cup upon one of the stones at his feet. As he straightened up, he said: "If you build shelters on someone else's land, Mister Langer, they'll tear them down."

"It isn't someone else's land," stated Henry Schmidt. "Do you want to see the patents they gave us in Denver?"

"No. I'm satisfied you got them, Mister Schmidt. But I'm not satisfied they're valid."

Otto Langer looked intently at Hatfield. "You a cowman, Sheriff?"

"No, I'm a lawman."

"But you worked for cowmen some time, Sheriff. This Douglas Hyland is a friend of yours?"

Evan could feel the color coming into his face. "Gents, let's get this out of the way right now. No matter who my friends are . . . or aren't . . . I administer the law. It's got not a damned thing to do with who my friends are. Now, let's get back to this other matter."

"First," stated Langer, shoving big hands into trouser pockets, "let me tell you that in Denver, when we asked if anyone else might be using our land, they told us we had a right to get the law out here to run them off. That's your job, isn't it?"

"If it is your land, Mister Langer. *If.*"

Schmidt jutted his heavy jaw. "We got the deeds to prove it."

"So does Mister Hyland!"

"His aren't any good."

Evan bit back his angry retort, paused, then in a calmer voice said: "Gents, he thinks different. What we're talking about right now isn't who owns the land. What we're talking about is . . . until it's settled whose title is right and proper you folks keep off Arapaho Creek. Stay plumb away."

Schmidt was red in the face when he sourly said: "Sure, we keep off our own land so that damned cowman can graze off all the grass we'll need for our horses this winter. We keep off it until winter, then it'll be too late to build cabins and we'll either starve or freeze, maybe both. You see those children over yonder?"

Evan held himself in check with an effort. He did not look toward the wagons, he looked directly at Henry Schmidt. "None of this is my doing, Mister Schmidt. I know it's going to inconvenience the hell out of you, but if you go over there and set up a camp, Hyland's riders will visit you, and that's not going to happen if I can prevent it. Any way you look at it, gents, this is a hell of a mess, and, if you think it's only bad for you, you're wrong. It's just as bad for me."

Henry Schmidt did not give an inch. "How bad for you? You got a stove in your office in town? You got a dry bed every night, Sheriff, and . . . ?"

Hatfield had had enough. With a hand resting

on his gun butt he said: "I'm not going to repeat it. Keep away from Arapaho Creek for the next two weeks." He waited, but neither of the men across the stone ring from him spoke. They looked steadily at him, though, without a hint of irresolution, as he thanked them for the coffee, removed the hobbles from his horse, swung up, and turned stiffly in the direction of town.

The best he could do was be hopeful, and, as he got close to Hyland's outskirts with his red mood diminishing, he thought Otto Langer might be reasonable. He did not believe he had made a favorable impression out there, and was disappointed about that. As for Henry Schmidt, he knew that type of man. Schmidt would probably never yield at all. If he did, he would never do it gracefully.

At the livery barn, Evan unbuckled the booted Winchester, left his horse with a hostler, and returned to the office. He was re-racking the saddle gun when Joe Lamont walked in, tugging off his riders' gloves. Joe said: " 'Afternoon, Sheriff. You got a few minutes to spare?"

Evan nodded and gestured toward a chair. As Lamont sat down and tucked the gloves under his gun belt, Hatfield said: "Did Mister Hyland get off all right?"

Lamont thumbed back his hat. "Yeah, he got off. He didn't tell me a hell of a lot, but I've worked for him a long time, and he was worried."

Evan thought that Douglas Hyland had reason to be worried, and sat behind the old flat-top desk. "Things'll work out, Joe, they always do."

The dark-eyed, graying range boss agreed. "Yeah, they always do." Then he sat a moment, probably organizing what he'd come here to say. "We're gettin' some trespassers over along the creek. It don't amount to much, I guess, except that Mister Hyland told me before he left not to let anyone hang around over there."

"Have you seen 'em, Joe?"

"No. We don't ride that part of the ranch very much, until we bring in the cattle for wintering. But there are some tracks, and I expect now I'll have to keep someone over there watching, and right now I sure can't spare the rider nor the time." Lamont's dark eyes came up. "I was wondering, Sheriff . . . if you was to be out there once in a while, if you'd sort of keep an eye peeled?"

Evan nodded because he had made up his mind on the ride back from the settler camp to do this. "Yeah. And there's something you can do for me, Joe."

"Sure. Shoot."

"If you find anyone over there, don't get all fired up. Don't let your men get fired up. I guess Mister Hyland told you about settlers coming around."

"He said something about a feller named Orcutt."

"There are two more, along with Orcutt. One's named Langer, and the other one's named Schmidt."

Joe Lamont gazed at Hatfield. "Settlers . . . three settlers bothering over along the creek? They think they got a right over there?"

"Yeah, they think so."

Joe Lamont kept gazing at Hatfield, then he abruptly stood up. "Maybe you'd ought to tell them not to go over there, Sheriff."

Evan also arose. "I've already told them, Joe. Now remember . . . if your men see someone out there, don't start something."

Lamont went to the door before replying to that. He frowned a little at Sheriff Hatfield. "When Mister Hyland's gone, I look after things for him, and that includes running off folks who got no business on the range."

He went out and closed the door after himself. He had not agreed to leave trespassers to the sheriff, and Evan stood at the desk remembering the look in Joe Lamont's dark eyes.

"Hell," he growled at the wall, and went over to dip up a drink of water before going out to make a round of the town.

He ended up at the café and Barley Smith brought him roast beef, tough enough to cover a saddle tree with, which was the way Hatfield liked his roasts, and some apple pie made from pithy little stone-sized crab apples that had to be

55

sweetened with their own weight in sugar, and still they were tart.

Barley related an incident that had occurred out front of Clampitt's store earlier in the day, and looked intently at Sheriff Hatfield as he mentioned it.

"That lanky gunman I told you about for drinking five cups of coffee. Well, by golly, he was coming out of the store this afternoon and one of Hyland's men was standing there in the shade, and said something. I don't know what, because I wasn't that close, but I tell you, Evan, that raw-boned feller in his new clothes and all . . . for a fact he sure did look green."

Hatfield listened. "Go on."

"Well, sir, the gunman made a remark back and that cowboy stepped off the boards into the dust and called the gunman a son-of-a-bitch."

Hatfield did not move. "And . . . ?"

"Evan, you never in your life saw a man with a draw like that. Button shoes and derby hat or not, I never saw anything like it, and neither have you. He had that shiny gun out and cocked, and aimed dead center on that cowboy's breast bone, before the cowboy had even cleared his holster. Then he says . . . 'You unbuckle that gun belt, let it drop, toss down the gun, and go out into the middle of the road and start walking, and, mister, when you're ready to apologize, come on back and I'll return the gun and shell

56

belt." And by golly that range man did it, hiking south to the livery barn without once looking back. Evan, I tell you, if that man's not a gunfighter, I'll eat my boots."

Hatfield shoved the pie away, swallowed a few more mouthfuls of tough roast beef, then paid up, and walked out of the café.

The day was ending; shadows slanted from building fronts across the way. The sun was masked by an afternoon heat haze that was lying far out. As Sheriff Hatfield turned in the direction of the rooming house, the evening stage arrived early, which was unusual, in fact for a stage even to arrive on time was unusual but, for one to reach town ahead of schedule brought a lot of heads around.

VI

By the time Sheriff Hatfield located Enos Orcutt there were shadows along the verandah of the rooming house, and out the front door came the smell of greasy cooking. There were only two other men on the porch, and, after the sheriff's arrival, they decided to cross to the saloon for a drink before supper. As they trudged away, one said: "Likely need more'n just one drink to screw up my nerve to eat supper in there again tonight."

For a fact the rooming house proprietor and

his wife set forth the worst meals anywhere in Lost Valley, and it might even have been as traveling men had suggested—that they served meals like that to discourage roomers from eating at the establishment. Sheriff Hatfield resided at the rooming house, and had not so much as entered the dining room there for five years.

Tonight, he went over where Orcutt was sitting, long legs raised, feet hooked over the verandah railing, dragged around a chair, and sat down as he said: "Nice night, isn't it?"

Orcutt turned slightly. "Very nice night. I'll guess why you're here, Mister Hatfield. That fracas out front of the store."

Evan liked directness. "I want the six-gun and shell belt, Mister Orcutt, and I want to tell you again . . . one more time . . . what can happen to folks who lock horns with Lost Valley Ranch."

Orcutt did not allow Hatfield the opportunity to explain what could happen. He shot up to his feet, murmured something about the shell belt and gun, and disappeared inside.

Hatfield rolled a smoke, watched them close the log gates of the corral yard southward, and speculated upon the identity of four range men who walked their horses toward the saloon tie rack, and by then the settler returned and handed over to the sheriff what obviously was someone else's holstered Colt and shell belt.

"It wasn't my doing," he said. "I was coming out of the store. There was a range man leaning there. He said . . . 'Mister, if you ain't careful someone'll take that shiny pistol and ram it . . .' "

"I heard what happened, Mister Orcutt. He called you a son-of-a-bitch."

"Not until after I told him no one as ugly and smelly as he was would take my gun. Then he called me that and stepped off the duckboards."

"And you outdrew him."

"Sheriff, gun peddlers only sell pistols if they can show how to use them. Draw faster than anyone else. Every town I've ever been in has got someone they figure is fast and accurate. Gun peddlers have got to beat that kind of competition wherever they go. Otherwise, they don't peddle guns."

Hatfield knew all this. He'd been marveling at the dead-shot, fast-draw gun peddlers since he'd been a boy. "Did you know that was a Hyland rider?"

Orcutt strung both long legs over the railing as he resumed his former position again. "Not right then I didn't. That man who runs the café told me afterward who the rider was."

"When he gets back to the ranch, he'll tell 'em. Tomorrow they'll be in town looking for you. Maybe even tonight."

"I can handle it, Sheriff."

"No you can't, Mister Orcutt, and, even if you

59

could, you're not going to try it . . . not in my town." Sheriff Hatfield turned. "Starting tomorrow, you go unarmed."

Orcutt stared.

"That's right, unarmed, Mister Orcutt, because around Lost Valley they don't shoot unarmed men. But you show up in the roadway tomorrow when Lost Valley Ranch is in town, and I don't care how fast you are, you can't make it against nine men. Now then, either I get your word about this tonight, or I'll waltz you down to the jailhouse right now, and keep you locked up for a spell."

Orcutt was aghast. "For what? All I did was protect myself against a damned bully. That's all."

"All right, Mister Orcutt, I'll accept that," stated Evan Hatfield. "Now then, you going to pass me your word or not?"

"Sheriff, the man was standing there to pick a fight."

Hatfield leaned, and Orcutt got a strange look on his face as something round and unyieldingly hard was pressed into his rib cage on the left side. "Stand up, Mister Orcutt. Stand up!"

As the raw-boned younger man arose that pair of roomers came back across the road from the saloon, ignored the pair of standing men farther along the verandah in the gloom, and went reluctantly inside.

Enos Orcutt felt Hatfield's big hand on his arm

as the sheriff turned him a little, then leaned and lifted away his nickel-plated six-gun. As he straightened up, Hatfield shoved hard with his pistol barrel. "Walk. Not a damned word out of you, just walk down to the jailhouse. If you get clever and try ducking between a couple of buildings, I'll aim low and break a leg."

"Sheriff . . ."

"I said not a damned word. Walk!"

A great many people around Lost Valley could have told Enos Orcutt this was exactly how Evan Hatfield operated. When he decided to move, he did not waste any time and he did not use one superfluous word. And he was fast, even in broad daylight Hatfield was fast and accurate with his six-gun.

Orcutt trudged toward the jailhouse as silent as a mute. When Hatfield opened the door, shoved him through it, and lighted a lamp, Orcutt finally spoke.

"Sheriff, I was absolutely justified in what I did. Any man would have done the same, except that most of them would have shot and killed that cowboy. I could have, but I didn't."

Evan motioned. "Shuck the shell belt."

It was like trying to reason with a stone wall. Orcutt let the bullet belt drop, and obeyed when Hatfield gestured him down the little corridor into one of the strap-steel cages in the jailhouse cell room. Only after he had Enos Orcutt locked in did the sheriff relax. He stood out front and said: "It wasn't just the business with the Hyland range rider. I talked to Langer and Schmidt. They had their backs up when I rode up. Mister Orcutt, I'll fill these damned cells if I have to. Yeah, I know what you're going to say . . . it was justified. I believe you." Orcutt stared, and Hatfield smiled at him before continuing: "I try to make sense to you people, and don't make a dent. For the last time I'll tell you . . . it's not title to that damned land along the creek that worries me, it's keeping a war from starting."

He turned on his heel and went back to the office, drew down the lamp, and for the first time in months, when he returned to the plank walk out front, Hatfield locked his jailhouse door. It did not occur to him that his prisoner hadn't had supper. He could not have done much about it if it had, because the café across the road was dark.

Ordinarily he would have headed for his room, but after the episode with Orcutt he was wide awake, so he stopped by the saloon for a night-cap, and ran into Joe Lamont with two Lost Valley Ranch range men, none of whom looked at Sheriff Hatfield with the easy amiability that had for years marked the association between Douglas Hyland's men and the local law. Hatfield nodded without smiling and stepped up along the bar for his drink. Until it arrived, Lamont remained in his place with his men, dourly pensive. But after

Hatfield had downed his shot of whiskey, Joe came down and leaned beside the sheriff.

"Those tracks goin' up along Arapaho Creek," he said, by way of openers. "Maybe they was made by that Orcutt feller, Sheriff."

Hatfield nodded. He knew what was coming.

"Today he jumped Arthur Daggett out front of the store here in town."

Evan shifted position, rested his stomach against the bar, and negatively shook his head when the barman came along to raise an enquiring eyebrow. As the barman departed, Hatfield said: "I think it happened the other way around, Joe. I think your man pushed that gunman into a fight. And, Joe, from what I've heard from folks who saw it, your man is lucky he's alive." Evan looked straight at the range boss. "I've got your man's gun and belt over on my desk. He can come claim 'em the next time he's in town."

Lamont's dark eyes were hard. "He'll be along. That gunman made him look bad, walkin' down the road like he done."

Evan shrugged. "He can come any time. But all he's going to get is his gun back. I've got the gunman locked in a cell."

Lamont's expression changed slowly. "Well, by golly, I'm glad to hear that, Sheriff."

Hatfield forced a small smile. He could have explained that the reason he had locked up Orcutt had nothing to do with the gun action out front of the general store that day, but he didn't do it. Lamont could believe anything he wanted to believe, and, if it happened to be that Sheriff Hatfield was sympathetic to the cattle interests, that was all right with Hatfield. All he wanted was—no trouble.

He left Lamont standing there, returned to the chilly late evening, and went on up to his room. He was tired, and he hadn't actually done anything to make him that way. He dozed off thinking of what those emigrants had said about needing feed for their livestock and shelter for their broods. In the morning he awakened thinking of Joe Lamont's misinterpretation concerning the incarceration of Enos Orcutt.

Evidently the news had spread. Barley Smith waited until Hatfield was nearly finished with his breakfast, then he asked if Evan wanted a| pail of coffee and some beef stew to take across the road with him. Evan nodded, expecting more, but Barley Smith was a discreet individual. He padded to his kitchen to fill the little pails and returned to stand them upon his counter, without once mentioning how he knew there was a prisoner in one of the cells across the road. If Barley Smith knew, then so did everyone else around town, not that it was a secret, but it intrigued Hatfield how the information had got around so swiftly.

He shoved the pails under Orcutt's cell door and

was agreeable when the prisoner asked if he could wash after he ate. Hatfield went out to the office to pour fresh water into the coffee pot atop his wood stove, fling in another fistful of ground beans, and was stuffing kindling into the stove when a woman walked in from the roadway. He looked owlishly at her. The number of females who had visited his jailhouse over the years he could have counted on the fingers of one hand.

She acted as self-conscious about being there as Hatfield felt about having her there. He got a chair for her and murmured something about the coffee being ready in a little while, and tried hard to remember where he had seen her before.

She dispelled the mystery. "Sheriff, I'm Missus Langer. I saw you at our camp yesterday."

Hatfield sighed, and went around to his desk chair to sit down. She was a tall woman, well put together, with wavy dark brown hair and eyes that matched. He would have guessed her age to be close to his own, and would have missed by five years; she was just barely thirty.

She blurted out the first words with both hands clasped in her lap. "I'm afraid, Sheriff."

To make it easier for her Evan smiled. "I am, too, ma'am, but with any luck at all nothing is going to happen."

She lowered her eyes to the clasped hands. "Last night another wagon arrived."

Hatfield's smile dwindled. "Settlers?"

"Yes. A family from Kentucky named Horne. Mister Horne, his wife, and their two half-grown boys."

Evan eased back in his chair. He could guess the rest of it. "You folks visited with them?"

Langer's wife kept looking down. "Yes. Last night and again this morning. Last night the men brought out a jug and talked long after Missus Schmidt and I put the youngsters to bed."

"This Mister Horne . . . how did he impress you, ma'am?"

"That's what worries me, Sheriff. He's a Southerner, a hard-fisted man with strong opinions. My husband . . . after you rode away yesterday, my husband told Henry Schmidt there didn't seem to be much else to do but wait the two weeks you mentioned. Henry is a little like Mister Horne . . . he's impatient and . . ."

"Willing to be a little troublesome?"

"Well, he's right, Sheriff. We have to build shelters before winter. But as I told my husband . . . this whole country is populated by people who will oppose us, and we're only two families." She finally looked up. Her face was pale and her eyes seemed darker as a result of that. "I told my husband this morning I'd rather go on, keep going until we got to Oregon even, because I was afraid. He said all we had to do was wait, there would be more emigrants arriving soon, then the cowmen wouldn't be able to bully us."

Evan went to the stove to poke in another couple of pieces of wood. When he turned back, the handsome tall woman was standing. He said: "This will be between us, Missus Langer. And I'm right obliged you came."

"Can you do anything to stop it before it starts, Sheriff?"

Evan's answer was quietly offered, but strong. "That's my plan. Whether your husband and Mister Schmidt believed me yesterday, or not, when I told them all I wanted was to make sure there was no trouble, it is the absolute truth." He went to the door with her and opened it. "Again, ma'am, I'm obliged to you."

After she had departed, Hatfield went over to sniff the coffee pot. The brew was not quite hot yet, but he drew off a cup anyway. It tasted terrible, but maybe that had less to do with the coffee than it had to do with the way Hatfield was feeling right then.

VII

The morning stage arrived an hour and a half late, which could have been important to the men who operated the company's corral yard, but not to anyone else around town. An aftereffect was that the mail was not sifted and sorted into its little cubicles over at the general store until about noon.

When Sheriff Hatfield strolled over, Steve Clampitt got his three letters, passed them over, and leaned in a conspiratorial manner to say softly: "Had three settlers in here this morning."

Evan nodded without much interest as he looked at his three letters.

"They bought bullets for handguns, some shells for shotguns, and two boxes of Winchester ammunition."

Evan looked up and Clampitt grinned bleakly across the counter at him.

Later, when Hatfield was out back at the wash rack with Enos Orcutt, he mentioned the newcomer, Horne, and Orcutt spoke from a face dripping with cold water. "Sheriff, there's bound to be more. They got big maps on the walls at the Denver Land Office showing all this country, and with the parcels in blue which can be homesteaded." As he reached for the grimy old towel, he also said: "You can't any more stop progress than you can fly, Mister Hatfield."

Evan grunted. "You think growth is progress, Mister Orcutt? I don't." He herded his prisoner back to the office, motioned for him to sit along the wall, and got them both cups of coffee. When he was handing a cup to the lanky settler, he said: "Two weeks isn't ten years."

Orcutt agreed. "I was willing to stay in town and wait it out. Sheriff, I don't think the cattlemen will wait. Why else did that range man try to start a fight with me across the road?"

"They'll wait," stated Hatfield in a growling tone.

"Tell me, Sheriff . . . did someone go up to Denver? Is that why all this waiting is important?"

"To Denver, yes, but down to Albuquerque first." Hatfield did not elaborate. He would not have explained even if Orcutt had asked him to. But Orcutt did not ask. He instead made a statement.

"I doubt that it'll turn out the way you hope, Sheriff."

Hatfield did not comment. If Orcutt was right, then the headaches were only just beginning for Hatfield, and he had known this since the day he'd last spoken with Douglas Hyland. "Finish your coffee," he said, and, when Orcutt put the cup aside and was herded back down into the cell room, he waited to speak until Hatfield had locked him in again.

"What about Schmidt and Langer?"

Hatfield pocketed the key. "They're unhappy. You knew that. Now, there's this other one, a feller named Horne who just pulled in yesterday."

Orcutt said: "I told you. And there'll be more."

Hatfield returned to the office, closed the damper on his wood stove, picked up his hat, and went out into the warming new day sunlight. A solitary rider was coming down past the rooming house from the north. Hatfield only recognized him when the rider turned in toward the jailhouse tie rack. It was the range man Orcutt had disarmed, Art Daggett, and, as he dismounted to tie up, he shot Hatfield an unsmiling look.

"Joe said you got my gun and belt, Sheriff."

Hatfield reached back, opened the jailhouse door, and led the way inside to his desk. As he picked up the holstered Colt and held it forth, he said: "Don't try that again."

The cowboy flung his shell belt around, caught the buckle, and made it fast. Then he hefted the weapon and looked straight at Sheriff Hatfield. "I guess I can't. Joe says you got that greenhorn locked up."

"He won't be locked up forever," stated the lawman, "and, when he comes out . . . he'll kill you if you try it again."

Daggett seemed about to speak, checked the impulse, and turned toward the door. "Thanks," he said, and walked out to his horse.

For the second time Hatfield returned to the roadway. Arthur Daggett was riding southward at a walk, down to the lower end of town, and on out. He did not cut westward the way a rider would have done who was going back to Lost Valley Ranch, and Hatfield briefly speculated about that, but had his ruminations interrupted by a red-faced, lanky man who was driving a wagon in from east of town, making enough noise to have been a herd of wagons. The sideboards rattled, the wheels ground over dry axles, and the tailgate chain was so loose it spanked wood with every chuck hole.

The red-faced man turned northward into the main road and saw Hatfield watching, sang out to his horses, kicked on the brake, and leaned to spray amber before calling over: "Which way to the buggy works, friend?"

Hyland did not have a wagon works, but it had a smithy where local wagon work was done and Hatfield pointed. "Yonder, that open gate south of the corral yard." As he dropped his arm, he saw the staring look the red-faced man was giving him. The man had evidently not noticed Evan's badge when he had first accosted him. Now, straightening on the wagon seat, the stranger showed clear, candid hostility as he nodded, yanked loose the brake, and started up his team. He turned once, a few yards ahead, and stared back.

Hatfield speculated that this might be Horne, the newly arrived settler. What made him inclined to believe it was the red-faced man's accent. He was a Southerner; he might not have been that particular Southerner, but he certainly had the drawl of the South.

Joe Lamont arrived in town from Lost Valley Ranch about the time Evan Hatfield was returning northward from looking in on his horse

71

down at the livery barn. Joe tied up in front of the jailhouse, waited, and, when Evan came along, Joe said: "Did you get a letter from Mister Hyland?"

Hatfield reacted with a grunt. He had tossed those three letters atop his desk before taking Enos Orcutt out back to wash and had not remembered them until right now. He led the way inside and, with Joe tugging off his gloves, picked up the envelopes, went slowly behind the desk as he opened them, and sat down when the last letter bore Hyland's signature.

Joe helped himself to a cup of coffee, and made a grimace after the first taste, but took the cup to a chair with him. Joe waited, and because Hatfield re-read Hyland's letter, Joe had plenty of time to finish his coffee before the sheriff spoke.

"He finished up at Albuquerque, and is now on his way up to Denver." Hatfield put the letter down and scowled at it. "He doesn't say a damned thing except that . . . he's finished at Albuquerque and is heading for Denver."

Lamont did not seem to be disappointed. "I got a letter from him, too, and he said he'd wrote to you."

"Anything in your letter?" the sheriff asked, and Joe answered almost indifferently.

"Not much. Some talk about the ranch, otherwise about what he told you." Lamont arose, plucking the gloves from under his shell belt. "Sheriff, I fired Art Daggett this morning."

That, then, accounted for the way Daggett had kept on riding south. Hatfield nodded but did not state that he thought the firing was a good idea. He did think so, though.

Lamont finished with his gloves. "I'm not plumb satisfied you and I look at this trespassin' business the same, but I know what you're trying to do. Mister Hyland would approve, so I guess I got to."

Hatfield arose, smiling. For a week now he had been fighting odds that had seemed to be multiplying right under his nose. This was the first encouragement he'd had, and, coming from Douglas Hyland's range boss, it was worthwhile. As he went around the desk, he said: "We got three separate views of this mess, Joe. Yours, mine, and the settlers' view. I'm square in the middle. But until Mister Hyland gets back, none of us is going to get off the hook."

Joe Lamont eased the door open slowly. "Maybe, when he gets home, Sheriff, it won't be any better. I can tell you one thing from working for him as long as I have . . . he don't give up."

They walked out front, stood a moment in overhang shade, then parted, and, as Joe Lamont rode away, Sheriff Hatfield walked up in the direction of the blacksmith's shop, a dingy, sooty building that was long and narrow and cluttered.

The red-faced man was there, with the black-smith. Neither of them heard Evan Hatfield walk up. They were discussing a badly worn axle. The blacksmith was of the opinion than unless it were removed completely, built up at the forge, and retempered, it would not last three months, but the red-faced, gangling man thought a flux weld with the axle still under the wagon but while the wheel was off would get him by. The blacksmith looked around, saw the sheriff, and said: "Evan, we need a third opinion." It was amiably said. The blacksmith was a good-natured, easy-going man by nature, but when the red-faced man looked around, he spoke sharply.

"I don't need no cowman sheriff's advice!"

The blacksmith's smile faded. He looked surprised, then he looked down at the worn axle and cleared his throat, plainly embarrassed.

The red-faced man said: "Just build it up right where it's standin' and I'll be on my way."

Finally, with his surprise gone and his next reaction taking its place, the blacksmith shook his head. "Mister, you better go somewhere else and get it fixed. Like I told you earlier, I don't have the time anyway."

The gangling man glared at the blacksmith. "You're like the rest, ain't you?"

Evan saw the smith's big fist tighten around the hammer he was holding. Before the smith could retort, Evan said: "Is your name Horne?"

The red-faced man swung around. "It is. And you're Hatfield. I heard about you last night."

Evan read the signs correctly. He had been facing things like this since the first week he'd pinned on his badge. In a quiet voice he said: "Mister Horne, I was going to ride out and visit with you this afternoon."

"You wouldn't be welcome at my camp, Sheriff."

Evan paused a moment. The blacksmith was staring at him. Hatfield and Horne understood all this, but the blacksmith, caught in the middle, was mystified. But whatever had brought this open hostility to the surface in his shop, he recognized the danger and resented it, so he said: "Mister Horne, I'm a busy man. I'll help you put this wheel on, then you can find someone else to build up the axle for you."

The settler was directly between them. They were both stalwart men, seasoned and oaken and one of them was armed. He turned, grasped the wheel in corded arms, and leaned to shove it over the axle. Not a word was said as he fitted the wheel, then twisted to snatch the nut from the blacksmith's outstretched hand.

Hatfield stood watching, and thinking. When the settler picked up the wrench to tighten the wheel nut, Hatfield said: "I aimed to come out to your camp and tell you what I've told the others . . . stay away from Arapaho Creek. By the

75

end of next week we'll most likely have this settled, but until then stay off Hyland's range."

Horne gave the wheel nut a vicious final twist, kept his back to Hatfield as he removed the wrench, then straightened around, clenching the big old wheel wrench, and glared. "I got title. All of us got deeds to that land. They're plumb legal and proper. I know what you're tryin' to do. We all know. You're owned by the cowmen. Hatfield, no one's goin' to keep us off land we filed on and got deeds to. No one."

Horne was waiting. Hatfield did not move. He had no fear of the man, or the wrench he was holding. "If you go out there," Evan said, "I'll lock you up for trespassing. Mister Horne, I don't personally give a damn who owns that land, but, until it's settled who does own it, I'm going to enforce the peace. That means, if you folks go out there, I'll be after you . . . All you've got to do is wait a week. That's not a very long period of time, and after that, if it's proved you got the right, then I'll work the same way to protect your legal rights."

Horne seemed to be balancing between a decision to attack, or not to attack. Hatfield knew this, and the blacksmith also recognized it. The blacksmith stepped over and reached for the wheel wrench. Now, finally, he had made up his mind about what he had to do, but the moment his hand closed down around the wrench Horne swung. He was fast and agile. He was also tough as rawhide, and strong.

The blacksmith smothered the blow by being too close, but it staggered him. As he caught his balance, he growled, released his hold on the wrench, and sprang at the settler. Horne was taller by half a head, but the blacksmith was built like a barrel. When he catapulted into the settler, Horne tried to swing the wrench. The blacksmith was even closer now; there was no way for the settler to do more than glance the wrench off, and the blacksmith's fists were pumping like cast-iron pistons. He was enraged and bore in at the settler with unstoppable power.

Evan Hatfield, instead of breaking it up, stepped out of the way as the blacksmith jolted Horne against an anvil stand, then, with Horne's back against something unyielding, the black-smith went after him. He made Horne's long arms turn loose and hang with a massive strike over the heart. He brought the taller man down in a knee-sprung sag with a fist to the side of the head, and, as Horne leaned, the blacksmith sledged him along the point of the jaw. Horne went down like a pole-axed steer, a trickle of scarlet at the corner of his mouth.

Hatfield finally moved between them, but the blacksmith was ready to stop. He looked down, breathed hard, looked up, and said: "He was mad at you, Sheriff, not me."

Hatfield was leaning to roll the unconscious

settler flat out when he said: "He's mad at the world. He's mad at everyone who doesn't have to live out of a camp wagon. Give me a hand. We'll take him down the back alley to the jailhouse."

VIII

Enos Orcutt leaned on the front of his cage, watching as the blacksmith and the sheriff eased Horne down upon the straw-filled mattress of the wall bunk. When they left the cell room, Orcutt still leaned there, staring into the cell opposite him.

In the office the blacksmith declined Evan's offer of coffee, heaved a mighty sigh, and flexed sore knuckles. "Tell me one thing," he said to Hatfield. "What the hell was that all about?"

"Settlers filed on homestead land along Arapaho Creek. They got their deeds at the government Land Office up in Denver."

The blacksmith was quizzical. "But that's Hyland's range."

"Yeah. Mister Hyland's in Denver now, trying to straighten it out. Meanwhile, I'm trying to keep those people away from the creek."

The blacksmith looked at his sore hands. "They just come along to grab someone else's land without knowin' who it belonged to?" He wagged his head. "How many are there?"

"Three wagons of 'em so far, and the feller in

the cell across from Horne. But there may be more on the way."

The blacksmith stared. "I never heard anythin' about this. I'll be damned." He went to the door and stepped out, then began wagging his head as he trudged back northward to his shop.

Hatfield returned to the cell room, but Horne was still as limp as a rag, so when Orcutt asked questions, Hatfield explained what had happened. Orcutt looked worriedly across the corridor. "He's been out a long time, Sheriff. Are you sure he isn't dead?"

Hatfield was sure. "He'll come around. He caught one hell of a punch on the jaw. When he sits up, I'd take it kindly if you'd try to talk sense into him. Just one more week, Mister Orcutt." Hatfield twisted to glance at the man on the wall bunk. "Maybe it'll be hopeless. I can tell you one thing about Mister Horne. He's got one hell of a temper." Hatfield faced forward again. "I'll go fetch you something to eat."

As he reëntered the office up front, the door was flung open from the plank walk outside, Otto Langer and Henry Schmidt stamped in, both of them wearing six-guns and shell belts, and there was no way to misread the expressions on their faces.

Hatfield was a believer in seizing the bull by the horns. Without waiting, he said: "If you're looking for your friend, he started a fight at the smithy, and now he's locked in one of my cells."

Schmidt glared, looking every bit as fierce and willing as Horne had looked an hour earlier. Otto Langer hooked thumbs in his gun belt and said: "We got a wagon outside. We'll take care of him back at camp."

Hatfield shook his head. "He stays, gents."

"On what charge, Sheriff?"

Hatfield stroked his jaw while replying. "Disturbing the peace, provoking a fight." He dropped his hand. "I'll think of something else."

Langer did not move. "He's entitled to bond."

Hatfield sighed. This was true enough. There was no justice court in Hyland. There was a circuit rider who appeared in town every couple of months, but short of murder, rustling, or horse theft, there were no common crimes that were considered serious enough for Hatfield to hold a prisoner that long. Moreover, he had a list showing a sliding scale of bail rates. Without consulting the list, Hatfield knew the fee for disturbing the peace—$3. For fighting it was the same, another $3.

But Hatfield had no intention of freeing Horne, so he said: "I can hold him twenty-four hours without a charge, gents."

Schmidt still glared, but he was silent. It was Langer, the taller man, who said: "We'll be back in twenty-four hours with the bail money. Right now, we're busy strikin' camp."

Hatfield knew better than to hope they were leaving Lost Valley. He studied the pair of them, had a bad premonition, and softly said: "What've you got in mind, gents?"

Now, finally, Henry Schmidt spoke. "We're goin' over onto our homesteaded land, Sheriff. We're going to set up camps and get to work. Summer don't last forever."

"Neither," responded Hatfield, "does my patience." He went closer to the desk and leaned there, big arms crossed over his chest. "One more week, gents. Make this easy on yourselves. I know you bought ammunition, and believe it or not I sympathize with you, but I've told you folks this until I'm getting tired of saying it . . . stay off Hyland's range until the matter of your deeds is cleared up. For your own sakes, stay away from there."

Schmidt turned fiercely toward the door, grabbed for the latch, and glared at Hatfield. "You're going to delay us as long as you can. One more week!" Schmidt sneered. "And next week it'll be the same . . . one more week. And after that . . ."

He wrenched the door open and stormed out, leaving Otto Langer behind. Hatfield turned slowly. "I was hoping you'd have enough sense to be reasonable, Mister Langer. I was sort of hoping you'd be able to hold your friend back."

"I'm reasonable," the remaining settler said.

"I'm even willing to sit doing nothing for another week. But like Henry said . . . after that week is up, there aren't any guarantees . . . are there, Sheriff?"

Hatfield side-stepped a direct answer. He had misgivings of his own, but he had no intention of sharing them with anyone, so he reverted to the main theme of their discussion by saying: "Don't cross the road, Mister Langer. Don't go over along the creek."

Langer remained motionless for a moment longer, then he also walked out of the office, but he did not say a word as he did so.

Hatfield leaned on the desk in thought for a while, then roused himself, went over to the café for beans and coffee for the prisoners, brought it back, and shoved two of the pails under Orcutt's door, then turned to face the venomous stare of the other emigrant. He leaned, shoved those two pails under, also, straightened up, and said: "You feel all right?"

Horne's response was savage. "You son-of-a-bitch. I'll get out of here one of these days, then you'll find out if I feel all right."

Hatfield considered the red-faced man. "The last man who called me that and meant it didn't wake up for two days. All right, Mister Horne, I'll be waiting when you get out."

He turned on his heel and went back up front, locked the cell-room door, and dropped the key atop his desk as he picked up his hat. He was not angry, but he was solidly convinced about what had to be done.

Over in front of the general store there were no loafers, which was unusual, it being still early with a warm sun shining. Up at the saloon he recruited two freighters, big bearded men in rough boots and checkered flannel shirts. He explained why he was rounding up a posse, but the freighters simply leaned on the bar, gripping beer mugs and grinning. They did not care in the slightest; all that mattered was that they would draw posse men's wages, four bits a day, ride livery horses they wouldn't have to pay for, and get an outing.

Over at the stage company's corral yard Evan had to explain to Frank Dimmer, the company's representative in Lost Valley, why he wanted to dragoon Frank's yardmen. All Frank said was: "Take 'em. I'll send all four of 'em down to your office. Just don't get 'em busted up because it's hard as hell to get good yardmen any more."

Hatfield trudged back to the jailhouse, took down his booted Winchester, stuffed vest pockets with loads, and went behind the desk, stooped far down, dug out a bottle of malt whiskey, took two swallows, again hid the bottle, then went out front where the hostlers from the corral yard were coming up, armed with saddle guns as well as belt guns, and cocked an eye at the sun. There was plenty of time. It would take the settlers at least an hour to strike camp, unless they had already taken care of that before Langer and Schmidt walked over to town a while back.

The pair of freighters ambled through roadway dust on a diagonal course from the saloon. They still looked like men going on a coyote hunt, and, although both wore belted six-guns, Hatfield had to go back inside and bring out a pair of Winchesters. Then he led his posse down to the livery barn. Behind him, up and down both sides of the road, people came forth to watch, then to gang together in little excited groups.

The liveryman listened to Hatfield, then went with his day man to bring forth enough horses. He did not say a word until Hatfield's six armed men were leading their animals out front, leaving the sheriff and liveryman standing alone in the runway. Then he spoke.

"It's them damned squatters, ain't it, Sheriff? I knew, even before I heard the talk around town last night, I knew them bastards would bring trouble with 'em. What folks ought to have done was ride out there some dark night, scatter their livestock, and burn their wagons."

Hatfield turned slowly. "You know a darned sight better'n to talk like that. There's not going to be any stampeding or burning. And if there is, I'll be after you first thing."

He led his horse out front, flintily looked at the grinning freighters, then swung up.

They rode northward up through town. People were ogling from the plank walk, and even more of them were doing the same from inside stores and from behind window curtains among the residences farther up toward the north end of town. Hatfield felt self-conscious, and just a little ludicrous, but there was no other way to get up along the north roadway, unless it was by riding several miles west, around town, then back again to the roadway, and that would take too long.

By Hatfield's calculations the settlers should be visible within the next hour or two. At the very most, two hours, and, because he felt confident they had struck their camp earlier, he thought now, as he led his riders up the stage road, the wagon tops would appear within an hour.

It was a long road and arrow-straight as far as the first rising swell of land eight or ten miles distant. Beyond that it ran onward for another sixty or seventy miles before coming into any kind of broken country. The real mountains were twice that far, but they were distinctly visible and seemed much closer. It was another beautiful day, which should have had some influence upon how the sheriff felt, but he scarcely more than noticed it where he left the road, angling eastward. From this point on, his posse men became less talk-ative; it had been a pleasant ride among convivial companions up to this point.

From here on, it might be different. Lawmen did not recruit posses for joy rides.

Finally Hatfield halted quite a way south of where he thought the wagons would cross, and, although there was no shade, the heat was not that objectionable. In fact, for a summer day, it was more like early autumn because there was a hint of briskness in the air.

One of the freighters piled off to lead his horse off a fair distance, then position the animal so that it was between the other posse men and his back. He stood wide-legged for a moment, then stamped his feet, and raised his head. The others were not interested; they were discussing with Evan Hatfield the possibility of having trouble with the emigrants. The man who had gone off to wet down the sagebrush turned to walk back as he called to Hatfield and gestured northward with an upflung arm.

"Wagon tracks yonder, Sheriff, and they're fresh."

The freighter was correct. Hatfield sat his saddle up there, frowning at the ground. Langer and Schmidt already had their wagons moving when they came down to talk to him about releasing Horne. They had stolen a march on him.

One of the corral yard hostlers spat aside, stood in his stirrups, and quietly said: "By God, there's white tops a hell of a distance north and west, Sheriff, headin' toward Arapaho Creek."

Now Evan Hatfield was angry. He led off at a stiff trot. The canvas wagon tops were visible upon the west side of the road, and obviously Langer and Schmidt had made a fool of him. One of the bearded freighters said: "Sheriff, them folks didn't waste no time. They must have headed over before sunup. You can't drive big wagons that far otherwise. I know. I been doin' it all my growed-up life."

Hatfield did not take his eyes off the distant wagons, strung out one behind the other, three of them moving like laden ships in a light wind across a calm sea. He boosted his horse over into a lope. The men behind him did the same, and now there was no conversation at all. Trouble was something that left its aura along the back trail for many miles. Nor did posse men have to be experienced at this sort of thing to realize that this was not, after all, any joy ride.

Hatfield hauled back down to a walk when he was about a mile and a half distant. The wagons had halted down along the creek where willow shade partially camouflaged them. They were not on the land Orcutt had a deed to, and they certainly were not far enough along to be on the land Langer and Schmidt claimed, which would be another mile or two westward, so what that halt signified was that the settlers had seen the horsemen coming, and had chosen the spot to make their stand.

Hatfield shook his head. He should have grabbed those two, Schmidt and Langer, when they were in his office. He should have jugged them both and flung the key out a window. He halted, raised a gloved large hand to halt the men behind, and sat on a low land swell gazing down where the settlers were occasionally visible, just the adults, which meant the children had either been told to remain inside the wagons, behind those musket-ball-proof oaken side-boards, or they had been hidden along the creek among the willows.

One of the bearded freighters made a shrewd study. "We can't hit 'em head on, and they got in among them willers, so's we can't sneak up ahind them. Who are they, Sheriff? There's one good head amongst them, I'd say."

Hatfield removed his gloves slowly, pocketed them without answering, and thumbed back his hat. The customary thing was to leave his guns behind and ride in down there with a hand in the air. A hell of a lot of good that would do. He'd already talked until he was blue in the face—and there they were, doing exactly what he had forbidden them to do. Talking was not going to do anything it had not accomplished before. He leaned and spat.

A corral yard hostler, dark with high cheek bones and black eyes, eased his horse around beside the sheriff. Hatfield knew the man; he was a Mexican who was reputed to have been one of the finest jerkline freighters in the business until a mule kick had broken his right elbow, leaving the arm partially stiff when it healed. Around town they called him Pancho, but his name actually was Guillermo. He jutted his chin as he said: "They got guns. I counted six by the sun flashes."

Hatfield looked around. "Six? There's only two men down there, Pancho."

The hostler grinned broadly. "They maybe got their woman armed, too. Anyway, you set here and wait. When one of 'em moves, you watch the sun flashes."

Hatfield sat and watched because he had not yet decided what else to do, and the hostler was correct. He caught reflections of sunlight off six saddle gun barrels.

Then he remembered that someone had told him the man he had locked up back in town, Horne, had two half-grown sons. Langer, Schmidt, maybe their wives, and those two half-grown boys would account for six rifle barrels.

Someone muttered crossly. "Hell, it's even numbers, and I didn't bargain for nothing like that."

Hatfield hadn't bargained for anything like this, either, but then he hadn't bargained for the blasted wagons to be on the west side of the road, and there they were, with the horses off, the tongues in the grass, and not a soul showing except for an occasional reflection of sunlight off gun metal.

IX

No one liked being made to look foolish and Evan Hatfield was not an exception. Not only had they made him look foolish, but now they were in a fair way to turn him back with his tail tucked, and that would be even worse. There were four hostlers and two freighters who would tell the story of Sheriff Hatfield's rout when the posse got back to town. On the other hand, he was stubbornly adamant about a battle. Not simply because he objected on moral grounds, but also because in the back of his mind there was the lingering doubt about who did actually own that land, and, if a settler was killed by a posse and it turned out he was entirely justified in what he had been trying to do when they had shot him, Hatfield would have the U.S. marshal to face.

Time was passing. His posse men were fidgeting. One of them dismounted and squatted like an Indian in the shade of his drowsing horse.

Hatfield had to ride down there, but he had no illusions. Even if he had been a man of eloquent persuasion, which he certainly was not, the memory of Henry Schmidt's stubborn jaw and hostile eyes would have discouraged him. On the other hand, sitting out here in the sun doing nothing at all was even worse.

He said—"Let's go."—and lifted his rein hand.

Now, the posse men were totally silent. One of the freighters surreptitiously raised his booted Winchester a foot and slid back the slide to make certain there was a bullet under the hammer, something he should have done back in town.

The wagons were lined out about two tongue-lengths from one another. There was not a person in sight as the posse men walked their mounts down from the land swell toward the creek, but, by the time they were two-thirds of the way along, a man stepped around in front of the foremost wagon, grounded a long-barreled rifle, and leaned on it, watching.

Someone said: "Damn, that ain't no carbine, that there is a rifle. He's got a quarter mile reach on us with that thing."

Hatfield answered curtly. "There's not going to be any shooting."

Again the posse men turned silent, but several of them exchanged looks. Maybe the sheriff did not want any shooting, but it always took two men with guns in their hands to make that binding, and the solitary tall man leaning on that rifle had a dampening effect.

It was Langer. Hatfield had thought it was

before they were close enough to recognize one another. There were other rifle barrels scattered among the three wagons, clearly visible now without the aid of sunlight.

Hatfield said: "I'll go on alone. You fellers sit down and get comfortable."

There was plenty of grass to sit on, one of the hostlers observed as Hatfield walked his horse away, but there wasn't a worthwhile rock or a tree for protection, and grass didn't stop bullets.

Otto Langer straightened up, stepped across a wagon tongue, and went as far as the south side of his big old wagon. There, he leaned on the fore wheel, this time with his gun held crossways in both hands, and, when Hatfield was close enough, Langer said: "We're in the right, Sheriff."

Hatfield rested both hands atop the saddle horn as he gazed at the settler. "I told you . . . that's not the issue. It's going onto Hyland's range before this mess is settled. Hyland's not around, but his men are, and they've been chousing trespassers for a long while."

"We're not trespassers, Sheriff."

Hatfield swore under his breath. He was going to have to go around and around again, using the same argument against their same arguments. He tried something fresh. "Mister Langer, let me put this on a personal basis. My job is to enforce the law. It's also to preserve the peace, and that's more important to me than enforcing the damned law. I'd like to ask you folks to do me a personal favor . . . go back east of the road and wait over there for a few more days."

From the rear of the wagon, back where the tailgate chains were dangling, Henry Schmidt appeared, carrying one of those long-barreled rifles. He stamped forward and shook his gun at Hatfield. "We don't go back! When we move from here, we go forward, over where our land is." Schmidt stopped a yard or two from Hatfield's horse, his face red and his eyes hot with anger. "Personal favor? That's why you come out here with a posse of men with guns . . . to ask a personal favor? Hatfield, you're a hypocrite. You snuck up on William Horne, you tried to hold us back so's we'd freeze this winter, and now, because you see we're going to fight you, you're going to try and jolly us."

Evan braced into the wrath of the square-built man waving his rifle. He waited until Schmidt had ceased to speak, and waited another moment beyond that, then he said: "You're going back. One way or another, Mister Schmidt."

The burly man suddenly stopped gesticulating and stood stonestill as he swung the rifle to bear on Sheriff Hatfield. If he was going to speak, he lost the chance by not doing it immediately. Langer hauled up off the wheel and said: "Lower that gun, Henry."

Schmidt acted as though he had not heard. Hatfield did not believe Schmidt would shoot him, but he did believe that Schmidt could be driven to it by more arguing, so he sat, looking down and saying nothing.

Two gangling boys, both with the same red-sorrel hair Hatfield's latest prisoner had back in town, eased around from the farthest wagon, and a raw-boned graying woman as flat in front as a man ducked from inside the wagon. She, too, had a rifle in both hands.

Hatfield's cheek itched, but he made no move to raise either of his hands. Langer was staring at Henry Schmidt. "He'll leave, Henry. Lower the barrel."

Schmidt finally did lower it, but not all the way, and his regard of Evan Hatfield was exactly as it had been before: fierce.

Hatfield looked at them both. He had lost. Everything he could think of to say had been said before. He lifted his reins to turn away, and caught movement as a second woman moved into view from behind a wagon. He recognized her. She walked slowly up to the side of the first wagon, then stopped there. She had no weapon, and, as she and Sheriff Hatfield exchanged a look, he saw the fear in her face. He touched the brim of his hat to her and turned the horse.

Not a sound followed his departure among those people back there, nor did Evan glance around. Dead ahead his posse men were standing beside their horses. They had risen from the ground at the loud exclamations of Henry Schmidt, and had almost held their breath when Schmidt had aimed his gun at Hatfield.

From a considerable distance someone fired a handgun. It ordinarily meant simply that someone was beyond shouting range and wished to attract attention. Right now, a gunshot meant something else, and Hatfield reined back to a halt, his posse men spun in a new direction, and the people back down along the creek who had been moving closer to one another now spread out again, straining to see where the gunshot had come from.

Hatfield saw them long before the settlers did— six riders loping from the southwest all in a bunch. Hatfield rode on up to his posse men, swung to the ground, and stolidly identified the newcomers as Joe Lamont and the Lost Valley Ranch riding crew. Ordinarily at this time of the season they would not be riding over here—not the entire crew, anyway—but as Hatfield stood, watching their approach, he was not surprised. Nothing had gone right since breakfast time. Even so, he expected no trouble, although he anticipated Joe Lamont's annoyance and the truculence of his riders.

One of the hostlers said: "Now things're looking better. Now we got some support."

Lamont led his men at a lope to within a couple of hundred yards of the posse men, then hauled down to a steady walk, and, as they approached, they looked northward down along the creek where the wagons were. Evan Hatfield made a smoke, lit it, and waited. When Joe came on up, Evan nodded quietly, trickled smoke, and considered the faces of the riding crew. There was not a smile showing, not even an expression of resignation or philosophical acceptance of those people being down there along the creek.

Evan said: "They got over here before I could stop them, Joe."

Lamont surprised Hatfield by saying: "Did you try to stop them, Sheriff?"

Hatfield dropped the cigarette and ground it out. The last time he and Joe Lamont had discussed emigrants, Joe had said he understood Hatfield's position, but right now he was not acting like he understood it, or wanted to understand it. Hatfield raised his eyes and said: "What do you think I'm doing out here with a posse? I tried to stop them, yes, and a while back I went down and talked to them."

"Talked, Sheriff?"

"Told them to get back east of the stage road, Joe."

Lamont turned, glanced down toward the creek, and said: "I don't see anybody puttin' horses on the wagon tongues."

"We'll give them some time," said Hatfield, beginning to feel animus.

Joe turned back. "I don't know whether we will or not."

The range men, sitting clustered around their range boss, were listening, and watchful. Hatfield's posse men were the same. Those two freighters looked over Lamont and his riders without a trace of fear, but two of the corral yard man were beginning to fidget a little.

Hatfield returned Lamont's stare without difficulty. "We're all walking a tightrope, Joe. It's not going to help if we start fighting among ourselves."

Lamont's expression did not change, nor did he raise his voice, but there was no way to mistake how he felt about those trespassers along the creek. Even when the sheriff reminded him of their last meeting when Joe had sounded tolerant, at least understanding, the range boss' expression underwent no change, and he said: "Sure, I remember that, but we were talkin' about those people stayin' over east of the road, Sheriff. And I know what you're tryin' to do. I figure you're mostly right . . . but look down there. They're defying you and the law. They're defyin' Mister Hyland's rule against this sort of thing." Lamont eased up slightly in the saddle to lean on the horn. "Sheriff, mostly there's folks in this world don't understand anythin' but a big stick. But they sure as hell understand that. Those folks are goin' back east of the road, and they're goin' back today."

What lent particular substance to Lamont's pronouncement was the very quiet way he made it. Evan Hatfield, in a quandary again, had a moment to think some very uncharitable thoughts about Douglas Hyland, then he turned, snugged up his *cincha*, and swung up across leather, facing Lamont: "Joe, you chouse those people and we're going to lock horns." Then he gestured. "Ride off with me a little ways."

Hatfield had no intention of laying down the law to Lamont in front of his riders or the posse men. That would put Lamont into a position where he would have to save face by bucking the law.

As they walked their horses side-by-side away from the watching posse men and range riders, Lamont said: "Sheriff, they got to move. We can talk all day and nothing's going to change that. They can do their waitin' east of the road, but they're not goin' to do it down along the creek. You know what'll happen to me if they're camped down there when Mister Hyland gets back? He'll fire me."

"He won't do any such a thing, Joe. He knows as much about this mess as anyone . . . more than you and I know about it. He and I had a private talk before he left. He knows damned well what he left for you and me to sweat over. He won't fire you, not even if I've got to yank some slack out of him about that. Joe, leave this to me. I'll get them back east of the road, but you leave it to me. All they got to do is see a bunch of armed range riders circling their camp, and they'll dig in their heels."

Lamont stopped his horse, leaned on the saddle horn for a moment, then said: "I got the riding crew to think about, too. They know Mister Hyland don't tolerate anything like this. If I tolerate it, they're going to . . ."

"Joe, damn it, I'm getting tired of sensitive feelings. You look them straight in the eye and say this is the law's business, and that's how it's going to be until Mister Hyland gets back." Hatfield turned his horse facing back the way they had come. "You can't run them off. Look down there. They're dug in and armed to the gills. If you make a fight of it, you're going to lose some men. Joe, you're also going to have the law against you, and the next time I ride out I'll bring half the damned countryside, and I'll haul the whole crew back and lock it up."

Lamont did not seem the slightest bit worried. In fact he sardonically smiled at Hatfield. "You couldn't raise ten men and you know it. Sheriff, I doubt like hell that you could raise two men to go against Lost Valley Ranch." Then, as Hatfield sat bitterly thinking that this was indeed true, and he had known it was when he'd been making his threat, Joe's sardonic smile lingered as he spoke again.

"But . . . all right, I'll take the crew home. We'll stay away from this part of the range until tomorrow afternoon. That ought to give you enough time to get those bastards out of here."

He and Hatfield exchanged a look, then the sheriff nodded, and they headed back where the other horsemen were waiting.

X

Hatfield was no better off after Lamont led his riding crew back in the direction of the home ranch than he had been before Lamont had arrived. In fact, he was in a worse situation, because now Lamont and his men knew the settlers were down along the creek. He had to take action. He'd made a promise to Lamont, and he'd issued a fiat to the emigrants. After watching the range men lope away, Hatfield left his posse men and rode back down to the wagons, and this time those two gangling sorrel-headed teenagers were alongside Langer and Schmidt and their women. That raw-boned, angular woman with the stringy iron-gray hair and the rifle was standing slightly apart from the others, bitterly watching Hatfield ride up. He

100

assumed she was William Horne's wife, and the sorrel-headed big lads were his sons.

Henry Schmidt did not allow Hatfield time to speak. He said: "Now you're goin' to threaten us with those range men."

Evan drew rein, considered Henry Schmidt, for whom he was forming a thorough and deep dislike, and said: "I don't make threats, Mister Schmidt." He turned slightly to gaze at Otto Langer. "You folks've had time to talk it over . . . ?"

Langer nodded. "We talked. We're not going back."

"Four or five more days make that big a difference, Mister Langer?"

Schmidt interrupted. "No, Sheriff, four or five days don't make that much difference. But you're not goin' to let us come back over here in four or five days, and once we're back east of the coach road, you'll set up some kind of patrol to prevent us from gettin' back over here ever. And, Sheriff, we're here. If folks got to fight for their own, they're a sight better off being on their own land when they do it."

"This isn't the land you folks filed on. That'll be another few miles westerly."

Schmidt leaned on his rifle. "We know that. And by tomorrow morning we'll be on our own land . . . if we got to fight you every single yard of the way."

Hatfield gave up. He ranged a slow look at the women, those two frightened-faced but resolute lanky youths with their rifles, and turned back as he said: "You dug the hole, Mister Schmidt, I didn't."

He left them watching him ride back to the posse. He did not say a word, but gestured for the posse men to follow along as he walked his horse back in the direction of town. When they had passed over several lengthy low land swells and could no longer see the wagons, or the willow tops down along Arapaho Creek, one of the freighters could remain silent no longer, and said: "Sheriff, I expect maybe you did the right thing, but it's strange how folks look at something like this."

Evan faced half around. "You mean letting them run me off?"

"Yes."

"Well, mister, I'll tell you something I learned long ago. The man who makes a fast judgment is usually wrong as hell." The bearded man puzzled over that, and finally asked what it meant. Hatfield gestured toward the undulating country on both sides and said: "You go west and your partner go east. Leave your horses hobbled and scout up northward on foot. You know how to do that?"

The freighter knew. "You mean . . . scout up them settlers?"

"Yeah. Scout back and do it mostly on your belly, because, if they see either of you, it's going to pitch a monkey wrench into the works. You boys scout up there and watch that camp."

Hatfield drew rein. His posse men, mystified, also halted. They watched the sheriff study the sky before lowering his head to speak again. "We got maybe three hours of sunlight left." He paused to let that sink in. "Gents, after nightfall there won't be a moon for a couple hours. We're going back down without our spurs, skulk westward up the creek, cross it, and get behind the wagons."

The second freighter grinned broadly, but no one else did. "Hit 'em like Injuns," he opined, clearly delighted. "Jump 'em while they're outlined around their damned supper fire."

Hatfield gazed at the freighter. "Mister, we're not going to touch those people. We're going to take our guns, but we're not going to use them unless we absolutely have to."

"What, then?" demanded the freighter.

Hatfield answered curtly: "Horses, mister. We're going to steal their horses."

For a moment the men sat staring at Evan, then that Mexican-looking black-eyed hostler slapped his leg and laughed. The others finally reacted favorably, too, but not as enthusiastically as the Mexican-looking corral yard man, probably because they had never stolen horses, had grown up looking on horse stealing as ranking right up there with murder as the worst of all crimes, and finally because they had to be shocked that a sheriff who was charged with protecting property, including horses, would suggest such a thing.

Hatfield smiled a little. "They figure to drive farther across Hyland's land in the morning. Sure as hell that'll bring Hyland's riders back, and this time loaded for a battle. We're going to strand them right where they are. Then we'll palaver. If they want to move at all, they'll have to make a trade with me first. Otherwise, I'll impound their damned teams and it'll cost them cash money to redeem them."

One of the corral yard men stroked his stubbly jaw. "But, Mister Hatfield, Joe Lamont wants them plumb off his range. You're goin' to fix it so's they can't go back east of the road."

"I'll talk to Joe after we have their horses. Right now, I want to stop them from moving any deeper into Mister Hyland's range. We'll worry about getting them east of the road after we've set them afoot." He paused, regarding the posse men. "Anyone want to drop out and go home?"

If anyone wanted to, they did not have the nerve to say so. Hatfield led them westward for a mile, down in a swale, then swung off, and gestured for the freighters to break away. His last admonition to them was to repeat the warning he'd offered earlier.

"Don't let them see you. Hobble your horses a long way back in a gully or a swale. And stay out there until sundown. I want to be sure those folks don't hitch up and start moving tonight."

The freighters left in opposite directions, riding in a stiff trot. The other posse men swung down, loosened *cinchas*, hobbled their animals, and removed the bridles so each horse could crop grass unimpeded by the bit. The men sank down in the grass, fished for their tobacco or eyed the position of the sun, then got comfortable for a long wait as someone said—"Damn, goin' to miss supper tonight."—and someone else answered that tartly: "What d'you care? Old Barley ain't cooked a decent meal in his misbegotten life."

Evan Hatfield removed his saddle to have something to do, and swathed off his animal's back with twisted handfuls of buffalo grass—and thought. To impound livestock legally the animals had to be on someone's land where they had no right to be, and they had to be running loose. They were loose, across the creek in the willows, grazing, but whether they were on someone else's land brought up the original question that had caused all this trouble. Hatfield told himself his conscience would be clear because as far as he and everyone else in the territory knew, that was Douglas Hyland's range. Even if it wasn't, Hatfield had no proof of it now—this afternoon—and he could therefore in clear conscience embark on what he intended to do.

He finished with the horse, laid the saddle blanket hair side up to dry as much as possible before dusk, and strolled out a way along a thin roll of land, looking for his freighters. Neither of the men was in sight, and only one horse, small in the westerly distance, showed against the pale land with its creeping shadows. At that distance it could have been a ranch horse, a loose animal, except that horses did not ordinarily go off to graze by themselves if they knew where there were other horses on the range.

He strolled back with dusk on the way, had a smoke for supper, re-saddled his animal, but left the *cincha* loose, then sank down where the posse men were speculatively looking at him. Hatfield said: "Well, short of having ourselves a war with those damned fools, I couldn't come up with any better way of neutralizing them."

A graying hostler commented dryly: "It'll neutralize 'em just fine, Sheriff. In this country a man can't go nowhere on foot. But they're going to come up screaming and clawing."

Hatfield smiled, leaned to stub out his smoke, and looked at the speaker. "It's a big country, *amigo*. They can claw and scream for ten miles in any direction." He yawned. "Sure wish I'd brought my saddlebags along. There's some mule jerky meat in them."

One of the freighters returned in a jog. He had

been east of the dry camp, and, until his partner also returned, they would have to wait. All he had to report was that the emigrants were gathering firewood for their supper fire, and, excepting one sentry atop a high wagon seat with a rifle in the crook of his arm keeping watch, the emigrants seemed to be going about their normal routines.

The Mexican-looking man said: "Where are their horses?"

The freighter was loosening his *cincha* and answered without turning. "All I could make out was a pair of big grays west up the creek a hundred yards or so. But I'd guess the other horses was up in there, too, somewhere, only dark colors don't show up like them grays."

Shadows deepened and someone muttered about the other freighter. If they were going back down to the creek, which was a fair distance, the sooner they started the better.

The second freighter came back in a casual walk as though he'd never been in a hurry in his life. "Nothin' much goin' on," he sang out as he dismounted and walked up to squat and lean on his carbine. "They're fixin' to eat supper . . . and right now I wish I was down there amongst 'em."

Hatfield arose, went out to pull loose his Winchester, then waited until the posse men were all making sure their horses would be here when they got back, then Hatfield sent the freighters back east and west again, each with a companion from the Hyland corral yard of the stage company. He elected to take that Mexican-looking hostler with him, and, before leading out, he admonished them again about being seen, or making any noise, or going close to the camp. They were to reach the creek on both ends of the wagon camp, cross it, and converge upon the far side with the other posse men, and they were to do it as prudently and warily as they could. They were not to hurry—what the hell, they had all night. He waited, and, when no one spoke, he gestured with his carbine.

The Mexican-looking hostler grinned as the other men faded away into the settling night. He said: "Sheriff, you ever sneak up and steal horses like this before?"

Hatfield looked down his nose. "No."

The hostler was not abashed to admit that he had. "When I was a buckaroo down along the Sonora border, I used to steal horses. Down there, it's how you make a living. Otherwise you starve."

Hatfield was not particularly interested so he said: "Come along."

It was a long hike. Hatfield had never cared much for long walks. Being a large, heavy-boned, muscular man he did not consider himself built for walking. One of the obvious natural laws of God, or someone anyway, was simply that horses had four legs and big stout bodies, along with very small brains, while men had only two spindly legs and much larger brains. It naturally followed, then, that men should ride horses. Hatfield had been riding horses, and avoiding this sort of walking all his life.

The hostler, though, was a wiry man who could keep up with Hatfield's longer stride and talk at the same time. He seemed to be enjoying himself.

It was farther than Hatfield thought. Or maybe it wasn't really any farther; it just seemed that way when a man had to cover all that undulating prairie land on foot, but by the time he was northward into the area where cooler air from the creek was noticeable, Hatfield felt that he'd probably covered more miles without halting to rest than he'd ever done before on foot.

The Mexican became quieter, more Indian-like in his attitude. He stepped close and spoke in a lowered voice as he gestured westward. "Got to go up there, Sheriff. I didn't see no dogs with them people, but a little breeze is blowing away from the camp westerly."

Hatfield leaned on his carbine, gazing down where a faint flicker of supper fire showed occasional sparks and a middling flame against the dark world along the creek. He sighed and straightened up to lift the carbine and move forward again. "You know," he said solemnly, "my daddy was a harness maker. He wanted me to follow the trade, too. He said there'd never be a day when a harness maker wouldn't be in big demand. . . ."

The hostler's white teeth flashed in the darkness. "But no, and here you are walking on foot like a peon, in the darkness, to steal someone's horses."

Hatfield saw the grin and smiled back.

They angled northward with the scent of creek greenery in their faces. Now and then a vagrant scent of wood smoke came up to them, also, but not very often until they were angling down the last slope before reaching the creek. There the smoke fragrance was steadier, which meant the hostler had been right back there, the little evening breeze did in fact flow from east to west.

Once Hatfield picked up a snatch of words, indistinguishable but unmistakable, and altered course so that they would reach the creek farther westward. They had to move more slowly, once they got into the spongy footing along the creek, because the grass was thicker than the hair on a dog's back and ten times as matted and wiry. One misstep would send a man sprawling into creek-side mud.

Hatfield paused to listen while the Mexican went forward. The night out here was as silent as the inside of a grave, and, while Hatfield had worried all the way down here that his posse men would make noise, now he was worried that they hadn't made any. The hostler returned from weaving back and forth through willows and thorny berry bushes to whisper that he had found a way to cross over. He also said—"I smell horses."—and pointed eastward.

Hatfield smelled nothing but rotting vegetation and mud. He followed his guide, got raked several times with berry tendrils that possessed dagger-like thick thorns, and smothered the natural profanity that arose to his lips each time it happened.

Then he stepped through a rind of mud into water and felt his way. Ahead, the hostler was moving like a leather-colored wraith. Arapaho Creek was not deep this time of year, although during winter snow run-off or spring deluges it spread a mile outside both its banks and drowned livestock every year.

They reached the far side, a matter of perhaps four or five yards, kicked off surplus mud and water, went ahead to the matted grass, and leaned to skive off the mud that had not been scuffed off.

Hatfield arose to look left and right, then walked farther northward to get clear of the willows and be in open country again. His companion brushed the sheriff's sleeve and made a gesture with two fingers. Hatfield nodded, and the Mexican turned southward, hanging close to the willows for camouflage and was lost to sight in moments.

Hatfield grinned to himself where he halted to lean on the saddle gun. The next time he had to do something like this he'd make a particular point of taking that Mexican with him.

XI

The Mexican found their posse men friends a considerable distance southward, and brought them back by going far out and around until, when they approached Hatfield, they were coming almost directly southward. He lay in the grass with his saddle gun shoved ahead until he was positive, then arose to ease down the hammer.

The other posse men, though, did not appear until Hatfield was beginning to mutter profanely, and even then the posse men skulked in one at a time as though they were scalp-hunting strong hearts making a stalk.

The Mexican knew where the horses were. He had encountered them on his southward search. He also knew something else. "There's a man in among the willows with them. He's got one of those long-barreled rifles."

Hatfield said: "Just one man?"

The Mexican elaborately shrugged, turned without a word, and faded out in gloom and tree shadows.

A thoughtless corral yard man leaned aside his gun to roll a smoke. One of the freighters did not open his mouth; he leaned and struck the troughed paper, sending flakes of tobacco to the grass. The corral yard man jerked indignantly upright, but all his companions were gazing stonily at him, so he turned away in mild embarrassment.

The Mexican returned. "They got the horses tied. Haltered and tied. They're standin' in there full as ticks."

Hatfield was more concerned with the sentry. "Only one man watching them?"

"Only one, and he's sitting down with his back to a willow. Maybe he's asleep."

Hatfield gestured. "Lead the way. Quiet now. Damned quiet."

They had close to a mile to travel before the Mexican raised a hand, then disappeared again, but this time he reappeared almost instantly, grinning. No one else was smiling. With both palms pressed together he put his hands to his cheek and leaned his head in the position of a sleeping person. Then he grinned again and pointed. Hatfield considered. Clearly they had to be sure of the sentry first, then get the horses. He motioned for the Mexican to head back, and now as each posse man walked through the spongy grass and creek willows, they particularly watched each step.

It wasn't a man sitting there asleep propped against a big willow; it was one of those gangling sorrel-headed youths, which disappointed Sheriff Hatfield. He had hoped the sentry might be Henry Schmidt. He would have no qualms about hitting Schmidt over the head with a gun barrel.

They got up to within twenty feet of the slumbering sentry, and halted, as motionless and silent as wraiths. The Mexican was grinning again. Evan Hatfield stepped closer, eased down to one knee, studied the raw-boned youngster, then slowly raised one hand to the slumbering sentry's face and the other one to his gullet. Then he moved, bearing the youth over backward and to one side into the spongy grass where Hatfield could smother the sudden wildly flailing of arms and legs until his companions could each grab an extremity and spread-eagle the youth, whose eyes were starting from his head.

Hatfield kept one hand over the youth's mouth and the fingers of the other hand closing around the youth's windpipe. He allowed air to pass into the boy's lungs but did not ease up his silencing grip until the youth stopped fighting. Then Hatfield said: "Son, not a sound out of you. Not so much as a sigh. You understand? Because we could have split your head open to keep you quiet, and we didn't, so now just sit up and be quiet. All right?"

For five seconds the boy was rigid, then

gradually, as his body loosened, Hatfield removed the hand from his gullet, grabbed shirt cloth, and pulled the boy up into a sitting position. Then he said: "Not a sound. Agreed?"

The lad unsteadily nodded his head.

Hatfield removed the remaining hand, heard the boy gulp air, and waited briefly. Then Hatfield rocked back on his heels. "Son, you got a choice. Go with us or stay here. If you want to stay here with your folks, we've got to tie you and gag you. If you go with us, you'll be taken to the jailhouse in town. Which'll it be?"

Perhaps Hatfield's calm words without menace in them helped the sorrel-headed youth recover, but in any event he said: "I don't want to go with you, Sheriff."

Hatfield was agreeable. "Give me your belt," he said, and leaned to wrap the boy's ankles with the belt and lash them tightly. Then he said: "Are any of these horses broken to ride?"

The boy, looking up at the closed-down faces of the posse men, two of whom were fully bearded and villainous-appearing in the darkness, swallowed with effort, then pointed. "That there bay horse, and the seal-brown ahind him, and that old gutsy gray mare. The other horses is only broke to pull."

The Mexican leaned to offer Hatfield a length of braided rope he used to keep his trousers up. Hatfield tied the lad's hands behind his back, eased him down in the grass, and felt for the youth's blue bandanna to use as a gag.

The Mexican used his own bandanna through two front loops to improvise a method to prevent disaster when he moved.

The boy's round eyes followed their moves as each man went toward a tethered horse. Hatfield chose the gutsy old gray mare, which turned out to be mean; she tried to bite his hand when he reached to untie her. Any other time Hatfield would have slapped her, but right now he did not want a horse fight on his hands, so all he did was call her a fierce name in a whisper.

It went off more smoothly than Hatfield had expected it to. They led the horses northward out beyond the willows, and kept leading them westward for a half mile before one of the hostlers turned the bay he was leading, wrapped a war bridle around its nose, made of the lead shank, and vaulted onto the horse's back. Nothing happened. The bay horse dutifully plodded along.

Twice Hatfield tried to mount the old brood mare, and both times as he turned to spring up, she bit his rear pockets. The third time he shortened the far side length of rope and made it up. The posse men leading team horses had to walk, but no one resented that now. All they wanted to do was get back across the creek and beyond rifle range of the wagon camp.

They probably would have made it except that

one of the thousand-pound light harness horses balked at wading out into what must have looked to him like a black morass of deadly quicksand. The hostlers swore and larruped him. He still balked. Hatfield and the Mexican rode their saddle animals up and leaned their combined weight forcing the team horse to yield, but he did it by sucking back and giving a tremendous leap, attempting to reach solid footing upon the far side. The man holding his shank was jerked a foot into the air, then was dragged belly down through mud and water and more mud, but to his credit he did not relinquish his grip. Then the trembling horse tried to kick free of the rope, and in this fit of anger he whinnied the shrill, high call of a horse in distress.

One of the hostlers rode up close, aimed a big balled up fist, and struck the horse squarely between the eyes. Only a very angry or reckless man would do anything like that, but it made the horse momentarily wilt and bat his eyes, and by then his mud-covered handler was able to stand up and renew his grip.

Hatfield motioned for them to move along. That soggy, muddy hostler accepted the offer of the bay horse from the Mexican, led his recalcitrant harness horse in close, and broke clear upon the south side of Arapaho Creek at about the same time the moon appeared.

They were about a mile and a half west of the

wagon camp when they left the creek riding southward—and heard a man's swift, high call of alarm back down along the creek somewhere.

One of the freighters abruptly changed course, heading more to the west. It was safe to assume he was thinking of the range of those rifles back yonder. But they got two miles southward with undulating land swells between them and the creek without another incident. Where they finally halted, they were beyond the sight of anyone back down along the creek.

That dragged man got down, pulled grass, and proceeded to rid himself of as much of the foul-smelling mud as he could. When he looked up and saw Sheriff Hatfield watching, the man said: "Somebody . . . you or them settlers back yonder, or the Hyland town council . . . owes me a new pair of britches and a new shirt."

Another posse man held up a hand. "I think I busted some knuckles on that damned horse back at the creek."

One of the bearded freighters shook his head. "Anybody'd know better'n punch a horse in the forehead, friend. If you want to get their attention like that, hit 'em on the nose where there ain't no bone."

Hatfield leaned to listen. He let the talk around him continue for a few moments before he growled for silence and got it. Then they all listened.

Not a sound came out to them although Hatfield had no doubt but that by now the settlers had found the terrified boy, and also had found that their horses were gone. He sighed and said: "Let's get our own horses and head for town, gents."

No one had much of an idea about the time, but, judging from the position of the moon as they plodded along, once astride their own saddles and leading the settlers' horses, Hatfield thought it had to be around midnight.

He was correct. By the time they had Hyland in sight the only lights visible were from two guttering old carriage lamps down at the lower end of town, one on each side of the broad doorless opening of the livery barn, and another brighter light in the front window of the general store. Otherwise, Hyland was not only dark, it was utterly hushed.

They corralled the horses in one of the public pens out behind the livery barn, routed out a night man to care for their own horses, and at his big-eyed stare the posse men turned their backs to walk up front to the roadway, following the sheriff.

Hatfield crossed on an angle in the direction of the totally dark café. He banged on the door until the entire wall shook, waited, then pounded again. A lamp flickered to life somewhere out back. Hatfield rattled the wall a third time, and now he got a reaction—an irate string of blistering profanity as old Barley Smith came charging forward with his lamp held high in his left hand and his old Colt .44 in the other hand, purple in the face. He flung back the door and jumped, wide-legged, into the opening, waving the six-gun. The man who was covered with creek-mud struck the gun aside, stepped in, and shoved his face within inches of Barley's nose, snarling furiously. They all bumped past Barley, bouncing him back and forth. Hatfield lit the counter lamp, set it down, hard, and turned.

"Just bring it out here. Whatever it is, just fetch it out here with some spoons to eat it with."

Barley let the Colt dangle at his side. His nightdress hung, slack and voluminous in the poor light, as he stared and wrinkled his nose. "You fellers smell like a tan yard, for Christ's sake. And I don't feed folks after nine o'clock, and by God every one of you know that!"

Hatfield looked steadily at his old friend. "Barley, we just stole a herd of horses, and we've been all day without a blessed mouthful to eat. Now you fetch it out. Never mind if it's in a stew pot, just bring it out here."

Barley stared from Hatfield to the other soiled, rumpled, muddy, tired, and beard-stubbled men. "You stole someone's horses? Evan, what in the hell . . . ?"

"Barley, if you don't bring out that food,

we're going to go back there and get it ourselves."

Smith shuffled around the far corner of his
counter, put down his own lamp while moving
toward the old blanket that cordoned off his
cooking area, and, as he passed Hatfield, he
rolled his eyes. "Stole horses . . . ? Evan, I can't
feed anybody cold stew. It'll give you the grip.
Set down and I'll warm it up. I'll fetch some
coffee. You been out tonight stealing horses,
Evan Hatfield?"

They eased down along the counter. When the
coffee came, they slid the pot back and forth
until it was empty. By then there was the aroma
of cooking food coming from behind the old
blanket.

Hatfield looked at the mud-stained corral yard
man and wagged his head. The corral yard man
shook his head, too, then he laughed, and they
all laughed at the grotesque sight he made.

XII

Hatfield fed his prisoners a late breakfast
because he had not awakened until long after the
sun had risen, and, while he was in the cell room,
he had to listen to their loud and indignant
imprecations because he had not fed them the
day before. To silence them he said: "Got sort of

busy yesterday and last night, trying to keep your friends from getting hurt. They moved your settler camp down along the creek. Hyland's riders found them down there. If I hadn't been down there, too, with a posse, there would have been some fur flying. Then, last night, I took all their horses and brought them here to town."

Horne and Enos Orcutt stared out of their cells, for the time being unmindful of the food at their feet regardless of their hunger.

Hatfield returned to the office to fire up the wood stove under his coffee pot. He had hardly got seated at the desk when Joe Lamont walked in, tugging off his gloves and soberly nodding at the seated lawman. Lamont kicked a chair around, dropped into it, and crookedly smiled. "I saw the horses down at the public corral, Sheriff. I left a man down there to keep an eye on them. We went down along the creek early this morning." Lamont's crooked smile widened a little. "You got some awful mad settlers down there. They had the gall to ask us to loan 'em some horses."

The office, which normally smelled of stale tobacco smoke, was beginning now to smell of heating coffee. It was a pleasant fragrance.

Hatfield leaned back. "They were going on westward to hunt up the land they got title to. I had an idea you might not take kindly to that."

"So you stranded them. All right, Sheriff . . . but that don't get them off our range, does it?"

"Joe, when I was a young man, I was in the war down South. An awful lot of men were struggling like hell to accomplish things that seemed to me never to get accomplished. Only part of them did. I came out of that war convinced of one thing . . . the best a man can do, if he's got other men doggedly set against him, is part of what he's trying to do. Last night I had to settle for keeping those emigrants grounded in place. It's a compromise, but at least it's holding them plumb still." Hatfield sniffed the coffee. "Care for some java?"

Joe was agreeable, and he smiled at Hatfield's broad back, not because he particularly sympathized with what Hatfield was trying to do, although deep down he did sympathize with it, but because he could still remember the footstamping wrath and exasperation of those stranded emigrants. He and his riders had laughed about that all the way to town.

When Hatfield returned with two cups, Joe accepted one of them with a dry remark. "They're madder'n wet hens."

Hatfield went to his chair willing to believe that. "Being mad's better'n being dead, Joe."

Lamont finally laughed aloud and Hatfield, sipping coffee, showed a twinkle in his eyes over the rim of the coffee cup. "Pretty mad, eh?"

Lamont lowered his cup. "Mad? I never saw folks so mad. There's a short, bull-necked feller, must weigh close to a hundred and ninety-five pounds, got arms on him like oak logs. He would have fought us two at a time if we'd've climbed down."

Hatfield said: "Schmidt."

"And there's a raw-boned gray-headed woman. She's got a temper like a tarantula. She blessed us up one side and down the other, until that feller called Langer stepped in."

"They thought you stole their horses?"

"Yeah. Sheriff, if I'd known anything about that, I wouldn't have rode down there. Those folks was mad enough to shoot someone. This Langer feller had a gawky big kid with him. The kid said it wasn't none of us, and after that things sort of settled down." Lamont drained his cup. "You're goin' to have trouble to your gills when they get to town and find their horses here. They don't much care for you anyway."

Hatfield could be philosophical about that; he did not much care for those emigrants. "It's a long walk, Joe."

Lamont did not dispute that. "Sure is. But they'll make it. People like that can walk all day, like an Indian, so they'll make it." Lamont arose and put his empty cup aside. "Sheriff, you better lock 'em up. That one bull-built feller is nothing but trouble four ways from the middle. The other feller's not as bad, maybe, but he was mad as hell, too."

Hatfield went to the boardwalk out front with Lamont. "I got two in the cells now, and I only have three cells."

Lamont turned and led his horse over to the tie rack in front of the general store, where several of his men were loafing, apparently waiting.

Hatfield was turning back into his office when two men rode up and swung down, and one softly said: "Sheriff . . . ?"

Hatfield turned. From their droopy hats to their flat-heeled heavy cowhide boots they were emigrants, although both rode good outfits and both carried six-gun leather shaped to the bodies of each wearer.

Hatfield nodded and held the door for the strangers to enter his office first, then he hospitably offered them coffee. Both declined. One of them was a broad-faced, slate-eyed individual with gray around the temples and a pleasant expression. The other stranger seemed more inward, more reticent and wary.

It was the pleasant-faced one who said: "I'm Cal Arbuckle. This here is Harry Dent. We just reached Hyland this morning." Arbuckle leaned to fish inside his coat. When he brought forth a folded, rough-textured map, Hatfield went wordlessly to his desk and sank down.

"You filed on some land," he said flatly. "Mister Arbuckle, I've seen those maps before."

The pleasant-faced man looked inquiringly at

the sheriff. "You don't like the notion of settlers, Sheriff?"

Hatfield side-stepped a direct answer. "Is your claim along a creek, Mister Arbuckle?"

"Yes, sir. Along an unnamed creek."

"It's got a name. It's known as Arapaho Creek. If those land people in Denver know enough to draw maps, I wonder why in hell they don't know enough to give the creek its proper name."

The second man shifted slightly in his chair. "Those are old maps," he said quietly. "By trade I'm a surveyor. I served eight years with the Topographical Corps of the Army. I been hiring out to make surveys ever since. They have old maps in the Land Office, but they're good. Just too old, I guess, to have proper names on them."

Hatfield eyed this quiet man more closely. "You're a surveyor by trade, Mister Dent?"

"Yes, sir. And a homesteader right now, by choice."

"Did they tell you fellers over in Denver that the title to the land along that unnamed creek was in dispute?"

Both the men stared. Evidently nothing like this had been mentioned in Denver, or anywhere else these two men had been. Arbuckle finally said: "Dispute with cattlemen, Sheriff?"

"With one cowman, Mister Arbuckle. With Douglas Hyland whose grandfather got title to it from the Mexicans before you or I were born."

Harry Dent looked slightly dolorous. "Sheriff, those old Mexican deeds about half the time were not worth the paper they were written on. After the Mexican War our government set up a commission to verify or deny the legality of Mexican grants. They verified very few, but they denied hundreds of them."

Hatfield was facing a different variety of settler this time. Neither of these weathered, seasoned men got angry, raised his voice, or showed solid intransigence. But Hatfield was not ready to let down his guard. If anything, he was particularly leery of these two. Men like Langer and Schmidt were predictable; these two were not.

"The problem right now is, gents, I don't want trouble on the range, so I'm forbidding settlers to go west of the stage road for another few days, until Mister Hyland gets back with the exact standing of his Mexican deeds. . . . I've got two settlers locked in my cells, and yesterday I stopped three wagonloads more from going any farther across Mister Hyland's range. You two . . . make it easy for me and for yourselves for a few days . . . either stay in town, or make a camp, whichever you have in mind, but don't ride west of the roadway."

Surprisingly both the armed settlers nodded their heads. Hatfield eyed them with suspicion. As they arose, Cal Arbuckle said: "We don't want trouble, Sheriff. How long before Mister Hyland gets back to town?"

"Couple of days, more than likely. He's been gone two weeks and that's all he expected to be gone."

Arbuckle accepted this. "Fine. We'll make a camp over east of town."

Hatfield stood in his office doorway, watching Arbuckle and Dent ride slowly back up through town, trying to decide whether he trusted them or not. From behind him on the plank walk someone said: "Sheriff!" When he leaned and turned, the fist was a blur. He had one second to react, which was not quite enough time, but instinctively he lowered his head and the rock-hard set of knuckles bounced off his skull, knocked his hat off, and made him see stars for a second, then he was moving away from the door, moving backward, yielding ground as the blurry distorted features of Henry Schmidt swam toward him through the momentary mist of being stunned.

Across the road where Joe Lamont and his riders were getting ready to mount up out in front of the general store, someone yelped in astonishment. Hatfield heard that, but it scarcely registered as he continued to give ground before the enraged settler.

Schmidt was after Hatfield like a badger. He came in swinging powerful arms, his body thrusting forward, his teeth bared in a soundless snarl. For the sheriff there was no time to over-come his astonishment; there was only time to try and avoid those granite fists and the onrush of the furious emigrant. Twice Schmidt scored, and each time Hatfield sagged. It was like being kicked by a mule. Schmidt had equal force in either hand, and clearly he was experienced at this sort of thing.

Evan Hatfield continued to give ground until his head was clear, then he pawed outward to spoil Schmidt's aim, stepped off the duckboards into roadway dust, and, when Schmidt launched himself forward, also stepping off the sidewalk, Hatfield caught the settler with one foot in the air. Hatfield, too, could hit hard. Schmidt grunted, temporarily lost his footing, moved sideways until he had regained it, and hauled up a curving shoulder to protect his face, and started in again.

Hatfield feinted, but Schmidt did not come ahead. Hatfield baited the shorter, thicker man, then side-stepped—and Schmidt was there to swing a punch that grazed Hatfield's shoulder. It dawned on the sheriff gradually that he was not fighting just an enraged settler, he was up against a man who knew more about this kind of fighting than Hatfield knew.

He kept away, pawed at Schmidt to keep him off, and tried circling to the left. Schmidt did not lift his feet to turn; he shuffled around in the dust, never being unprepared. Hatfield tried circling in the opposite direction. The same thing happened again. Hatfield stepped two paces to the right, one back to the left, and fired a fist straight through Schmidt's guard, and that time the heavier man wilted. Hatfield went in fast, swinging hard and trying to get the full weight of his entire body behind each blow. He was fighting desperately now.

Schmidt weathered most of the blows, massive arms up to protect his face and jaw, but Hatfield aimed lower, hit Schmidt over the heart with his body twisting in behind the strike, and that time Schmidt's arms dropped, his face contorted, and his eyes mirrored pain.

Until this moment Hatfield had heard nothing and had seen only Henry Schmidt, but when he stepped back to gulp air and lower his arms for a moment of respite, the cries of Lamont's riders and a dozen or so townsmen, along with their motions and contorted faces coming into focus, showed Hatfield that he and Schmidt were in the center of a ring of excited spectators. Evan raised his arms with an effort, and went in again. Henry Schmidt was slow to react, but he got his guard up, only this time it was lower to protect his body, and Hatfield aimed higher.

Hitting Schmidt along the jaw was like hitting a stone wall. Most other men would have collapsed. Schmidt bobbed and weaved, took the blows and tried to protect his chin within the bend of a hunched-forward shoulder, but now he was on the defensive. Hatfield was still not angry, but his arms felt as though each one weighed a ton, and his lungs were afire as he continued to push forward. Finally Henry Schmidt gave ground for the first time, and the spectators yelled and roared, gesticulating with their fists and stirring dust as they moved around to see better.

The sheriff battered away, never missing, but no longer with the power he'd had earlier. Then he suddenly stepped back and dropped both arms. There was blood at the corner of Schmidt's mouth, and his right eye was puffily closing.

Hatfield sucked air a moment, gazing at his adversary, then he said: "Go on into the jailhouse, Mister Schmidt."

Without a word or another gesture, Henry Schmidt turned none too steadily, and, where the crowd parted to let him through, men hooted their derision that he ignored. He groped for the door latch. A spectator leaned, opened the door, and stepped back.

Men thumped Hatfield's back as he, too, walked across to the door and went inside. They probably would have also crowded in, but Hatfield kicked the door closed at his back.

Schmidt sank down upon a bench, hung his face in both hands, and faintly blood trickled to the floor. His breathing was as loud as that of a wind-broke horse.

Hatfield went behind the desk, leaned far down to rummage, and brought up his hidden whiskey bottle. He filled two glasses, topped off the upper half with water, and went over to push a glass at the settler.

"Take it," he commanded. Schmidt complied, straightening up as though his ribs and stomach pained him.

Hatfield went over to the edge of the desk, leaned, gulped air, shook off sweat, and gazed at the heavier man. "Drink it," he said. Again Schmidt complied.

Hatfield sipped his branch water and whiskey, remained silent until his breathing got closer to normal, then he went to the desk chair and eased down. He knew how Schmidt felt because he did not feel any better.

The whiskey helped. Hatfield put the glass aside and examined his skinned, battered hands. Schmidt was sitting up now, drinking as though the glass held medicine. His eye was almost closed. It was also turning slightly blue above and below. There were other contusions, but the broken lip at the corner of his mouth was swelling and it lent him the appearance of a man ready to sob.

Hatfield finally said: "Where's Langer?"

Schmidt's answer was prompt, but his injured mouth made the words thick. "Back at camp. I came alone. Langer didn't know I was coming."

Hatfield looked up. "Alone? You came in here looking for a fight, alone?" He wagged his head. "You're not very smart, Mister Schmidt. If you'd put me down, they'd have probably strung you up."

"You stole our horses!"

"Sure did. They're down at the public corrals, impounded by the law."

"You're the one that broke the law!"

Hatfield finished his whiskey and water and eased back in his chair. He steadily gazed at the battered, square-jawed settler, then he said—"Hell."—in a tone of monumental disgust and arose. "Empty your pockets on the desk, and hoist your britches legs so's I can see if you've got any hide-out weapons."

Schmidt was slow to arise, but Hatfield was in no hurry. Maybe Joe Lamont had been correct; maybe he was going to have to lock up every blasted one of them.

XIII

It was said that trouble, like rattlesnakes, came in pairs. Evan Hatfield was out back at the wash rack in the alley, using cold water on his bruised face and hands when Steve Clampitt came into the empty office and sang out. Hatfield stepped to the open back door and growled, then stepped back to his basin of cold water.

Clampitt had his storekeeper's apron rolled up and tucked into his belt. He looked in awe at Evan's bruises, but tactfully did not mention the fight, which he had seen through a window across the road. Instead he said: "There was a feller looking for you over at the store, Evan."

Hatfield reached for the towel. "What feller? Is he blind? The jailhouse has a sign over it."

Clampitt digested this surliness with a flinch. "Federal lawman, Evan."

Hatfield lowered the towel and turned. "Did he say that's what he was?"

"Well, no, but when he fished in a pocket to pay for the stogies he bought, I saw the little badge on his vest under the coat."

Hatfield leaned to peer in the wavery mirror at his face. "You want to know something, Steve? That little sawed-off son-of-a-bitch can hit like a stud horse."

Clampitt, about to comment on Hatfield's bruised face, changed his mind at the last moment and said: "I guess that deputy federal lawman was over here, looked in, and you was out back. Anyway, he asked about you . . . where you might be and all."

Hatfield reset his hat, flung away the water, hung the basin from its nail, and turned with the towel in his hand. "Thanks. I'll look him up. Care for some coffee?"

Clampitt declined the coffee but trooped inside behind the sheriff, then went out the roadway door back across to his store, having done his good deed for the day.

Hatfield went over to the café, had Barley fix three pails of stew and coffee, and, at the inquiring look he got, Hatfield said: "For the battling settler. Now I got every cell full."

Barley was not and never had been a tactful man. Unlike Steve Clampitt, Barley cocked his head, squinted, then said: "He got you a few times. Want to know what I think?"

Hatfield sat down at the counter. "Sure."

"That feller's fought for money, somewhere."

Hatfield had arrived at this same conclusion during the battle. "Fill me a cup of stew first, and I'll be eating it while you're making up the pails."

Barley nodded, making no move to depart. "But you gave one hell of an accountin' for yourself. Fellers around town are saying you're just as good now as you was ten years ago."

Hatfield sighed. "The stew, Barley." There was no one in the town of Hyland who knew how good Evan Hatfield had been ten years ago.

He was eating his bowl of antelope stew when the stranger walked in, nodded amiably, sat down. When Barley poked his face around the blanket partition, the, stranger said—"A bowl of the same."—then he watched Hatfield for a moment, considered the purple splotches and swellings, and said: "You're a hard man to get hold of, Sheriff."

Hatfield did not look up. He knew who the stranger was. "Not if you holler when you poke your head in the office doorway."

The stranger smiled. "I'll remember that." He extended a big hand, palm up, holding the circlet-and-star badge, so Hatfield could see it. "Deputy U.S. marshal from Denver." He closed his hand and pocketed the little badge. "Name's Charley Wheaton."

Hatfield finished the stew and shoved away the bowl as he straightened back for a look at the federal officer. Wheaton looked average in just about every way, except in the dead-level, stone-steady way he returned Evan's look. He was perhaps forty years old, tanned, lean, and loose-looking. Hatfield, who was a good judge of men, had no trouble coming up with his assessment this time—calm, straightforward, and deadly.

Barley brought the pails and the federal deputy helped Hatfield carry them across to the jail-house, but the federal officer lingered in the office, over by the rack of guns, until Hatfield returned from poking the little pails under each cell door. Orcutt and Horne were hungry, and silent. Henry Schmidt's mouth was too sore, and he did not appear to have much of an appetite anyway.

When Hatfield returned and closed the cell-room door, he gestured for Charley Wheaton to have a chair, and went over to sit at the desk, and wait.

The federal peace officer offered Evan a cigar, which was declined, then lit one for himself, and with a bemused expression gazed over at Sheriff Hatfield. "A week back the Land Office in Denver got a letter from some settlers, Sheriff. It said the law down here in Lost Valley wouldn't let the homesteaders go onto their land. The federal marshal sent me down to look around."

Evan eased the chair around a little so he was fully facing the federal officer, then he leaned back slightly to get comfortable, and started reciting everything that had happened up to the battle in the roadway this morning. The only thing he left out was his last discussion with Douglas Hyland. When he had finished, the cigar-smoking, calm man over by the door said: "Well, Sheriff, those people have title to the land."

"So does Mister Hyland, Marshal. I just told you . . . all I'm trying to do is keep the peace until Mister Hyland gets back. Then we'll know whose title is good."

"I saw the maps of government land up in Denver, Sheriff."

"Fine. Did you look up the titles for the land down here?"

Wheaton removed the cigar before replying. "No. But the clerks up there told me . . ."

"Marshal, clerks make mistakes. We all do. But even if they didn't make any, until Mister Hyland gets home with the results of his title search, no one trespasses on Hyland range, because, if they do, Mister Hyland's range riders are going to chouse them off, and that's exactly what I'm trying to prevent . . . someone getting killed."

Charley Wheaton examined the gray ash of his cigar for a moment before speaking again. "When will Mister Hyland get back, Sheriff?"

"By my calculations, maybe tomorrow. I sure hope to hell it's tomorrow. I'm getting worn to a frazzle keeping people apart. And you might as well know, because the settlers'll tell you anyway, last night I led a posse to steal their horses, fetch them back to town, and impound them."

Wheaton's gray eyes lifted from the end of his cigar. "You served impounding papers on them?"

Hatfield curbed his rising temper. "No, sir, and, if I had, they'd have shot me off my horse. One son-of-a-bitch was ready to shoot me yesterday just for trying to talk sense to them."

Marshal Wheaton went back to examining the cigar ash as he quietly said: "You better make out those papers and serve them, Sheriff, otherwise those people can swear out a warrant against you for horse stealing."

Evan smiled without a shred of humor. "There's no one to serve it, Marshal. I'm the only lawman in Lost Valley."

Wheaton's gray eyes swept up again. "You *were* the only lawman in Lost Valley, Sheriff."

Hatfield's antagonism was increasing by the moment. Marshal Wheaton's hint of condescension, his imperturbability, and now his hint about using his federal powers in something he knew almost nothing about, while Evan Hatfield had been bearing all the danger—and pain—made the sheriff sit there, staring at the other man. Finally he said: "Marshal, did you ever hear the story about that old Texas Ranger who rode over a hill with his men and came onto a big band of Mex raiders?"

Wheaton shook his head.

"Well, Marshal, the old Texan looked at the Mexicans, who were looking at him and his men, then the old ranger looked up and said . . . 'Lord, please be on our side, but, Lord, if you can't do that, then please, sir, go over and set under that tree out of the way, and watch the damnedest fight you ever saw.' "

Wheaton smiled, removed his stogie, and unwound gracefully up out of the chair. "I gather from that, Sheriff, that you're telling me to go sit under a tree, and stay out of this until it's settled."

Evan stood up, too, and smiled back. "Something like that, Marshal."

They went out front where afternoon shadows were thickening. The federal officer looked up and down the roadway, plugged the stogie back into his mouth, and said: "You have a nice town here, Sheriff." He strode northward in the direction of the rooming house.

Hatfield returned to his chair, gingerly probed some sore ribs, then searched among his drawers for one of the blank printed forms to be filled out for the impounding of livestock. He took fifteen minutes to fill the thing in and make a copy of it, then he went down into the cell room, and, when Henry Schmidt responded to Hatfield's order to approach the door of the cell, Hatfield shoved the paper through. Schmidt took it, frowned downward, then looked out at Hatfield. "What's this?"

"Legal notice that I'm going to impound your livestock."

"You already have them."

Hatfield leaned on the door. "Yeah. But this makes it legal." He and Schmidt exchanged a long look, while behind them across the little aisle Orcutt and William Horne were hanging on each word. Hatfield said: "You feeling all right?"

Schmidt's one good eye hardened. "Better'n you're feeling!"

Hatfield smiled a little. "You might be right at that. You hit hard."

"So do you."

"You're more experienced at that kind of fighting than I am."

"I've done my share of it, Sheriff."

"For money, Mister Schmidt?"

"Yes."

Hatfield and the bull-necked man continued to regard each other for a moment, then the sheriff said: "You want another drink of branch water and medicine?"

For the first time since they had met, Henry Schmidt's gaze showed something else besides violent dislike and antagonism. Even his voice was different. "I'd admire that, Sheriff."

Hatfield fished out the brass key, wordlessly unlocked the cell door, and led the way back up to the office. Orcutt and Horne watched in silence, then exchanged a long look of disbelief.

Henry Schmidt went to the same wall bench where he had sat before, and waited until the sheriff had doctored two glasses of malt whiskey with creek water, then Schmidt tasted his, licked his lips with care because one side of his mouth was swollen, and fixed Hatfield with his one good eye. "You could fight for money," he said. "You gave me the best fight I ever had from someone who's never climbed into a ring."

Hatfield chuckled. "No, thanks. About one more like that, Mister Schmidt, and I'd be riding a wheelchair." He sipped his drink. "Not bad whiskey, is it? I get a bottle every now and then when a freighter named Gallatin comes through the valley."

Schmidt ignored the comment about the whiskey. He drank it slowly, and leaned against the wall, gazing over at Hatfield. "You trying to soften me up, Sheriff?"

"Nope. I just figured you might ache as much as I do."

"But you're still Hyland's man."

"I never was Mister Hyland's man. I've known him a few years. He's tough, but he's fair and honest as the day is long. I've said it a dozen times, but I'll say it again . . . all I'm doing is keeping the peace. That's all I aim to do until Mister Hyland gets back. After that, if his title's no good, I'll personally ride with you folks to your homesteads. If it is good, I'll give you back your horses along with one day to get off his range. Care for a refill?"

Schmidt looked into his empty glass for a moment before answering. "No thanks. One more and I'd have to crawl back to the cell down on all fours." He looked up. "I think you're going to win, Sheriff."

Hatfield swished the dregs in his glass. "Mister Schmidt, pass me your word you won't make any more trouble, and I'll loan you a horse to get back to your family." Hatfield put aside the glass.

The battered settler was slow to answer. "You got my word, Sheriff."

Hatfield arose, fished in his desk for Schmidt's personal possessions, then waited, and, when the settler had everything shoved back into his pockets, Hatfield led the way down to the livery barn. Over in front of the general store several loafers slouching in the shade, stared, and one man said: "I'll be damned, will you look there? They was trying to beat each other to death this morning."

XIV

Without Hatfield's knowledge the federal deputy marshal hired a horse and rode down along Arapaho Creek. He spent a couple of hours there and was making a leisurely return to town when he was halted by converging range men. Joe Lamont led them, and evidently Joe had watched the marshal go down to the creek, and had waited to waylay him on the ride back.

By the time Charley Wheaton reached Hyland, it was suppertime, and, although Marshal Wheaton ate at Barley Smith's counter, he missed encountering the sheriff by a half hour. They did not meet until after nightfall when Marshal Wheaton visited the saloon for a nightcap and met Sheriff Hatfield at the bar. Wheaton took a bottle, invited Hatfield to a table, and, when they were comfortable, Wheaton related his adventure.

143

Hatfield sat in silence until Wheaton was finished, then looked stonily at the federal officer. "I thought you were going to stay in town, Marshal."

Wheaton was refilling his little shot glass when he answered. "That was your idea, not mine." He leaned also to refill Hatfield's glass. "My job is to find out what's happening down here. I got your version this morning and their version this afternoon." He raised his glance, smiling. "And while I didn't figure on it, I got the cattlemen's version, too." Wheaton raised his head, dropped the whiskey straight down, and did not even blink as he set his empty glass aside, and felt inside his coat for a stogie. "If you're waiting for my judgment, Sheriff, I don't have one. Nobody around here seems to be exactly wearing a halo." He lit up. "And if Hyland returns tomorrow, that should pretty well settle the main issue."

Hatfield raised his glass, downed its contents, and blew out a flammable breath. "If . . . ," he said. Wheaton gazed over at him so he finished it. "If Mister Hyland returns tomorrow."

"You got doubts, Sheriff?"

"No, not about his intentions, but things don't always work out the way we want them to, do they, Marshal?"

Wheaton trickled smoke. "I sure hope he returns tomorrow, Sheriff, because an awful lot of people are expecting him to, and, if he don't, it's going to aggravate conditions, isn't it?"

Evan did not answer the question. He had just glanced up in time to see those two settlers named Dent and Arbuckle walk in. There was something about those two. There had been something when they'd first walked into his office, but he could not pin it down except that they only half resembled settlers; otherwise, they left Hatfield with a feeling that they were stockmen, or at least had been stockmen. Nor was it simply because they wore shell belts and six-guns. It was the way they wore them.

Marshal Wheaton caught Hatfield's attention with a question. "Those two are men you know, Sheriff?"

"Met them this afternoon. They're settlers. At least that's what they told me, but the settlers I've met lately don't commonly carry guns or look quite as natural atop saddle horses."

Wheaton watched Arbuckle and Dent approach the bar, removed his cigar, and said: "Up north, where there's a lot more homesteading, we see quite a few like that pair. Range riders turned settlers. A hundred and sixty acres of decent land beats riding in blistering heat and blizzards for ten dollars a month, Sheriff."

Hatfield shoved out his legs under the table and continued to watch Arbuckle and Dent, but only peripherally because Marshal Wheaton was speaking again.

"You remind me of the little Dutch kid who shoved his thumb in the dike, Sheriff. You're stopping settlers from going up Arapaho Creek, and meanwhile more settlers are arriving . . . like those two at the bar. It's called progress."

Hatfield shook his head. "Growth, Marshal, not progress."

Wheaton accepted that in his unruffled manner. "Growth. All right, we'll call it growth, and, Sheriff, I can tell you that for every one you hold back, ten more are on the way. By next autumn you'll have 'em camping around your town like honey bees at a rose bush. You can't dam them up east of the stage road."

"I don't mean to. I wouldn't have done it this time, if there hadn't been damned good reason to do it. By next summer we'll know where they can squat and where they can't."

Wheaton's steady gaze was unwavering. "That's not exactly what I meant, Sheriff. I mean that right now you're protecting Hyland's range. Next summer it will be other cowmen. Maybe Hyland, too, but the other stockmen in Lost Valley. You'll be standing there with your thumb shoved in the dike trying to hold back the sea."

Hatfield sighed. "You didn't understand a damned thing I told you today, Marshal. I'm not protecting Hyland as much as I'm trying to protect those damned settlers. As for the other cowmen . . . if settlers roll in with clear titles to

146

land, legal titles, my job will be to see that their legal rights are protected."

"Can you do it, Sheriff?"

"Why don't we wait until it happens and see if I can do it, Marshal?"

Wheaton removed his stogie to comment when several loud, rough voices over at the bar over-rode all the quieter voices in the room and Hatfield swung to look. He knew the angry cowboy, not by name but by sight, who was easing away from the bar as he faced Arbuckle and Dent. The man worked for an outfit called Cedarbrake, which lay about twelve miles south-east of town and was owned by a corporation of Eastern investors. There were two other Cedar-brake range men along the bar, but they were northward, behind Dent and Arbuckle, and, although they had turned at the sounds of friction, so far they had not moved. Still, what bothered Evan Hatfield was that this was how killings occurred—one man in front holding attention, and two men behind in the crowd.

Hatfield shoved up to his feet as the angry cowboy said: "You god-damned squatters got no right in here anyhow. You're supposed to be drinkin' swill at the trough with the other pigs."

Hatfield was moving before Cal Arbuckle, who was closest to the red-faced Cedarbrake rider, stepped sideways away from the bar in order to have moving room. Into the sudden barroom

147

hush Arbuckle said: "You're forcing this, mister."

The cowboy sneered. "You clod-hopping bastard!"

One of the other Cedarbrake riders farther along the bar raised a hand in warning, trying to convey by gesture that someone was coming up behind the settler-baiting range man.

Arbuckle took down a shallow breath. Hatfield could see that while he was still ten feet from the Cedarbrake rider. Arbuckle was going to fight. In a clear, rough voice of command Hatfield closed the distance in three big strides and rammed a six-gun muzzle into the back of the Cedarbrake range man. "You get on your horse, mister, get out of Hyland, and don't you ever come back."

No one moved. The other patrons were as hushed and motionless as stone. Harry Dent, behind Arbuckle along the bar, had a hand on his gun butt. Those other two Cedarbrake men were standing the same way, undecided and intently watchful. One of them moved a little and from over by the door a voice came as distinct and cold as steel balls falling on glass spoke.

"Take your hand off that gun . . . you, with the red shirt!"

Eyes swiveled in that direction, but otherwise none of the patrons moved. The cowboy in the red shirt lifted his gun hand very slowly and draped it over the bar top. The man by the door shifted his stogie from one side of his mouth to the other side. He was holding a long-barreled Colt.

Hatfield reached around to lift away the gun of the man he was covering, and the cowboy whirled with a haymaking wild swing. Hatfield was already leaning so he simply leaned lower to allow the arm to sail above, then he caught cloth in his reaching hand, yanked the red-faced man around, and swung his six-gun sideways to the temple. The Cedarbrake cowboy went down in a heap in the sawdust of the barroom floor.

These other two Cedarbrake men wilted. They hadn't really been prepared anyway when their half-drunk friend picked the fight.

Every eye in the crowded saloon went from the unconscious man at Hatfield's feet to the cigar-smoking stranger over by the door with the long-barreled six-gun.

The barman made a perfunctory sweep of the worn wood in front of him with his bar rag, then leaned to look down at the unconscious man. "He always drinks too much," the barman plaintively said into the silence.

Hatfield ignored that and growled at the pair of Cedarbrake men behind Dent. "Pick up your friend and haul him back to the ranch. And keep him there. Tell the range boss I don't want to see him back here in town. Get him out of here!"

Gradually, as the unconscious man was hoisted and balanced between his friends to be taken out into the star-bright night, the saloon returned almost to normal, but it would not actually be normal again tonight. Hatfield's annoyance, the efficient way he had downed the fighting cowboy, was only part of what superseded all other matters under discussion along the bar and among the tables. The other subject was the identity of that cigar-smoking stranger with the fast draw and the long-barreled Colt.

But Wheaton seemed ignorant of being the focal point for a lot of sidelong looks as he resumed his chair at the table and poured both their glasses full again. Then he smiled over at Hatfield and said: "Here's hoping you'll always be able to get a handle on them, Sheriff. You did that right well."

Hatfield did not smile back as he ignored the glass and said: "Thanks for the help." Then he leaned to arise and head for the rooming house. "And I'm right obliged for the whiskey."

Charley Wheaton nodded, pulled on his cigar, and watched the sheriff's departure through narrowed eyes, impervious to the glances he was getting.

Hatfield paused to breathe deeply of fresh night air when Cal Arbuckle walked out behind him and said: "I guess that was the best way to end it, Sheriff, but the damned fool deserved shooting."

Hatfield turned. He was tired, his body ached, and right now he was sick and tired of looking at settlers, so he said: "Mister, no half-drunk feller deserves shooting, not even a silly one like that bastard. Good night."

Hatfield crossed the road and went up to the rooming house. The uppermost saving thought in his mind as he got ready for bed was that tomorrow Douglas Hyland would return. Then, one way or the other, this whole damned over-size headache would be resolved. And if he didn't return?

Hatfield dropped his head upon the pillow completely unwilling to believe that. When Douglas Hyland said he would be back in two weeks, a man could count on it to the day. With that thought firmly in mind, Hatfield fell asleep—and snored.

When he awakened, hours later, and moved, his muscles ached almost as much as they had right after the fight, but by the time he had shaved, dressed, and was ready for breakfast down at Barley's place, he had warmed out of the stiffness like an old horse.

Orcutt and Horne greeted him with loud demands to be released as he had released Henry Schmidt, and he ignored them until the pails had been shoved under each door, then he stood up, looking benign, said nothing, and retreated back to the office. Not until the liveryman came shoving in breathlessly to report that someone had stolen those impounded settler horses did

Hatfield's firm conviction that this was to be a good day for him begin to waver.

He returned southward with the agitated liveryman, walked all around the empty corrals, decided that reading sign in an area where everyone wore those flat-heeled freighter-type cowhide boots was a waste of time, and growled for his horse to be saddled, then strode back to the jailhouse for his Winchester.

He was emerging with the booted saddle gun draped in one bent arm and encountered the federal marshal. Wheaton raised one eyebrow. "Indians coming, Sheriff?"

Hatfield was not in a facetious mood. "Those blasted settlers stole back their horses last night."

As he turned to stride southward, Marshal Wheaton fell in beside him. "Could it have been someone else, Sheriff? It didn't have to be the squatters, did it?"

Hatfield turned a vinegary expression upon the marshal. "No, it didn't have to be. It could have been the Four Horsemen of the Apocalypse. They got bucked off while riding through the sky last night and stole the settlers' horses for replace-ments."

Wheaton said no more. When Evan Hatfield buckled the boot into place on the underside of his rosadero, then led the horse out back before mounting, Marshal Wheaton stood like a preacher with both hands clasped together under his coat in back, watching. As soon as Hatfield rode away, the marshal collared the liveryman and ordered a livery animal brought up and saddled for him.

Hatfield looped his reins, rolled and lit a smoke, and sniffed the morning air. It had a slightly metallic scent to it. He scanned the sky, found some soiled remnants of clouds a long way off northward, and decided it was going to rain, if not tonight, then tomorrow.

The land was empty as usual; the grass was beginning to head out and cure on the stalk. Autumn was not far off, a couple of months away. Hatfield decided to follow the land swells and, while doing this, caught sight of distant movement, men and horses heading in his direction. He walked his horse along, watching in puzzled interest because, although he could make out the horses fairly well, they did not all seem to be under saddle. Perhaps four or five of them were riderless among a pair of riders. His first thought was that Lamont had led a raid and had come off second best. Then, as he stood in his stirrups, something compelled him to look back. Marshal Wheaton was cantering easily along in Hatfield's wake.

He halted, sat flat down, and waited. By the time the federal deputy came up, those other horsemen were a mile closer, and Wheaton pointed in their direction. "Bringing them back, Sheriff."

He was correct. Hatfield said nothing as the two of them turned to intercept the distant horses. Henry Schmidt, unmistakable in build even in the saddle, was herding the same livestock ahead of him that Sheriff Hatfield and his posse men had gone to such trouble to steal a couple of nights back. Riding in the drag, looking dejected, was one of those sorrel-headed gangling youths, the son of incarcerated William Horne.

Hatfield halted, looped his reins, and leaned upon the saddle horn, waiting. When Schmidt arrived, he looked with interest at Marshal Wheaton, then ignored him to nod to Hatfield as he said: "Our horses must have got out last night and headed for home."

Hatfield was staring at the crestfallen youth. No horse got out of those public corrals without some two-legged help.

"We caught them a couple of hours back," stated Henry Schmidt, "and was bringing them back."

Hatfield continued to lean and gaze at the self-conscious tall youth. Then he shifted his attention to Schmidt, whose closed eye was purple and slightly less swollen today, but was still tightly closed. For a moment they regarded one another before the sheriff gruffly spoke.

"Take 'em back with you, Mister Schmidt. It's too long a drive back to town, so keep them down there with you folks."

They continued to look at one another. Schmidt finally said: "We're right obliged, Mister Hatfield."

Evan ignored that to say: "Don't drape any harness on them."

Schmidt nodded. "We'll be right where we are now when you come back, Mister Hatfield." Then he considered the federal officer and said: "The womenfolk are getting breakfast, if you gents are hungry."

Hatfield lifted his reins. "Thanks all the same but we've eaten." Then he looked stonily at the gangling youth. "Boy, the next time you get a bright idea like that, you ask some older man first. You understand me?"

The sorrel-headed youth got red in the face. "Yes, sir, I understand you."

Hatfield bobbed his head at Henry Schmidt and turned to ride back toward town. Charley Wheaton, who had not opened his mouth back there, did not open it now until they had roof tops in sight. Then he yawned, stretched, looked at the sky, the rolling miles of rangeland, and said: "Sheriff, like I already said, I think you'll make it work."

XV

Something happened before noon that ordinarily did not bother folks in Hyland. It rarely bothered the sheriff, either. The morning stage from the north was late.

Hatfield stopped by the corral yard and spoke briefly with the company's local supervisor on his way back to the livery barn. All the stage man could say was that he'd been told by the previous driver from up north that there had been some bad flash floods over in the direction of Denver. Hatfield and Wheaton walked their horses down to the barn, handed them to the day men, and started back toward the jailhouse. Wheaton said: "It's still early, Sheriff."

Hatfield fired up his stove, put new grounds in the pot, filled it with water, and set it atop the solitary burner of his wood stove, then he tossed down his hat and gazed at Marshal Wheaton. "And suppose Mister Hyland's titles are good?"

The marshal's concern had never been anything but clinical. "Then the squatters along the creek will have to leave."

Hatfield went to his desk, sat down, heard noise in the roadway, and sprang up to step to a front window, and peer out. The morning stage had just made its big swing up the road to enter the palisaded corral yard. He stood a moment in thought, then went to the stove to poke in another piece of wood, which was not needed, lifted the lid of the coffee pot, peered in, replaced the lid, and went back to his desk. Marshal Wheaton watched all this wearing an expression of faint amusement.

Minutes passed before Hatfield heard boot steps approaching out front. They stopped, a strong hand lifted his latch, and shoved the door in. Hatfield started to arise, then froze where he was standing. The newcomer was a total stranger. He was pale-eyed with a droopy cavalryman's moustache, and had an ivory-stocked six-gun tied to his right leg. He held the door aside, nodded at Wheaton and Hatfield, then moved slightly to one side as Douglas Hyland walked in.

Hyland looked drawn. His clothes were rumpled. His normally craggy, rough-set features were flaccid as he stepped into the room and nodded at Evan Hatfield, then eyed Marshal Wheaton. Before he could speak, the stranger with the cavalryman's moustache said: "Charley . . . they said you'd be down here."

Wheaton arose. "Sheriff Hatfield, this is Sam Hinkley, deputy U.S. marshal out of Denver. Sam, Sheriff Evan Hatfield."

The pale-eyed man stepped ahead and pumped Hatfield's hand, then stepped back as Douglas

Hyland pulled a chair around and sank into it. "Evan, everything all right?"

Hatfield felt for the chair behind him. "No, everything isn't all right."

Hyland accepted that as though he had expected no other answer. "Do you have a shot around the office, Evan?"

Hatfield leaned far down, drew forth his malt whiskey, and set up a couple of shot glasses. Hyland came over, poured himself a jolt, swallowed it, refilled the glass, and returned to the chair, holding it.

Hatfield was beginning to feel as though someone had yanked out the ground from under him. Hyland motioned for Marshal Sam Hinkley to help himself to a shot, too, but Hinkley remained over by the door, evidently willing to be an onlooker now, as Douglas Hyland reached inside his rumpled coat and brought forth some carefully folded papers that he held on his lap as he said: "Mister Hinkley and I've been riding stages since day before yesterday. When I was thirty years younger, getting bruised and shaken didn't bother me. I could sleep on a stagecoach. But not any more." He leaned to pitch the papers atop Hatfield's desk, downed his second jolt of whiskey, and seemed to revive.

Evan considered the folded papers, several of which were maps. He knew the answer was in them, but he preferred hearing it from the man they called the lord of Lost Valley. "Did you get it settled?" Hatfield asked quietly, clasping both hands atop the desk.

Hyland blew out a whiskey breath before answering. "Yes. It took three days but it's settled. My deeds are perfectly legal."

Hatfield loosened slightly. "Those land people up in Denver were wrong, then?"

"Not exactly, Evan. In fact, the titles they issued were proper and all . . . they just were issued for the wrong township. Someone didn't complete a file search of old deeds. In Denver they said that happened in Omaha, but my guess is that in Omaha they'd say it happened in Denver, but the main point is my land legally belongs to Lost Valley Ranch."

Charley Wheaton glanced up at Marshal Hinkley. "They sent you along to verify this, Sam?"

Hinkley's answer was ambiguous. "They told me to come down here with Mister Hyland to verify it, yes, but they also said you were likely to need help. How many settlers have we got on Mister Hyland's range?"

Wheaton looked at Hatfield for the answer to that. Evan let go a long breath, then eased back in his chair. "They won't be troublesome, Mister Hinkley. There are three wagons of them along Arapaho Creek on Mister Hyland's range, and I've got a couple more locked in my cells."

Douglas Hyland stared at Hatfield. "Three wagons of them on my range, Evan?"

Charley Wheaton spoke first. "Mister Hyland, Sheriff Hatfield did a hell of a job keeping your riders and those settlers from going at it, and in the process he got threatened with guns, and damned near whipped in a fist fight. I'd say you owe him a big load of thanks."

Hyland listened to this, then gripped the little shot glass in his fist, and scowled at it.

Hatfield, who knew Douglas Hyland as well as anyone did, guessed what thoughts were going through the older man's mind. Douglas Hyland might be tired, worn down, and right now feeling the subdued fire of two jolts of whiskey, but he was still flinty, unyielding Douglas Hyland, and trespassers on his range, regardless of the circumstances, were intolerable to him. When he raised his eyes, Hatfield was waiting to say: "You don't just climb on a stage and head for Albuquerque, then over to Denver, and expect everything here to remain the same when you damned well knew there were settlers coming. Maybe someday when I feel like it, I'll tell you the whole story. Right now, Douglas, we'll ride down there and let the marshals tell those folks they're in the wrong township, and you can get a little taste of how they feel."

But Hyland was not ready to go anywhere except to his home place. As he arose, he pointed to the copies of maps and deeds atop the desk. "Keep them, Evan. Right now I'm going home to sleep for a couple of days." He turned toward the door, then glanced back. "Step out front with me for a moment, will you?"

Hatfield arose and walked around the desk to comply. Outside, those distant soiled clouds were beginning to fill up and broaden, otherwise the afternoon was a little warmer than the morning had been and everything else seemed about the same.

Inside, Marshal Hinkley finally stepped to the desk to fill a glass from Hatfield's bottle, then he faced Charley Wheaton. "That's a tough old man, that Hyland."

Wheaton had a judgment of his own to offer. "Hatfield's more than tough, Sam. He's tough and sensible."

Hinkley downed the whiskey and made a face. Then he said: "How many of these clod-hoppers are we going to have trouble with?"

"Serious trouble, none, Sam. Hatfield broke 'em to lead one at a time. I'll tell you about it on the ride back to Denver."

Hinkley considered refilling his glass, gave up the idea, and said: "You're to go back, Charley. I'm to go on down to Raton where a pair of Chihuahua renegades named Jensen and Rowe have been stealing horses and cattle and driving them down over the line."

Outside in the pleasant sunlight with the busy town handily ignoring them as they leaned upon the tie rack, Douglas Hyland was frowning at the ground as he spoke.

"It was a damned close thing, Evan. My grandfather recorded the old Mexican deeds in Albuquerque . . . in Spanish. Just by damned good luck did those old files get turned over to the Americans when we took over this country out here, but no one could read them and some got thrown out and burned. Mine happened to be saved. It was nothing but luck." Hyland raised his face. "I worried about you and Joe up here. That feller inside was right, I'm sure of it . . . you kept the peace. About those squatters along the creek . . . I'll ride down there with you tomorrow."

Hatfield said: "No, you won't, Douglas. So far I've been getting by on the skin of my teeth, because I could guess about how people would act. It's been touch and go, but so far no one's got shot."

"What's that got to do with me going down there with you tomorrow?"

"A lot. I know you as well as I know myself. Those folks aren't going to like what the marshals tell them. If you were along and they got rough in their talk, you'd send your riding crew to visit them. That's been your reaction to trespassers ever since I've been in this country. But not

162

tomorrow, Douglas, not any more at all. I'll go down there with the marshals in the morning. We'll get it all settled and get those folks to move back east of the road."

Douglas Hyland said nothing for a long moment while he gazed at Evan Hatfield, then slowly his craggy face split into a rare, flinty smile, and he pushed out a hand. "I never doubted for long that you'd be able to handle it, Evan. Not for very long. Come by the ranch in a day or two and we'll have supper and some whiskey afterward, and talk. Agreed?"

Hatfield nodded, watched Douglas Hyland head south to hire a horse at the livery barn, and remained standing in the warming sunlight for several minutes afterward, before he reëntered the jailhouse office to make plans for the morning ride down along Arapaho Creek with the two federal deputy marshals.

Maybe he should have been a harness maker, after all. It was going to be raining cats and dogs in the morning, and he knew it. Harness makers did not have to ride through rainstorms to carry unwelcome news to folks.

IRON
MARSHAL

I

It rarely happens in life, and yet it has been recorded that occasionally a man lives on past his functional usefulness, and in his sundown years finds that he has become a legend. Texas Jim Collins was such a man. From the oldest to the youngest there was none in New Mexico who had not at one time or another encountered some saga relating to Texas Jim, but particularly was this true of the people of Anza County. It was especially true of the residents of Buellton, seat of government for Anza County, for Buellton, aside from being the town of the powerful Setter family, was Jim Collins's bailiwick; he had administered the law in Buellton for twenty-five years. He had without help cowed wild Texans up from the mesquite country with their trail herds. He had faced down Wes Hardin, Bill Longley, and Diamond Dan Duryea of the short-gun fraternity.

He had not always triumphed, but he was still alive, which was victory, because the others weren't. Texas Jim had a bad shoulder, the result of a notched bullet. This shoulder sat a little lower than its companion. He also had a limp, the result of a slightly stiff knee wound. Altogether, he had eleven gunshot- and knife-wound scars on his body. Once, he'd been creased above the temple by a .44-40 ball. He combed his gray hair over that gouge because the normal hair did not grow back after the wound had healed, leaving a long, pink, shiny scar.

Jim Collins was not, as most gunfighters were not, a complicated man. He feared nothing on this earth; he believed implicitly in a right and a wrong that had no shades of gray. A man did right or he did wrong; he stole or he did not steal; he killed or he did not kill. Jim, possessing no fear, had no patience, either. His enemies—and he had his share of them—said he never thought for himself, that his gun thought for him. But his friends said simply that Jim was the straightest-shooting lawman New Mexico had ever known, not excluding Pat Garrett, and they meant this two ways: the obvious way, because he never missed what he shot at, and the less obvious way, meaning that he was as honest as the day is long.

This was the way Jim Collins's world regarded him after twenty-five years of unrelenting law enforcement. He had never married, and as far as anyone knew he had no relatives living; at least he'd never mentioned any. He was a raw-boned, loose-moving, high-headed man with a yeasty flash to his light blue eyes. He drank a little—more now than he had a quarter of a century before—and he gambled a little. But he had only one or two close friends, lived in the same backroom at the jailhouse he'd taken up residence in when he'd first pinned on the marshal's badge in Buellton, and was just as much an enigma to the folks of Anza County now as he'd been the day he first rode into town, up out of some backwater town down in Texas.

Every four years someone had filed to oppose Jim at election time, and every four years the Setters had exerted their power to have him reëlected. But despite this, no one in Buellton believed, although sometimes disgruntled people said it, that old John Setter owned Texas Jim Collins.

Old John owned everything else, though. He had arrived in Buellton two years ahead of Texas Jim, and in many ways these two were much alike. Neither of them feared man or devil—or each other. But where they differed primarily was in the core of their unshakable convictions. Jim believed in right for right's sake. John believed in money and only money. Inevitably then, since both these cold-blooded men had spent a quarter century serving the things they fanatically believed in, their paths had steadily diverged until Texas Jim ruled Buellton so undeviatingly that it was a model of orderliness during times as stormy and violent as anyone had ever known in the gunfighting West, while John Setter acquired a cattle empire covering thousands upon thousands of grassland acres, blocks of town property, and the wealth that went with such substantial foundations as these—plus political power as well, that ordinarily accompanies ruthless men in their relentless search for great gain.

They were alike, and yet those twenty-five violent years had made them different, too. For example, the time John's oldest boy Carlos splintered the arm of an itinerant faro dealer at the Golden Slipper Casino in a drunken shooting spree. Carlos was brought down by an overhand, hard-arcing slash from behind. Texas Jim had simply drawn his gun, stepped up close, and struck. Carlos had lain unconscious with a mild concussion for two days and old John had sent for three killers; he kept them on a leash until it was certain Carlos would recover, then he had paid them off and sent them on their way. He never said a word to Jim, and afterward, when they had met, they were civil. But Jim had known about the gunfighters, and, although he never said it, he had expected John Setter to act no differently. In reversed circumstances he would have acted exactly the same way. But that's how it was; Jim did not temporize and John accepted no excuses. They were alike and yet they were different.

Buellton, in its hell-roaring past, had been simply a cow town. The spur track of the Texas-Northern Railway had brought trail herds initially, but after the Panic of 1893, when the

170

bottom dropped out of the beef market, Buellton, under Jim Collins's guns and John Setter's calculating shrewdness, did not die as did Abilene and Dodge City. It had retrenched for a few years, then it began once more to grow. Slower this time, but more solidly. The freighters came. Setter built warehouses for them. Wells were dug, and settlers trickled in to take up| land. Merchants came to supply settlers, and wagon mechanics, blacksmiths, wheelwrights came to service the freight lines.

When cattle came back strongly again, John Setter owned more range, more she stock, and good Durham cross bulls than a man on a tall horse could begin to count. Livestock buyers from Kansas City and Chicago opened offices. Buellton came out of the doldrums bigger, more prosperous than ever, and John Setter sat on his verandah up on Setter's hill, surrounded by his three sons and one daughter, as hard and as uncompromising as ever, exulting in his wealth and his blessings, while down in town Jim Collins strode the plank walks, undisputed gunfighting king of all he surveyed, but twenty-five years older.

Texas Jim's legend never diminished. It was a thing of iron; there were times when it was almost a millstone, too, for it attracted other men who thought their gun prowess superior and whose restless spirits could not rest until they had tried

Texas Jim. South of Buellton, beyond the tar-paper shacks down there, was the boot hill cemetery. Jim Collins's guns had planted a number of that graveyard's permanent guests; each one adding fresh luster to the iron legend of unbeatable, incorruptible Jim Collins, marshal of Buellton, New Mexico.

Buellton had another cemetery; it was east of town upon a little, tended hill. Here the respectable people were buried. The people of substance and industry such as John Setter's wife Nettie, dead seven years the spring that Christel, old John's only daughter, was nearly killed by a runaway.

It happened in this manner. Christel was twenty at the time, and, as old John had once said proudly, she was "as pretty as new money." She was spoiled, too. John had done that even before Nettie died, but afterward people said, if old John Setter had a blind spot, it was his girl Christel. She wasn't just willful, though, she was also beautiful. Along with these things she was proud, as yeasty in her own high-breasted, breathtaking way as old John was in his way. She had a phæton buggy imported from back East; it had sparkling yellow wheels and a glossy red undercarriage. Christel drove it to a matched Hamiltonian team of chestnuts with flaxen manes and tails, and she drove it like she was going to die tomorrow and everything had to be done today.

Most folks felt they were entitled to half a roadway; Christel also felt this way, but she took her half out of the middle, sometimes with painful results to the settler wagons with their plodding teams that could not get out of her way in time. Then she had the runaway.

It was a warm spring day with a water-blue sky overhead and the air was as clear and heady as good wine. Christel took a drive down from Setter's hill southward, out and around town, and was flashing back northward toward Buellton up the north-south stage road, running with the sunbeams. She saw the horseman dead ahead, going toward town, also, and, if she'd looked, she'd have noticed that he was riding his horse in a hackamore with the *mecate* tied close so the animal could not suddenly duck its head for bucking; in other words, the stranger was riding a green-broke colt. She didn't heed these things; she didn't give an inch, even when the swift rattle of her buggy and the racing breath of her team made the colt tuck its tail and roll big eyes as she swept in from behind him.

She did see the stranger twist to look back, but he was only a man to her, a stranger in the town that belonged to her father. She cracked her whip with a pistol-shot sound and started past. At that second the stranger's colt exploded, got his head down and bawled once, then bucked for all he was worth. The stranger rode him straight up and scratching. His sun-darkened face was nearly black with fury and he turned the littlest bit as Christel's team came even, lashed out with his heavy, shot-loaded bronco-buster's quirt, caught Christel's near side horse across the jaw—and the runaway was on.

Buellton did not forget this for a long time because the bolting colt kept even with the runaway team right up through town, scattering people like quail out of the roadway, causing wagoners and riders to saw frantically out of the way, then passed northward on out of town for a quarter mile with dust rising up the full distance of Main Street.

Then the stranger got his colt run down and controlled, and he also jerked Christel's team to a slamming halt. What he did next put an abrupt silence to all the angry profanity back in town among the watching people. He piled out of his saddle without a word, caught Christel Setter by the arm, jerked her down, and bent her powerfully over one bent knee, and used the palm of one gloved hand to give her a licking. He then, still without saying a word, threw her back into the buggy, mounted his colt, and rode all the way back to Buellton, swung off at the livery barn, and told the slack-jawed hostler to rub his horse down, box stall it, and give it the best hay available—but no grain.

No one knew this man. They watched him step

across to the Golden Slipper and disappear inside, his face still as black as thunder. He was a tall man with the flare of shoulders tapering to small waist and lean-downed flanks that indicated a born and bred range man. He wore black trousers and a black shirt. Even his stiff-brimmed hat was black. So were his eyes, black and as steady as stone.

At the Golden Slipper bar this stranger leaned down to order ale. Where the saloon's other customers slouched easily where they stood or sat, this newcomer kept his shoulders straight as though that searing anger would not let go, as though fiery energy and fulsome wrath were the only emotions he now experienced. He was drinking the ale when Jim Collins strode in, studied the stranger briefly from the doorway, then crossed over to stand beside him, and also order ale. In the background, townsmen and range riders glided in, too; they wanted to see this; it was going to be something to remember.

Jim got his ale. He put his blue gaze upon the barman until that functionary took the hint and walked clear to the north end of the room. Then Jim turned, leaned there, and gauged the stranger in his dark clothing with his lashed-down ivory-butted six-gun, and he said: "Mister, that wasn't the smartest thing you ever did, so, when you're finished with that drink, you get back on that colt and ride on out of Buellton."

The stranger might not have heard at all; he didn't face around toward Jim, he just went on cooling himself out with that ale. His half-handsome face with its layer upon layer of suntan did not change one bit. Then he said: "You her father, Marshal?"

"No. No relation at all."

"I see." The stranger put his empty glass aside, turned from the waist, and regarded Jim Collins for a long time before he quietly said: "What crime did I commit?"

"None," said Jim just as calmly. "But I don't want any killings in this town, mister, so you just ride on and there won't be any."

"You mean her husband'll come after me?"

"She's not married, mister."

"Then who . . . ?"

"She's John Setter's daughter," pronounced Jim Collins, and paused, waiting for that to take effect. When it did not, when the tall stranger's smooth face showed nothing, Jim said: "Her paw's a big man hereabouts. He's got about fifty cowboys riding for him, and unlikely to overlook what you did to his girl."

The stranger faintly nodded. He thought on what Jim had said a moment, then he spoke plainly: "I see. Her paw's got a spoiled daughter and he thinks the sun rises an' sets on her. Well, Marshal, it's not a new story. The trouble with folks like that is they don't study out in advance who they can walk over and who they can't. Maybe she was a mite old for an old-fashioned spankin', but will you honestly tell me you don't think she had that coming?"

Jim gazed at the stranger with no expression showing. "The only thing I'll tell you," he said, "is keep on riding. Like I said, I don't want any killings in Buellton."

Jim pushed off the bar, nodded to the stranger, and started across the totally silent roomful of spectators. No one said a word until Jim was at the door.

Then the stranger called softly: "Marshal, I put a lot of miles under me today. That colt is tired and so am I. I thank you for your advice, but we won't be leaving for a day or two."

He then turned his back on the room, beckoned the barman back, and said loud enough for Jim Collins at the doorway, and everyone else close by to hear: "Bartender, another ale. But this time take it from the bottom of the ice bucket, not off the top."

Texas Jim stood quietly considering the stranger. He seemed to be balancing some notions in his mind. But he said no more, and a moment later he continued on his way out into the golden brightness of this fateful day, walking easily along toward his jailhouse.

It mattered not one whit to Jim Collins what the dark-garbed stranger did. He had delivered his ultimatum. The stranger could abide by it or not, as he saw fit. Boot hill always had an open grave waiting.

Buellton, fastening upon this bizarre affair, had a field day with it. Some shrugged over the foolishness of the stranger. A few deplored what was now certain to ensue. But on one score you couldn't get an argument—Christel Setter had gotten something she'd been needing badly since the day her mother had died.

II

A little after 11:00 three horsemen came quietly walking their horses side-by-side down Main Street. They didn't look entirely alike, yet there was an unmistakable stamp of kinship to them. They were of a size, about average, and they were all in their twenties with the fair-haired one appearing closest to thirty. This was Carlos Setter; he had a square jaw but a loose mouth. His eyes were like old John's—pale and frosty and shadowed with pride and toughness. The next brother was Reginald—called Reg. He seemed an easy-going, good-natured man; he was known far and wide for horsemanship. It was known that when the Mexican bronco-busters couldn't take the snap out of a horse, Reg could. He had a way with him; some said, who should've known, that he got this unique gift from his mother. Old-timers remembered Nettie as a woman who had, in her youth, made some of the finest reining horses in Anza County. The last of the Setter brothers was Frank. He was the least talkative of the trio and in many ways most like his father. Frank was barely twenty-four, yet he had a knack for seeing straight to the point of any discussion. And he was very good with a gun; all the Setter boys, though, were top-notch pistoleers. Still, when the three of them were out for some such purpose as the one that brought them to Buellton today, it was Frank who made the decisions and who gave the orders.

They passed along under half a hundred sly-watching pairs of eyes as though unconscious of the whispers passing in their wake. They halted at the Golden Slipper's tie rack, got down with calm deliberation, tied up, and stepped across wood to push on inside. The barman saw them instantly; so did the dozen or so loafers at the gaming tables or over at the bar. No one said anything until those three men leaned over the bar, standing casually, casting their rummaging gazes over the room's occupants. Then the barman, making elaborate swipes with a damp rag, said: "He ain't here, boys. He left about an hour ago."

Frank finished his study and faced around. "Where did he go, Sam?"

"Dunno. The marshal told him to ride on. He said he'd leave in a day or two. Did you try the hotel?"

Frank shook his head, looked at his brothers, and the three of them pushed clear of the bar, strode across the room, and out into noon's bright sun smash. They turned south, and, across the road inside the livery barn's gloomy maw, a tall man dressed in black said to a watery-eyed palsied man at his side: "Is that them?"

The alcoholic nodded, blinked furiously, and put out a hand. The tall man dropped a double eagle into it and kept his assessing gaze upon the Setter brothers. His companion went in a beeline for the Golden Slipper, clutching that coin in his sweaty fist. He had a terrible burning in his throat.

A hundred yards south from the hotel, across the road, Marshal Jim Collins, leaning motionlessly in the shade under his plank walk overhang, watched the Setters, too. He had his bad leg stiffly set and his good leg crossed over it at the ankle. Collins drew in a deep breath and slowly let it out, then he started for the hotel. He did not see the tall stranger step forward, too, northward, spy Jim, and quickly step back again. He wasn't thinking about the stranger at all.

Before Jim got to the doorway, the Setters came back through again. They passed up the plank walk, looking north, looking south. They saw Jim approaching and kept their eyes on him. From across in the barn's gloom, the stranger saw all this and watched it. He heard Collins say flatly: "Never mind. I know what you're in town for, and I'm telling you to leave it be."

Carlos, the fair-haired one, said: "You don't know the straight of it or you wouldn't say that, Marshal."

"I know the straight of it, boys. I saw it, just like a lot of others did. And I'm still saying for you three to leave it lie. I'll handle it. I don't need your help at all."

"Well, now," drawled Reg Setter, looking steadily at Texas Jim, "this is different from stealin' Setter beef or rustlin' Setter horses, Marshal. That man struck Christel. That's a lot different."

"I told that stranger," responded Jim in a voice getting thin with impatience, "I'd have no killings in my town. I meant it, and that same warning applies to you three."

"You also told him to get out of town, we heard, and he hasn't gone." This was young Frank speaking.

"You don't see him, do you?" demanded Jim.

"No," Frank conceded, "but he's still around."

"How do you know that?"

"Because, before we left the ranch, I sent ten men to patrol the stage road both above town and below it. If they catch that man, they're to send us word here and hold him." Frank raised his shoulders and let them fall. "They haven't sent us word, Marshal, so he's still around, you can bet money on that."

Marshal Collins's patience was at its absolute limit. He regarded the Setter brothers over an interval of silence, then he jerked his head sideways, saying: "Get!"

The Setters did something now they had never before done, something old John would never have sanctioned, either, had he been there, but he wasn't there; they split up, leaving young Frank, reputedly the fastest of them all, to face Texas Jim. Reg turned and paced fifty feet north of Collins. Carlos walked fifty feet southward. Then they all turned and waited, their bodies unmistakably loose and ready, their unafraid stares unwaveringly upon Jim, and their purpose glaringly clear.

Frank, less than three feet in front of Texas Jim, said: "Marshal, you've trampled us roughshod ever since we were kids. All that's changed, starting right now. From today on you get it through your damned skull that we're not kids any more at all, and you won't be riding herd on us from here on." Frank paused; it was evident, though, that he had more to say.

Jim didn't give him the chance to say it; he curled his lip and he looked his solid scorn. "You're punks," he ground out contemptuously.

"Even three to one you're punks. You think by getting me in a cross-fire you'll back me down?" Collins said a deriding word; he looked north and south, then back to Frank again. His pale gaze wasn't angry; it was bitter with clear ridicule, clear contempt. "Why, if there were three more of you, you couldn't win. Now get on your damned horses and get out of town before I do to you punks what that stranger did to your sister. I'm going to tell you something else, too," Collins said, throwing his customary caution where old John Setter was concerned to the wind. "Your sister had that spanking coming. She's had that coming for a long, long time. And you can tell your paw that if you want to, I don't care. Now get!"

Carlos shifted stance the slightest bit; his right shoulder settled low, and his right arm swept back until the hand was no more than three inches above his holstered six-gun.

Frank said nothing; he was closest to Marshal Collins. He would be the first target. He could have been carved of stone, so still did he remain. Reg, always the least tense of this trio, was standing easy, both arms down, both hands hanging, but the fingers of his right hand were slightly bent.

There were many witnesses to this; mostly they were so astonished at the Setter boys chousing Texas Jim that they forgot to duck when gunfire seemed imminent. The full length of Buellton's roadway was without sound or movement. The sun beat down and somewhere west of town a cow bawled, and some boys made a quicksilver, fluting call to one another.

On across the road a tall shape stepped clear of barn shadows, pacing forward to halt in the roadway's center. It was the lean-downed stranger. He also took a fighting stance, but here, every witness saw at once, was no novice; here was pure death in black clothing that made the white-ivory butt of his holstered handgun stand out with deadly significance. Those who had not considered it before, now did—this man was a gunfighter.

"Boys, you heard the marshal. You'd better get back on those horses and slope, because the odds don't favor you at all, now."

Frank, seeing that newcomer out in the dazzling golden roadway light over Texas Jim's shoulder, kept still, kept absolutely motionless. Reg and Carlos also swiveled rapid glances outward, but Collins, with the stranger behind him, did not move at all. He did, though, recognize the menace in the stranger's tone. He waited a second longer, then, when near thirty years' experience in such matters told him the danger had passed, he said once more: "Get!"

Frank teetered a second longer before coming to his hard, his bitter decision. Collins they might try; they might, he thought, even top old Texas

Jim because he was far from a young man any longer. But that other one, that black-eyed deadly man out in the road, that was something else altogether. As the stranger had said, the odds were even now, although the numbers were not. Frank's nostrils quivered, his breath ran out, and he brought both arms forward, hooked his thumbs in his shell belt near his front buckle, and considered the stranger.

"Are you the one?" he quietly asked.

His words dissolved the last of that tension; a sigh seemed to pass the full length of Buellton. Carlos and Reg emulated young Frank; they came out of their crouches gradually and stared over at the stranger. Texas Jim stepped away from in front of Frank and turned.

"Yeah, sonny, I'm the one. Your fight's with me, not Marshal Collins there."

The stranger had not moved; he was still prepared to fight. Everyone could plainly see this. Texas Jim cleared the plank walk and strode forth to brace the tall man from a distance of five feet. "There's going to be no killing," he said. "Take your hand away from that gun."

The stranger obeyed. He straightened up, put a sardonic look upon Marshal Collins, and stood out there with a brittle little humorless smile tugging at the outer corners of his wide, tough-set lips.

"Sure not, Marshal. There'll be no killing.

The odds weren't great enough for those three."

"You," snapped fair-haired and fiery Carlos. "Take off that gun!"

The stranger looked past Texas Jim, then back again. He said, still with that hard little faint grin: "You got any objections to the boy there getting his satisfaction with his fists, Marshal? After all, he's entitled to that, at the very least."

Jim kept eyeing the stranger. This was one of the few times in his life when he was having trouble correctly gauging a man. It had happened before, but very rarely, and each time it had happened, the man under study had turned out to be something very unusual, very special.

"No," said Jim forthrightly. "I have no objection, stranger. Not if it'll clear the air a little."

The tall man bent, untied the leg lashing of his holstered weapon, unbuckled the heavy belt, and handed these things to Marshal Collins. Across the way, still upon that shady plank walk, Reg and Frank were helping Carlos prepare. Carlos's face was eager; it showed with those primeval, cruel lights of ancient anticipation. His eyes were smoky and darker by shades than they normally were.

Jim Collins went slowly back to the walkway, stepped into shade there, and turned his back on the three Setters to consider thoughtfully that tall man out there dressed in black. He was a gunfighter, but there was more to it than that. Something tugged in a distant part of Texas Jim's brain, something elusive that skittered away when he tried to pin it down.

A man passed out of the Golden Slipper, brushing against Collins. Texas Jim did not turn, not even after this man hissed in his ear.

"Marshal, old John'll raise Cain if you let this go on."

Collins swiveled his head, saw Sam the bartender, and grunted. "You peddle your whiskey. I'll handle everything else."

Sam subsided; he shuffled back along the building front and joined the slowly congregating crowd of other men who had materialized along the roadway, on both sides, to stand silently watching this unprecedented affair.

Frank Setter stepped in front of his brothers to the plank walk's very edge. He said to the waiting man out in the roadway: "When this is over, stranger, you're leaving town one way or another."

The tall man eyed Frank; he then did an unusual thing under the circumstances, he chuckled. It was a deep sound full of genuine amusement. "Listen, little rooster," he said pleasantly to Frank, "let's just worry about one thing at a time."

Frank stood on, glaring. His face paled to a stone-gray color and fire points danced in his eyes. He had been talked down to; he had been deliberately and casually belittled in front of the people of Buellton. Texas Jim, watching him, saw the vein in Frank's throat swell and pound; Jim was prepared to move if Frank moved. But Carlos was ready now, divested of gun, shell belt, hat, and neckerchief. When he walked forward, young Frank was no longer the center of all that expectant attention. He moved back to stand with Reg.

Carlos Setter was a powerfully built man; his shoulders and arms were tightly packed with muscle. He was as quick as a cat on his feet and he didn't know the meaning of fear. But there was one thing about Carlos most of the folks of Buellton knew from his past brawls, which the tall stranger could not have known: when Carlos lost his temper, he also lost his head. He had in the past come within an ace of killing men he'd beaten in fist fights. That's it had been that time he'd shot the faro dealer. Carlos was more than just dangerous; he was deadly.

Texas Jim watched him go out to meet the stranger; he saw how Carlos moved, up on the balls of his feet, his mighty arms swinging easy, his fists balled and ready. Texas Jim made a private bet with himself about the outcome of this, but wild horses could not have dragged this secret out of him.

III

It was a battle of titans. For a generation yet to come folks in Anza County would relish the recollection of it. Carlos went on, and, although he looked resolutely wrathful, actually he was not angry; he was eager. Because he was not angry he was doubly dangerous. Waiting for him, the tall stranger stood out there in blazing sunlight making his assessment of Carlos from the half droop of lids, his black eyes missing nothing. Then he shifted stance, went up onto his toes, and hung there as though an instantaneous flash of warning had struck every nerve, every muscle, leaving him cold in the heat of this summer day. In the stranger's dark face was also that expression of ancient, brutal eagerness. Then he twisted the smallest bit sideways, showing that he knew what Carlos meant to do. It was like a soft call in the stillness. The stranger reddened a little from the sturdy sloshing of his heart, from its increased tempo. His black stare turned cruel. He lifted his fists, finally, when Carlos was near, and he shuffled his booted feet in roadway dust.

Just before he halted his approach Carlos said: "Mister, have at it." Then Carlos paused for the smallest part of an indrawn breath, and drove his powerful body straight on, throwing a fist. The stranger, already half twisted, sucked back from that blow, letting it pass harmlessly. Then, as Carlos's momentum carried him up, the tall man flicked his hand out three times as fast as the strike of a snake. Over on the plank walk breathless onlookers heard each of those little flicking jabs strike. Carlos was past; he came around and flung his head up. Now he was mad; he hadbeen stung and he had failed to smash the stranger, and now he was furious. He launched himself forward once more. The stranger did not give ground again, but this time he should have because Carlos had corrected to the other man's profiled stance. He came in shooting another balled fist, got past the tall man's guard, and ripped across a strike that cracked solidly and sent an electric shock all the way up to Carlos's shoulder.

Now the stranger gave ground. That blow alongside the head had shaken him. He rolled right and he rolled left. He weaved and bobbed, staying away from Carlos's seeking hands. When one blow crashed through his guard again, the stranger caught it on his elbow, deflecting it. But Carlos's rush was carrying him backward; it was the rush of a blind bull. The stranger halted then, let Carlos get almost to him, and jumped side-ways, letting Carlos rush on past. He might have struck as his enemy went by, but he was instead content to take this little respite and use it just resting.

Carlos grunted each time he put everything behind a punch. He grunted now as he squared around and, digging in with both heels, catapulted himself forward. This grunting was the only sound; so silent was the roadway that it seemed inordinately loud.

The stranger dropped down flat-footed. If Carlos had noticed this, it might have warned him, but he did not see it; he was glaring from pinpointed eyes only at the tall man's face as he jumped in, sank a fist wrist-deep into the other man's belly, and started to jump out again. An arcing short blow came out of nowhere, cracked against Carlos's jaw, and both men reeled there, hurt, the stranger gasping from the belly blow, Carlos furiously blinking away the haze before his eyes. The stranger took two long steps away and again paced himself, resting. He might have been able to finish Carlos then and there, but he declined to make the effort. His face was shiny with sweat and paler than it had been. There was a roaring in his ears that no one but himself heard.

Carlos recovered and, moving slower now, stalked ahead. Once more the tall man waited, both fists up and cocked, right shoulder down a little behind his right arm. Carlos whipped out; spectators saw this blow only as a blur. The tall man rolled his head, turned his left shoulder to take the edge off this strike, then turned back with smoothness and let go that poised right. Once again Carlos leaned into punishment. But now the blows did not cease; the stranger was using his hoarded reserve strength now. He was after fair-haired Carlos Setter like a panther, shifting, dropping back, stepping in, going far down under Carlos's pawing, and coming upright again with both arms whipping in, whipping out.

Carlos reacted instinctively to this beating. He turned to take those powerful blows along his side; he was absorbing terrific punishment and a groan went up from the spectators—all except Texas Jim Collins. He hadn't moved, and his expression was identical to what it had earlier been. Carlos rolled his shoulders; he dropped his face behind a thick forearm. He pushed one leg back for balance, and he tried to reach the stranger with groping hands. He never contacted and those flashing fists exploded high against him, then lower down. He stood on, stunned and hurt, seeing those blows only as they were hitting him and whipping back to hit him again, never as they came in. For that reason Carlos could not protect himself or escape.

The stranger tired; he stepped back, lowered his arms, and squinted. Carlos brought his head up; he peered over his forearm, and he sprang, trying to smother the other man, trying to get hold of him with scrabbling fingers and bear him down by brute weight alone. Carlos's breathing bubbled and blood dripped from torn lips. He sobbed with effort now, threw wide both reaching hands—and a blow with all the power of a down-swept axe exploded alongside his temple.

A lesser man would have gone down at once. Carlos's arms dropped away, his mouth opened, his jaw sagged, but he rocked there like a tree in a high wind, unwilling to drop. Once more the stranger danced back. His breathing sawed in the absolute silence. Every eye was upon Carlos. For a long moment everyone waited to see what would now happen; scarcely a spectator could draw a full breath, so great was the power of this high moment.

Carlos's head sagged, heavily weighted. He loosely brought up his guard again, and he loosely weaved forward, too. The ability to feel bad pain was gone out of him; he moved like a dullard, his co-ordination was badly impaired, but his spirit would not stop pushing. From ten feet off the stranger turned, ran a calculating look over at Jim Collins, and the brothers of the man shuffling forward. There was not one whit of rapport in any of those faces; they were staring out of brutal eyes; they would not stop this fight regardless. The stranger turned back to his work.

Carlos stopped, he measured the taller man, he pawed at him. He got hit over the bridge of the nose; he was rocked by a blasting strike that slid over his sweat-greasy jaw. Then he was paralyzed by a sledging blow that dropped Carlos's mouth wide open and sent his eyes turning aimlessly from side to side. The beaten man's arms dropped, his fists, battered and bloody, gradually opened. A strange, wild look twisted Carlos's face, and he gently fell against the earth, making a soft rustling sound as he collapsed.

The stranger turned. His mouth was smashed a little and there was an angry red burn alongside his right jaw. There was a strong, smoky flare to his gaze when he put it toward Reg and Frank and Jim Collins.

No one said anything. Someone back along the wall of the Golden Slipper Casino shuffled off for a bucket of water. That was the only sound, and yet the crowd was sizeable.

Carlos lay crumpled. The stranger bent, rolled him upon his back for easier breathing, then he placed one of Carlos's arms up to shield the hurt man's eyes from a pitiless sun. After that, he stood briefly gulping air, and he finally passed over to halt before Jim Collins, holding out one hand.

Texas Jim wordlessly handed the stranger his shell belt and gun. Over the stranger's shoulder he saw Reg and Frank start out into the roadway. Jim watched them.

The tall man finished buckling his belt and bent to fasten the holster thong to his leg. He straightened up, finally, dusted his hat against one leg, and dropped it on to the back of his head. Forty feet onward Reg and Frank were struggling forward into shade with limp and battered Carlos between them.

Without taking his eyes off the Setters, Jim Collins spoke softly from the corner of his mouth. "All right," he told the tall stranger, "you wanted him to have his satisfaction and now he's had it. This will be the last time I'll tell you to get on your colt and get out of Buellton."

The stranger stood, also watching the Setters and deeply breathing through parted lips. He, once more, might not have heard what was said to him. Moments later he turned, ignored the staring spectators to all this, and paced on through the Golden Slipper's spindle doors to halt at the bar, to hook both elbows there, and call to Sam for cold ale.

The yonder crowd drifted away in twos and threes. Finally there was talk. Some two dozen men drifted into the saloon and took up places here and there, covertly studying the tall man. Jim Collins was not among these men. He went along to the bench bolted to his jailhouse front and eased down there in hot shade to make, and quietly smoke, a brown-paper cigarette. He was thoughtful.

It took a little time for Buellton to resume its normal life. Down at the livery barn, for instance, which was the center for Buellton's idle set, bets were grudgingly paid and fresh bets were offered. The stranger, even money had it, would not live two more days even if he rode out of town right now.

At Balinger's saddle shop, another favorite hang-out for range men and loafers, the talk was less concerned with odds and more concerned with the battle. Hoag Balinger said that within four walls Carlos could've whipped the stranger, that Carlos hadn't used his head, or he wouldn't have let the fight take place in the roadway where the stranger could dance around like he'd done. Toby Hostetter, night barman at the Golden Slipper, said that Carlos had been too upset over what the stranger had done to Christel to think straight, and this put a pause to the conversation. The men at Balinger's shop turned privately to their own thoughts concerning the spanking of Christel Setter. Some were convinced it was the best thing anyone had done to Miss Christel in years. Others, more sly in their thoughts, thrilled to the notion of bending that handsome girl over their lap and doing what the stranger had done.

Then Pete Sloat, a stump rancher from the back country, a raffish, grizzled and weathered older man who had very little use for any of the Setter clan, summed it up succinctly. "Say what you want an' think what you want. That big feller the same as stepped barefoot into a rattlesnake pit. I been in this country within a few years o' old

John Setter and I can't recollect, ever, anyone ever doin' to him and his'n what this man done today . . . all in the space of a few hours. I figure, if it takes old John the rest o' his life and half his fortune, he'll bust that tall feller down to his knees and make him beg for mercy, an', if any o' you think it's all over now, you're crazy. I figure it's just commenced."

And it had.

IV

Texas Jim Collins was making his final round of the late night when he found the stranger, lying in black shadows, half in, half out of a dirty alleyway. For a moment Jim just stood there, looking down. Then, with a rattling sigh, he knelt, rolled the tall man over onto his back, and considered the black clot of dried blood. He leaned with both arms crossed over one knee gently shaking his head. The fool. No matter how wily or how tough an individual man was, he remained only an individual man, while John Setter, in his mansion atop Setter's hill, had more arms than an octopus.

One or more of those night-riding arms had patiently waited in the night for the tall man to pass, and had come within a hair's breadth of crushing the tall man's skull. Of proof, of course, there was none. But over a quarter century Jim had seen this identical thing happen before to the enemies of John Setter. The fortunate thing was, Jim now thought, that this man, unlike some others, had a skull made of stone; otherwise, he'd now be dead.

Collins got help, had the stranger borne to the hotel, and bedded down there. Then Jim went on to his own room and also bedded down. Before dropping off to sleep, he saw now that the stranger would be unable to leave Buellton for several days, and this irritated him. As long as this man remained in town, serious trouble was not far off. The stranger was one of those men who gravitated toward trouble—or perhaps it was that trouble gravitated toward him. In either case, it meant the same thing; this was at the root of Texas Jim's annoyance. He fell asleep, thinking about this, and the following morning, after he'd breakfasted, Jim went to his office, pushed through the slightly open door, and eyed the medical practitioner, sitting patiently there, awaiting him.

Jim nodded, went to the hat rack, and hung his Stetson there. Then he turned, eased down at his desk, and silently waited. The doctor smiled. Jim thought this was a malicious smile. The doctor did not like him and Jim was aware of it. But it wasn't only Jim; the doctor did not like gunmen of any kind.

"I think old John's bitten off about all he'll

want to chew this time," said the medical man, still looking malicious. "I'm referring to Mister Black."

"Mister Black?" queried Texas Jim, not very interested yet.

"He didn't tell me his name. When I asked, all he said was hurry up with that bandage and shut up."

Jim gradually fixed his stare upon the doctor, something unbelievable firming up in his mind.

"I call him Mister Black because he was dressed in black." The doctor was enjoying this; he was playing with Jim Collins. "You know, Marshal, I've buried 'em for a lot less than that man took yesterday. Yet here he came, along before dawn, with his torn scalp and bashed-in head, routing me out of bed to sew him up, bandage him, and set him on his way."

Collins wasn't even blinking now. "Are you talking about the stranger who spanked Christel and whipped Carlos?" he demanded.

"I am."

"He came to you under his own power, this morning?"

"He did."

Jim Collins rubbed his jaw and gazed out a window. "He was limp as a rag when we put him to bed," he said pensively.

"Marshal, that man's got a skull like iron."

"He's trouble," murmured Collins, ignoring what the medical man had said. "Pure trouble. I hope he doesn't cave in before he's a hundred miles away."

"He wasn't going that far, Marshal."

"What do you mean?"

The doctor's malicious smile came again. "He asked me the way to John Setter's cow camp."

An old wall clock rhythmically ticked. Texas Jim kept his gaze upon the doctor for a long time, then he said: "He'll be killed."

"Probably. Only, before that happens, John Setter's going to know he's around, cracked head and all."

Jim started to arise. "You could've told me the minute he left your place."

"Yes, I could've. But I had my reasons for not telling you."

"What reasons, Doctor?"

"That man is a gunfighter. It's marked out plain to see. I'm in favor of his kind going up against others of the same breed."

"Yeah," said Texas Jim, a trifle tiredly, "I've heard you say that before. Something about gunfighters killing other gunfighters so decent folks can live in peace."

"That's right, Marshal."

"Well, Doctor, there's just one thing wrong with that kind of an idea . . . it shows how little you know of human nature. You see, for every gunfighter that's downed, there have always been two to step forth into his tracks. Now, this tall

200

stranger you call Mister Black, happens to be a pretty fair sort of a man. He's not a killer, I can tell you that. He's trouble, sure, but I like his kind of trouble a heap more than your kind."

"My kind?"

"Yes, Doctor, your kind."

Texas Jim let it rest there. He got up, took his hat, and walked to the office door. He swung the panel inward and stood stonily, waiting. The doctor crossed over, passed out into morning sunlight, and halted to look back at Collins.

"You'll be too late," he said. "Mister Black has a good three-hour lead on you."

Collins closed and locked the door with his back firmly to the doctor. He said nothing. When he finally turned, he considered the doctor's back, on down the walkway, and he said a fierce word. Then he went around back to the horse shed, got his mount, and rode out of town through the rear alleyway.

The springtime sun was hot and yet it was also pleasant because, from some far-away snowfield, there was also a sharpness to the felt warmth. Texas Jim rode along unhurriedly. There had been a time, in his youth, when a mission such as this one would have sent him headlong down the land. No longer. On the sundown side of fifty a thoughtful man knew nothing ever happened in life because one hurried, or because one did not hurry.

Jim did not ride the long miles to the Setter cow camp anyway. If that was where Mister Black had gone, a three-hour head start was too much of a lead for him to be overtaken, and whatever was to have happened out there had already occurred.

Jim rode instead to Setter's hill. He passed along the great curve of graded roadway all the way to the top; he passed through an ornate arched gateway and onward, where several gnarled and very ancient black oaks grew. Here, in blessed shade, he left his animal at a tie rack, turned, and for just a moment looked at the baronial home old John Setter had built atop this knoll. Then Texas Jim went along to the pillared porch, gleaming white and immaculately kept, and stopped where five men stood in deep silence at the side of a battered ranch wagon.

Old John was there, his shock of nearly white hair faintly moving in the breeze. Carlos and Reg and Frank were also there, peering over the side down into the wagon. And John Setter's range boss, Dave Wesson, was standing back a foot or two, red-necked and white up around his narrowed eyes, looking as grim as death.

The wagon had been deliberately driven up in front of John Setter's house and stopped less than a foot from the stone steps. It had come a goodly distance, and, judging from the glistening coats of its team, it had come fast.

Texas Jim, being solidly ignored by those five

men, passed quietly over the grass and came to rest across from them on the wagon's far side. They looked up and over at the same time Jim looked downward into the wagon.

There was a dead man lying there, all loose and easy, with a soiled bedroll tarp thrown back so that sunlight struck pitilessly into his sightless eyes. He had one puckered purple bullet hole visible, equal distance between both eyes and two inches higher.

"Bull's eye," murmured Dave Wesson, looking solidly at Texas Jim. "Dead center as neat as you please."

Collins knew the dead man. His name had been Mark Leffingwell. He was a hard drinker, a hard fighter, and an old Setter cowhand.

Collins leaned, staring at Leffingwell, thinking that Mister Black had wasted not a minute. Jim could believe implicitly, without asking a single question about it, that Mark Leffingwell had been the man who had stepped from a black alley after the tall stranger had passed in the night, and struck him down with a pistol barrel. Leffingwell had done worse upon other occasions in the service of the Setters. Collins could find no sadness for this man's passing anywhere in his mind or his heart.

Jim raised his glance, put it upon John Setter, and waited. He had felt the smarting lash of old John's tongue before. Those other times he had borne this with fortitude and he was prepared to do the same now. But old John ignored Collins completely. He had something brassy clutched in one fist. When he finally moved, it was with uncertain steps. He simply turned his back on all of them and went up on to his porch, felt along to a chair next to a table, and sank down there. He raised that fisted hand, opened the fingers unsteadily, and stared at the massive gold watch in his palm.

Texas Jim looked at the others. All but Carlos were watching old John in uneasy bewilderment. Carlos was glaring across the wagon bed at Marshal Collins. His face was a healing shambles but his eyes were evilly bright and hating.

"God Almighty," said John Setter from fifty feet away. He had flicked open the back of that massive gold watch and was staring at an inscription there. "God Almighty," he said again, and seemed stricken, seemed suddenly bereft of the iron-like fiber that was both his character and his personality.

"What's wrong?" Reg asked, starting forward.

Old John looked up. He appeared to notice Texas Jim for the first time. He said: "Go away, all of you. Leave me alone. Dave, take Leffingwell to the private plot. Have the men bury him there." When no one moved at once, John Setter's seamed old face darkly colored. "I said go on. That's what I meant!" This was an unmistakable command and the men moved. Wesson got back to the wagon seat. As he stooped to unloop the lines from a brake handle, he said quietly to Texas Jim: "Come around to the barn." Then he drove off.

Reg and Frank started toward waiting horses at a tie rack, and Carlos went sullenly into the house, slamming the door hard behind himself.

Texas Jim stood his ground. He said—"John." —and got no further.

"Leave him be, Jim," exclaimed the slash-mouthed other man from upon his porch. "He didn't murder Leffingwell. Dave saw it. Leffingwell went for his gun. He was outdrawn and outgunned. Dave said it was a fair fight."

"What I want to know," said Jim quietly, while considering in his mind reasons for John Setter's peculiar behavior, "is Leffingwell the man who tried to kill that stranger last night in town?"

Setter shot a close look outward. "What difference does that make now?" he asked. "Leffingwell is dead."

"I see," stated Texas Jim. "It was Leffingwell. One more question, John. Whose watch is that in your hand?"

Setter's fingers closed convulsively around the gold watch. "Mine, now," he said. "Go on back, Marshal. This thing is finished."

"Finished, John? How . . . finished? That man struck your girl, he beat hell out of your oldest boy, and he killed one of your oldest riders. You're going to let it end here?"

"Yes. Now go on back. I don't want you up here."

Texas Jim nodded. He lingered a moment longer, staring, then he returned to his horse and rode on around the house and across to the gleaming white barn. There, he sighted Dave Wesson and beckoned from the saddle. Wesson came at once. He was sweating and he was troubled. He would have spoken the instant he was beside Texas Jim, but he didn't get that opportunity.

"Whose watch is it John has?" asked Marshal Collins.

"I never saw it before Mister Setter took it off Mark's body. But it didn't belong to Mark, I can tell you that, Marshal. Hell, Mark never had enough money at one time in his lousy life to buy a gold watch like that one."

"Dave, where was Mark last night after sundown?"

"In town, I reckon. He left the cow camp about sundown. Carlos rode in. I didn't see them talkin', but not ten minutes after Carlos come, Mark rode out."

Jim regarded Wesson steadily. "How is it," he asked, "that as range boss you don't keep a tighter rein on your men?"

"I do, dammit. That is . . . with one or two exceptions."

"Mark Leffingwell was an exception?"

"Well, yes. He's been with the Setters a lot longer'n I have, Marshal. They sort of favor him. I never made no big issue of it when he came and went. Especially, like last night, when I figured Carlos told him to go do something."

"Like maybe riding to Buellton and braining someone?"

"I don't know where he went, Marshal. That's gospel truth."

"All right, Dave. But he didn't have that watch when he left?"

"He didn't have that watch ever, Marshal. I've bunked with Mark for five years. If he'd had a gold timepiece like that, he'd've shown it to me a long time ago."

"Then," said Texas Jim, "it's not hard to figure where he got it. Off the man he came within an inch of killing last night. The same man who hunted him down and killed him." Collins studied Dave Wesson's anxious expression. "Dave, tell me about the fight."

"We were bedded down, Marshal. This feller came ridin' in. He got down and he said to Jasper Jones, the horse wrangler . . . 'Feller, which man is Leffingwell?' Jasper was fixin' to get up. He had to go run in the remuda before break-fast. He points to Mark's bedroll, then, as this tall feller walks over, Jasper grabs me by the shoulder and liked to yanked me plumb out of my blankets, pointin' at this big feller's back. I was just sittin' up when that feller kicked Mark in his blankets. Mark was plumb asleep. He didn't get back from town till way late. He kicks Mark awake, and he says plain as day . . . 'Leffingwell, get up out of there.' Mark wakes up, sits up, rubs his eyes, and looks upward. That's when it happened. I reckon Mark recognized that tall feller, for all at once he dives for his gun in his holster. The butt of it was stickin' out of Mark's boot top beside his bedroll. He had the gun, Marshal, was swingin' around with it when . . . you'd never have believed it . . . that tall feller just seemed to tilt his wrist an' there was an explosion. Mark got slammed near out o' his blankets. The rest o' us was plumb froze, it happened that fast."

"And," said Jim Collins, "he got back on to his damned horse and just rode out of there?"

Dave Wesson heard the incredulity. He avoided Texas Jim's gaze and dolorously wagged his head. "Marshal Collins, you never in your whole life seen a man draw an' fire a gun like that feller did. That's why none o' us moved so much as an eyelash. But it wasn't fright, Marshal. We was just plain stunned."

"So he rode away."

"Yeah. He rode away."

"And you brought Leffingwell to old John."

Wesson nodded. "As fast as I could whip up

208

the team." Wesson raised his eyes. "What the hell came over the old man when he took that watch off Leffingwell? He looked to me like he was goin' to throw up or fall down in a faint, or something. What the hell you reckon was wrong with him? You expect Mark Leffingwell meant that much to him?"

"It wasn't Leffingwell at all," said Texas Jim quietly. He turned in the saddle to look outward and downward from Setter's hill where the land ran on to earth's farthest dim merging with the springtime sky. "Which way did that tall feller ride, Dave?"

"As far as I know, Marshal, he rode back toward town."

Collins's head whipped around. He stared at Wesson. Then he lifted his rein hand and rode away from Setter's hill without a backward glance. He got all the way down to the plain before he turned, for some inexplicable reason, and looked back up to the big white house, to its broad verandah. There, he saw old John still sitting, stricken-looking and loosely slumped as he'd been before Collins had left his hill. But now John Setter was not alone. Christel was there with him. Collins knew it was the beautiful, willful girl by the way hot sunlight flashed flame-like over her red-gold hair.

V

Marshal Collins made the rounds as soon as he returned to Buellton, but he found nothing relating to the tall stranger until he walked into Joe Karns's livery barn. There, he interrupted a fierce tongue-lashing that Karns was delivering to his drunken hostler. At sight of Texas Jim, Karns turned, still angry-looking, and the hostler fled.

"That feller that whipped Carlos," said Jim. "I'm looking for him, Joe. Is his horse here?"

Karns pointed. "Yonder in that stall, Marshal. He come in a little bit ago." Karns let his arm drop; he screwed up his face. "Say, there's a rumor goin' around that this man shot someone out on the range. Is there any truth in it?"

"Mark Leffingwell," mumbled Jim Collins, passing across to the indicated stall and leaning upon its door. "Quite a horse," he said, drumming with the fingers of one hand upon wood. "Joe, where would you say that brand came from?"

Karns came up and looked, also leaning upon the door. "Danged if I know," he said, studying the horse's identifying shoulder brand. "If I was just guessin', I'd say maybe Mexico. It's too fancy, got too many curlicues, for this side of the border. Some o' those Mex brands are artistic as all hell."

Jim continued to scrutinize the horse and drum with his fingers. Finally he said: "I was hoping it wouldn't be Mexico. I was hoping it'd be Texas or Arizona or even California. Those places a man can get answers from . . . but not Mexico."

"Marshal . . . ?"

Jim turned, gazed at Joe Karns, and said: "Yes, it's true. This feller killed Mark Leffingwell."

Karns's mouth formed a perfect O and his eyes popped.

Jim Collins walked on out of the barn, turned right, and kept going as far as the last small wooden structure before he encountered an intersection with Main Street. Here, he entered without knocking, nodded to a young woman sitting at a table, and strode past to push into a second room. This time he did not knock, either.

Two men looked up. One of them was the doctor. The other man was the tall stranger; he was having a dressing changed on his head. Neither of them spoke to Marshal Collins but both watched his every move.

"How's his head?" Collins asked the medical man as he crossed away from the door, passed around so that he was facing the injured man, looking down into his face.

"He's not favoring it any," snapped the doctor, obviously irritated by Texas Jim's abrupt entrance into his inner private office.

"I expect he isn't," said Jim, and leaned upon

the wall, crossed his arms, and put his steady gaze upon the stranger. "Did you know," he said, "that doc here has given you a name? Mister Black. How do you like that . . . Mister Black?"

The wounded man considered Texas Jim for a while without speaking. Then, ignoring the question, he said: "What's on your mind, Marshal?"

"A killing, Mister Black."

The doctor's hands stopped moving. He looked startled.

"The killing of Mark Leffingwell, Mister Black," went on Texas Jim. "Care to tell me about it?"

"Sure not," said the stranger, matching Jim's quiet tone with a voice just as silky. "I was on my way to the hotel to get my bedroll and saddlebags . . ."

"You were fixing to leave Buellton?"

"Not exactly, just changing rooms was all."

Texas Jim sighed. "Go on," he said.

"I stepped across an alleyway opening . . . and the world fell on me."

"You didn't see who struck you?"

"No. When I came around, I was in bed at the hotel. A friend came and told me how I'd gotten to the hotel. Thanks, Marshal Collins. I never forget a favor."

"This friend," said Jim. "Who is he?"

Mister Black slowly wagged his head. "It's a conviction of mine, that, if a feller never implicates other folks in his troubles, he makes no unnecessary enemies."

Texas Jim did not push it; he had an idea about the identity of this informant. The same "friend" he'd just seen Joe Karns verbally skinning alive down at the livery barn. The reason he suspected the old derelict drunkard was because this wasn't the first time that old devil had offered to sell newcomers to Buellton information for the price of a few drinks.

"For the time being," said Texas Jim, "we'll let that lie. There's one other thing, though. How did you know it was Mark Leffingwell who crowned you?"

Once again the stranger wagged his head. "Like I said, Marshal, I don't like to get other folks involved."

Texas Jim nodded, saying softly: "That friend of yours again. He's pretty observant, isn't he?"

"I didn't take his word entirely, Marshal. I didn't hunt Leffingwell up half cocked. You see, when I came to at the hotel, I'd lost something. I knew you hadn't taken it, and I knew my friend hadn't because he never had the chance. So, when I found Leffingwell, there it was, hanging in plain sight from one of his boots beside his bedroll so that when he looked around . . ."

"Yeah, so that when he looked around, he could see what time it was."

The stranger's lips closed. He regarded Texas

Jim stonily, then he said: "Have you got it, Marshal?"

"No, I haven't."

"But you've seen it. You know where it is?"

"Yes."

"Mind telling me?"

Texas Jim's expression did not alter at all when he said: "A friend of mine has it, Mister Black. I'd tell you, only I don't want to implicate another person." He unfolded his arms, crossed to the door, put a hand upon the latch there, and looked back to find the tall man's black eyes hard on him. "Where are you from, Mister Black? Or have you some scruple about that, too?"

Mister Black said nothing; his face was smooth and expressionless. He continued to stare at Marshal Collins over a long silent moment. It was clear that he was not going to speak, so Marshal Collins opened the door, passed through, and continued on out to the roadway. There, he stood a moment looking at Buellton's morning traffic, then he started southward toward his office. Not until he was several hundred feet along did he falter in his stride, staring dead ahead where a handsome phæton with a matched team of chest-nuts stood at his jailhouse hitch rack. He did not increase his pace at all, but strong curiosity rose up in him. It remained high, too, until he entered the office and saw Christel Setter standing there, obviously awaiting his arrival.

Jim removed his hat, hung it up, faced the lovely girl, and said without any greeting at all: "You've brought me something, Miss Christel?"

The girl's liquid gaze rose to Texas Jim's face and lingered there. "No," she said. "Why did you ask that?"

"No gold pocket watch, ma'am?"

Christel swung her eyes to the wall and back again. "You saw it?" she asked.

"Not up close, just in your father's hand. I figured maybe your paw'd sent it on to me."

Christel looked surprised. "Why would he do that, Marshal?"

Jim, regarding Christel, saw that he had taken a wrong lead in this conversation. He pointed to a chair, saying: "Have a seat, ma'am."

Christel sat. She put both hands in her lap and gravely studied Jim Collins. "My father sent a message for you, Marshal. He wanted me to tell you he would hold you responsible for anything that happened to Chris Madsen while he's in Buellton."

Texas Jim raised a hand, began to drum with it on his desk. He eventually nodded his head at John Setter's very handsome girl, and, for some reason she could not fathom, Texas Jim looked suddenly pleased about something. "All right, ma'am, you've delivered your paw's message. Now I'd like you to take one back to him for me. Mister Madsen was leaving Buellton when Leffingwell attacked him."

"Is that all, Marshal?"

"Not quite. I'm going to try and talk Mister Madsen into staying on now, maybe as my deputy, Miss Christel."

The girl's hazel eyes widened. "No!" she burst out. "My father doesn't want you to do that."

"Oh?"

"He wants Chris Madsen to leave."

"Did he ask you to tell me this, too?"

"No, but that's what he wants. I know it is."

Texas Jim leaned back on his desk. He pursed his lips and he rocked back and forth, then he said: "Miss Christel, your paw owns Buellton, but he doesn't run it. From the law's standpoint I run it. If Chris Madsen wishes to stay, I'll back him in that."

Christel swiftly rose up. Her willful jaw jutted; her gold-flecked eyes flashed at Texas Jim. "You're up to something, Marshal. You've never before let a killer stay twenty-four hours in Buellton. My father won't . . ."

"Madsen's no killer, Miss Christel. He shot Leffingwell in a fair fight. Your paw's own range boss swore to me that's how it was."

"My father won't like this. I'm warning you, Marshal."

Texas Jim stopped rocking; he put a deceptively mild gaze upon Christel Setter. "No threats," he told her. "I've gotten along passably well with your father for a quarter century, girl. There've been no threats before. There won't be any now."

Christel's nostrils flared. She stood stormily glaring, but she seemed to Texas Jim also to be uncertain, to be suddenly very troubled about something.

He said: "I think your paw knows he can trust me, Miss Christel. I don't know what's going on here, but your paw ought to know by now that he can . . ."

"He can break you, Marshal, that's what he can do."

Now Texas Jim's marginal store of patience was exhausted. He stood up to his full height, hitched up his bad shoulder so that it was nearly even with his other shoulder, and he put an icy look upon John Setter's daughter, saying in an entirely changed voice: "I don't figure we have anything else to say to one another, ma'am. Thanks for bringing me your father's message . . . and thanks for carrying mine back to him."

He opened the door and held it thus until Christel had passed out. She turned upon the plank walk, saying hotly: "My brothers told me what you said about my deserving that . . . that spanking, Marshal. I won't forget you said that, Marshal Collins."

Texas Jim's brittle gaze almost softened. He was not so old a man that the beauty of this handsome girl did not stir his male instincts to life. "I hope you don't forget it," he stated. "But I hope, when you remember it, Christel, that you think on it the way I meant it. It's in you, girl, to be so much finer than you are."

He watched her stride out to her phæton, fling up into it, and dash away southward, driving furiously through morning's brilliant sunlight.

A man's dry voice from some northward shadows spoke up quietly, breaking in upon Texas Jim's thoughts. "They tell me, Marshal, you've got a knack for rubbing folks the wrong way."

Collins turned in his doorway, recognized the tall stranger, and without showing any surprise at this unexpected meeting, he stepped aside and said: "Come on in, Mister Madsen. It's hot out in the roadway."

The tall man checked himself in mid-stride. He looked steadily at Collins, then he made that near-to-smiling little quirked-up expression with his lips, and passed on into the jailhouse. There, he turned as Marshal Collins went past to his desk, and said: "You didn't know my name twenty minutes ago, so it probably was the girl who told you. But how did she know it?"

Texas Jim squared around. "That's what I'd like to know. Seems like there's something going on that's being kept a secret from me."

Chris Madsen faintly frowned. He stood lost in

thought for a time, then he started in his tracks, saying: "Of course, my watch."

Jim nodded. "Is there an inscription in that watch?"

Madsen did not answer this at once. He appeared to be piecing his thoughts together to form an understandable pattern. Then he looked up, saying: "Who has it?"

"John Setter has it. He took it off Leffingwell's body."

"I see."

"Maybe you see," stated Jim laconically, "but I sure don't. John Setter's been riding roughshod over this country for a long time, Madsen, then you come along, spank his daughter, beat one of his boys senseless, and kill an old trusted cowboy of his . . . and he told me this morning to leave you alone."

"He told you that, Marshal?"

"He did. And he meant it, too. Will you tell me why?"

Chris Madsen moved; he went to the chair Christel had occupied, and dropped down into it. He sat on for a while without raising his eyes to Marshal Collins, then he slapped his leg, got up, and went to the door. There he smiled thinly back at Texas Jim, and passed on out of the building.

Jim's reaction, initially, was one of indignant anger. Then he turned calculatingly thoughtful and pensive. He had thought, and with what had then appeared to be good reason, that the tall stranger had been a drifter, one of that innumerable brotherhood of men who made their living in the West when and where they could, and who drifted into places like Buellton, then drifted on again within a day or two.

Now, though, Texas Jim changed that notion. He felt quite certain that Chris Madsen, for some reason Jim could not yet imagine, had deliberately come to Buellton, and whatever that reason was, it vitally concerned old John Setter. "And that," Jim said aloud in the privacy of his office, "will be worth finding out about."

He was puzzling over this riddle later, when he went to the hotel dining room for his midday meal, and even later, when he went through town on one of his periodic but irregular rounds of the saloons, variety houses, and gambling rooms. When he encountered Dave Wesson coming out of the doctor's embalming shed, behind the doctor's combination office-residence, he nailed him before Dave could climb into the wagon and drive off.

"I thought old John told you to plant Leffingwell up on Setter hill," said Texas Jim. "I heard him tell you to bury him in the ranch's private plot."

Wesson put a pained expression up for Texas Jim to see. He said: "Marshal, I quit trying to figure things out after what happened at the big house this morning. All I can tell you now is that Miss Christel come to me about an hour ago . . . when we had the grave near dug . . . and said Mister Setter'd changed his mind. That I was to fetch Leffingwell here for doc to embalm. Then he was to be buried down here at boot hill."

Wesson took up the lines, flipped them, and drove on with a solemn nod at Marshal Collins.

VI

Texas Jim Collins was not a man whose patience permitted him to live for long with a riddle. He survived the second night with this one, then, directly after breakfast of the third day since Chris Madsen had arrived in Buellton, he saddled up, rode resolutely to John Setter's mansion atop its knoll, and told Miss Christel he wished to see her father—privately.

Old John was in his office, a bare, scarred room that had survived unchanged since John Setter had amassed his wealth. Here, Texas Jim was received by the powerful old cattleman; here he walked through the doorway into an atmosphere of cold and antagonistic resentment thick enough to cut with a knife.

John Setter was behind his large old desk. Only those brittle, uncompromising eyes moved, and they followed Texas Jim all the way forward, the brows above them rolling together the closer Jim came to Setter's desk, until John Setter's expression was as dark and dangerous as thunderclaps.

"Marshal," said John Setter, almost before Jim had halted in his onward stride, "I told you I didn't want you up here. I also told you that other thing was ended. Now, Marshal, I meant exactly what I said, and you'd best get that through your head." Setter paused; his bloodless slash of a mouth thinned out and turned downward at its outer corners. He fixed Texas Jim with his cold, cold stare. "We've come close to clashing a few times, Collins. God only knows why we never did. Don't make this the occasion for our clashing now. I said that thing is over . . . and by God it *is*."

Texas Jim, from his standing position, returned John Setter's unfriendly look with a look of his own. He said: "Mister Setter, I got your message yesterday. I also sent a message back to you. Did you get it?"

"I got it."

"Mister Setter, I meant that message, too."

Setter leaned back; his chair squeaked. He locked his fingers across a flat stomach and studied Texas Jim a moment before saying: "Collins, you're a fool. Any man with good sense would heed my warning, would be discreet an' sensible. Not you. You're going to push. You're going to push until someone goes down into his grave."

"No," said Texas Jim quietly and softly. "No. I'm not pushing. You are. All you've got to do is tell me what this is all about. Then, if it makes sense, I'll back off. Like I told Miss Christel, you should know now, after a quarter century, that I can be trusted."

"Trusted, hell!" exploded John Setter, glaring his indignation. "Why do I have to trust you, Marshal? Who the hell do you think you are anyway? You're just a lousy eighty dollar a month cow town law officer. I pay my range boss more than you get for wearing that silly nickel badge. You came here the same time I did. What've you got to show for it? A knocked-down shoulder, a bum leg, and a quiet town . . . and nothing in the bank, no property, nothing for your old age. Trust you? Collins, you make me laugh. I don't have to trust you. I don't have to tell you a damned thing, ever. To me, you're nothing . . . you're less than nothing. I can buy and sell a hundred men like you any day. . . ."

Setter ran out of breath, but the biting scorn remained up like a flag in his glare.

Texas Jim was pale around the mouth. His eyes were misty. "You've had your say," he retorted, his voice roughened by emotions that never showed on his face. "Now I'll have mine, Mister Setter."

"You'll get out of here, that's what you'll do."

Collins let this go by. He said: "You're right, I

have nothing in the bank. As for my old age . . . I don't expect to have an old age. Maybe everything you said about me is correct, Mister Setter . . . but the day you get some idea about being bigger than the law, that's the day you make your biggest mistake."

"Collins, I'll . . ."

"Mister Setter, I want that watch you took off Leffingwell."

"Marshal, by God, this is absolutely the last warning I'll give you. Get to hell off my hill right now and stay off!"

"The watch, Mister Setter."

John Setter leaned forward with both elbows upon his desk. He was black in the face, his hands shook, but when next he spoke, it was in such a quiet, husky tone Texas Jim scarcely heard his words.

"All right, Jim Collins. You've called it. Now I'm going to give you a promise, and I think by now you know John Setter's word is never broken. Marshal, by this time tomorrow you'll be dead."

Setter arose, he put out a hand to steady himself for a second, then he passed unseeingly out and around Texas Jim, and passed completely beyond his office, leaving Marshal Collins quite alone.

For some little time Jim simply stood where he was. Then he paced back the way he'd come, left the house, and breathed deeply of the good spring air upon John Setter's porch before going to his horse, mounting up, and reining downward and around to the flat land below Setter's hill.

It's come, he told himself, the showdown with John Setter that had been postponed one way or another for a quarter century had come. He thought about this all the way back to town and it made him bitter. He could recall many near clashes such as the shooting of that tinhorn gambler by Carlos; it had very nearly come then. Collins thought, as he passed along toward town, that of all the times when he and John Setter should have clashed, this time appeared the least formidable of them all. Actually he had nothing against Setter, or for that matter he had nothing particular against Chris Madsen. He only wanted to know what lay between those two. And for this, John Setter had threatened his life.

It had to be a vitally important secret to Setter, he thought. It had to be close to the old highbinder's heart, otherwise he never would have taken the affronts Madsen had given him. He'd seen John Setter turn his wolves loose on men over the long years for much, much less than this tall stranger with the ivory-stocked gun had done.

"Hey, Marshal . . . !"

Texas Jim reined up in the roadway. Joe Karns loped toward him from the livery barn doorway. Joe's face working agitatedly.

"What do you want?"

"Pete Sloat's lookin' for you. He's over at Hoag Balinger's saddle shop."

"Thanks," said Texas Jim, and started away.

"Setter's riders pushed cattle through Pete's meadow fence and the critters trampled down all Pete's standin' hay."

Texas Jim nodded and kept on riding.

Karns drew in a big breath. "Marshal, Pete shot six head of 'em."

Texas Jim stopped his horse. He twisted to look around and down at Karns. "Killed six of John Setter's cattle, Joe?"

"That's right."

Texas Jim slowly righted himself, kneed out his animal, and rode along to the tie rack before Balinger's shop. He swung out and down, took his thoughtful time at the rack, then crossed through overhang shade and stepped into the saddle shop.

There were several men here, and not one of them looked pleased at Texas Jim's appearance; they simply looked up at him, then down again. Toby Hostetter, night barman at the Golden Slipper, cleared his throat and spat into a box of sawdust provided for that purpose. Pete Sloat, looking gray and worried, as though now, in calmer moments, the enormity of what he'd done had just struck him, sat on Hoag Balinger's cutting table, listlessly swinging his legs.

"Why," demanded Texas Jim at once, scowling

at Sloat, "didn't you just hurrah them out of your meadow? Why did you have to go and shoot them, Pete?"

Sloat looked up. "You heard, eh?" he said, sounding weak. Marshal Collins stood on, awaiting his answer. Sloat fidgeted, he opened and closed his hands, then he said: "I been takin' it for a long time, Marshal. For years, in fact. If they don't run cattle into my meadow, they cut my fences or dump salt in my water holes. Old Man Setter told me once I'd sell to him. He told me that, sittin' in his damned buggy and grinnin' at me like an ape, an' ever since then it's been like this . . . one damned lousy thing after another."

Sloat paused; he looked around at the solemn ring of faces; he lifted his shoulders and let them fall. "This mornin' I just saw red. I run an' got my Winchester an' rode down there and commenced chargin' them damned cattle. I run most of 'em back through the break in the fence, but six real spooky ones scattered . . ."

"So you rode 'em down and shot 'em."

Sloat nodded, looking uncomfortable under Texas Jim's stare. "So I shot 'em," he echoed the law officer. Then he rallied, dredged up his weak anger and his defiance, and spoke on: "An' Setter's cowboys seen me do it, too. They heard the shootin' an' rode up on to that ridge east o' my place an' sat up there, watching. They didn't

227

have the guts to ride down at me, though, an' there was five of 'em."

Collins shifted his glance; he looked at the other men in the shop. All but Hoag Balinger were watching him; Hoag was sitting at his sewing horse, mending a leather trace with two needles and an awl. He seemed quite absorbed in what he was doing.

Texas Jim put his gaze back upon raffish Pete Sloat; it was a contemptuous look. "Didn't have the guts," he said in a scornful tone. "Who are you trying to fool, Pete? John Setter's riders aren't the least bit scairt of you."

"Then why didn't they ride down when I was shootin' their critters?"

"Because they didn't give a damn whether you shot Setter cattle or not. Likely they even laughed about it, because they know how old John reacts to things like that. They just waited until they knew how many head you'd shot, then high-tailed it for Setter's hill and reported to either Carlos or Dave Wesson. And you can bet your damned boots, by now John Setter knows about it, too."

Toby Hostetter bobbed his head gravely up and down in agreement with this. Hoag Balinger, finally rocking back from his work, looked over at Pete Sloat; it was a pitying look.

"You should've sold out to Setter," Hoag pronounced, then returned to his sewing.

Texas Jim, concentrating his full attention upon this new dilemma, made a decision. He crooked a finger at Sloat. "Come on, Pete, I'm going to lock you up."

"For what, Marshal?" piped up the stump rancher. "I got a right to defend m'property. The law says a man's . . ."

"Don't quote law to me," snapped Collins. "Just come along. Pete, I'm doing you a favor by locking you up. Now get down off there and come along."

VII

Carlos Setter, Dave Wesson, and four riders appeared in town at Marshal Collins's office an hour after Texas Jim had locked Pete Sloat in a cell. Texas Jim, coming back from his room at the hotel, met them on the plank walk outside his jailhouse. He read in their faces that they were geared up for trouble, so, as was his custom, he met this trouble head-on and immediately seized the initiative.

"Sloat's locked up," he said to Carlos, "and, if you fellers have some notion of taking him out, or threatening him, forget it . . . unless you want to try walking over me to get at him."

Carlos glared but it was Dave Wesson who

spoke. Dave said: "Marshal, Mister Setter wants payment for them critters Sloat shot, and he wants Sloat prosecuted for shootin' 'em."

Texas Jim nodded over this. "He'll be tried in court when the circuit judge comes to town. You can tell Mister Setter that, Dave, which is the way it should be done." Jim looked over at fiery Carlos; he cocked his head a little when he said to Carlos: "Are we going to let it stand like this, or aren't we?"

Carlos started to speak, checked himself, and stamped out to his horse. From the saddle he growled downward: "Sloat's a damned fringe-ranch rustler. He's been sneakin' a calf off us now and then for years. No, Marshal, we aren't goin' to let it stand like this. Come on, Dave, let's get out of here."

Wesson looked distressed; he jumped his gaze from Texas Jim out to Carlos and back again. As he was turning to leave, he said: "I'm only the range boss, Marshal."

The six horsemen went loping northward out of town, and once again, as he stood quietly in thought, Jim heard that dry, nearly amused voice come out of some northward shadows.

"I don't see how you've done it, Marshal, staying out of a showdown fight with that Setter outfit all these years."

Jim turned, not surprised at the sight of tall Chris Madsen standing there. He said in reply:

"I got to admit, Madsen, I don't know how I've done it, either. But now . . . ."

"Yes?"

"Nothing."

These two stood looking at one another for a full sixty silent seconds, then Texas Jim said in his usual blunt manner: "Madsen, I need a deputy. You want the job? It pays sixty a month, horse feed, and ammunition. You'll be on call any time of the day or night."

Chris Madsen stepped closer to Texas Jim in the overhang shade. He had a twinkle in his dark eyes. "One day you're thinking you might have to kill me, the next day you're offering me a job. Why?"

Jim went to the wall bench and sat down. "I want you to hang around," he said forthrightly. "I want to know just what the hell is going on here. But that's not all of it, either." He looked up at the much younger man. "John Setter threatened my life yesterday. He's not a man who ordinarily makes idle threats, Madsen."

"Why did he do that?"

"I don't honestly know. I wanted to see that watch he has that belongs to you. That triggered it, somehow. I never saw him get mad so quick. Tell me, Madsen, what's written inside that watch?"

The tall man was no longer smiling; he was regarding old Texas Jim Collins with a peculiar expression. "Nothing important," he eventually said quite softly. "But I'll tell you one thing, Marshal. There's more to this mystery than either of us knows. I'm going to keep quiet until I find out more about it. After that"—Madsen shrugged—"after that, Marshal, I got no real objection to you knowing about the watch."

Texas Jim looked up the roadway. He said: "All right. I guess patience is something that comes to a man as he gets older. I'll wait. Now, about that deputy's job . . . ?"

"I'll take it, Marshal. What've you got in mind?"

"You've probably heard about a feller named Sloat shooting six head of Setter cattle?"

"I heard. In Buellton here, the livery barn's better for getting fresh news than the telegraph office."

"Yeah," replied Collins dryly, "I reckon it is. Well, I want you to go out to the Sloat place and sit there."

"You're thinking Setter will send a crew there?"

"With torches," said Texas Jim in the same dry tone. "It's happened before to the little cow outfits on the fringe of the Setter range. I've never been able to tie John or Carlos to those burn-outs, but old John always winds up owning the land afterward."

Chris Madsen stood on, gazing over at Marshal Collins. After a time he said: "Sure, I'll do it.

232

But it looks to me as though I'd be better off hanging around town."

Texas Jim understood the thought behind these words and shook his head. "No," he softly said, "that threat don't scare me a whole lot. Anyway, if John is dead set on keeping that promise, two of us wouldn't stand any more chance than one of us, because he's got about thirty men working for him."

Madsen's gaze sharpened. "You don't believe he'll keep that promise, do you?"

Texas Jim got up, steadied his stiff leg, and said with an air of finality: "I don't know, exactly. I don't think he'll keep it today, like he said. I think he's got something else on his mind he'll want to attend to first."

"Like me leaving Buellton?"

"How did you know that?" asked Texas Jim.

Madsen's faint grin returned; it hovered down around his lips. "A girl told me, Marshal. Just about the most beautiful girl I ever saw in my whole dog-goned life."

Collins showed surprise, which was unusual for him. "Christel Setter?"

"Yes."

"You mean you met her again?"

"Well, not exactly met her, Marshal. It took a little figuring. That's where I've been all day . . . out on the range watching Setter hill and waiting for her to drive down in that fancy rig of hers. I had some questions I needed answers to. About my watch, for one thing."

"Did you get your answers?"

Chris Madsen shook his head. He put up a hand and touched his cheek. His black eyes were pensive, yet at the same time they showed faint merriment. "I got slapped. Miss Christel's got more power to her than a man'd think. The only thing she told me was that I had to leave the country."

"Did she say why you should leave?"

"No, and after she hit me, I didn't ask."

"Why did she hit you?"

"Marshal," drawled Madsen, "I don't figure I can rightly tell you that. If Miss Christel wants to tell you, why that's all right, but it wouldn't be right for me to tell you."

Texas Jim stared. "You tried to kiss her," he said. "You idiot, you tried to kiss old John Setter's girl."

Madsen hesitated. He lowered his hand and drew upright. In some ways he had characteristics that were very like Texas Jim's personal ways. He said: "You want me to go out to Sloat's place right now, Marshal?"

Texas Jim didn't immediately reply to this. When he did, he looked a little grim. "And take your carbine, if you have one," he said. He put a frosty look upon the younger man. "Let me give you some advice about Christel Setter. Her pappy's an old terror and her three brothers aren't easy men to calm down once they've got their backs up. And if that isn't enough, in the way of trouble for you, why just you remember that girl's had her own way so long she'd drive a man out of his mind."

Madsen squinted at Texas Jim. "Once," he said, "I met a stud colt with just about the same antecedents, Marshal."

"And? You couldn't ride him, could you?"

"I'm riding him right now, Marshal."

Madsen nodded, and strolled along up the plank walk toward the livery barn. Texas Jim stood back there, gazing after him. He puckered up his brows and he said a mild cuss word.

The day wore along. Texas Jim waited; he felt that John Setter might do something. He'd been uncontrollably angry when he'd made that threat and perhaps he'd spoken out of his thick rage, not entirely meaning everything he'd said. But, still, he was a proud man and he'd do something.

Texas Jim, better than anyone else, knew just how proud John Setter was. He sat in his office, thinking back to the revealing past, thinking back to a full-breasted, flashing-eyed woman who had lived in Buellton some twenty-odd years earlier, when he and John Setter had been much younger than they now were. Her name had been Rosalia Bent. After she'd left Buellton, word trickled back to Texas Jim that she'd married a rich sheepman out in Nevada.

But what Texas Jim was now remembering was how things had been before Rosalia Bent had departed from the Buellton country. He and John Setter had been fiery, too, in those days. But John had been married. Still, John Setter, being as he was—willful and yeasty and headstrong, and callous, too—hadn't let that stop his paying court to Rosalia Bent.

Texas Jim had been indignant that John had wanted to have his own woman and another one, too. They'd had a few words about that, but nothing had come of it because beautiful dark-eyed Rosalia had preferred Texas Jim. For more than a year the white-hot romance between Rosalia Bent and Jim Collins had been the source of much talk, much speculation. Then Rosalia left Buellton. People wondered about that; Jim remembered the whispers. He'd never done anything about them, though, and no one ever spoke to him about them because Texas Jim Collins was not the man to make fun of.

Of course, as the years passed, folks forgot Rosalia Bent. But Jim Collins never forgot her; he didn't re-live those secret times together so much now as he once had, but he never forgot them nonetheless. Especially on fragrant spring nights. But Jim Collins, even as a young man, was dedicated to his work. That, in one sentence, was what kept him from ever marrying—Rosalia Bent or any other woman.

He thought back now to the times when he and John Setter had walked stiff-legged around one another, how they had come near to drawing against each other over luscious Rosalia Bent, and how John's yeasty pride in those days had been keen-edged. But that was a long time past.

Still, he told himself in the quiet atmosphere of his noon-day office, men don't change basically from what they are in youth. It was true, what old John had said: he made no idle threats. He would do something, if for no other reason than because the fiery pride of youth, which was now the crusty determination of late age, would demand that he not go back on the unshakable belief he had in himself that when he said something, he meant it.

Texas Jim had never, in that intervening quarter century since they'd first met, actually made a deep analysis of John Setter. He had never done this for a very elemental reason: Jim Collins, the iron-legend of Anza County, had not, up to now, been a deep-thinking man. He'd had no need to be; he was the top-notch gunfighter of his part of the country. Gunfighters, with badges or without them, were not complicated men. They arrived at decisions largely through instinct, and after that they acted.

That's how it had always been with Texas Jim.

Up to now, anyway. But now he tried to plumb the depths of John Setter; he sat there remembering things and seeking to ascribe motives to them. Their competition for the heady favors of Rosalia Bent was easily figured; they had in those days both been virile men with the woman hunger of all virile men. But from then on it was not always easy to understand why Setter had done many of the things he'd been involved in.

He had squeezed out a number of little fringe ranchers. He'd done this for the best possible reason: to acquire contiguous lands. And Texas Jim didn't condemn him for this, really; stump ranchers like Pete Sloat could not make a living off their little starve-out places. They existed, was all. Too, they had a monotonous habit of living off beef from their larger and more powerful neighbors. This was an accepted fact in any cow country.

As he sat there thinking back, it gradually came to Texas Jim that granite-like John Setter had a streak in him Jim had never once thought he'd had. He arrived at this conclusion by accident. In thinking back to the stump ranchers John had frozen out, he remembered that in each instance Setter had given the fringe rancher top dollar for his acres. He also recalled how old John had given his sons and his beautiful daughter everything they had also wanted. And John had never deprived dead Nettie Setter of anything, either. He'd imported blooded Kentucky horses for her to ride; he'd even once sent to Boston in far-off Massachusetts for furniture Nettie had admired.

Slowly all these things and many others that he'd paid no heed to at the time began to make an image of John Setter in Texas Jim's mind that left him a little breathless, a little shocked, because icy-eyed John Setter was now emerging as something altogether different from what Jim would have sworn he was and always had been. He was so wholly lost in this bizarre rationalization that, when the liveryman, Joe Karns, poked his head in at the doorway and called out, Jim did not hear him the first or second time.

"Hey, wake up, Marshal. You sleepin' with your eyes open or something? I said John Setter hisself is ridin' down the road with his three boys and what looks like half his cow-camp crew."

Jim blinked. He brought his face down and around. He stared at Karns.

"You sick or something?" Karns demanded, looking worried, looking perplexed.

"No," murmured Texas Jim, pushing up out of his chair. "I'm all right, Joe. Thanks for the warning."

Karns's head disappeared from the doorway, his hastening footfalls dimmed out, and Texas Jim stood up, flexed his arms, and started forward.

From across the room Pete Sloat bleated behind his cell bars: "For God's sake, Marshal, don't let 'em in here! They've come to lynch me. I know they have. Marshal, you got to keep them out . . ."

"They won't lynch you, Pete. They don't even want you. They want me."

"Tell Mister Setter I'll pay him for the six critters, Marshal. He can pick out six from my herd as replacements if he wants them. Tell him that, Marshal."

"Rest easy," said Texas Jim, regarding the nearly panicked fringe cowman. "Mister Setter's not thinking about any six lousy cows. He's thinking about principle."

"Well, you tell him what I said I'd do anyway, Marshal," croaked the imprisoned man, not sure at all what Texas Jim Collins meant by *principle*.

Jim nodded. "I'll tell him," he said quietly, "if I get the chance." He cocked his head to listen, heard the sudden loud silence out in the roadway where moments before Buellton had been bustling with activity, and also heard that steadily approaching large body of mounted men.

He went to the door, passed on out, and took his stance on the shaded plank walk.

VIII

John Setter did not very often ride horseback any more. In fact, he only rarely went into Buellton. He had no need to, hadn't had any such need in many years. For this reason the townspeople gaped now as old John paced past with his sons and his range riders around him. Word was flashed from mouth to mouth of his coming, of his grimmer-than-usual look, and of the guns riding with him. Hoag Balinger, when he heard, rose up, shed his apron, resolutely took down his Winchester, and went to stand silently in the doorway of his shop. Hoag was a quiet man and a tolerant one; he was also an admirer of Texas Jim Collins. So was Joe Karns, and Joe was in his doorway, too, but with a double-barrel shotgun charged with lead slugs, a terrible weapon at no greater distance than the width of Main Street.

John Setter saw Marshal Collins standing there. He kept his eyes steadily upon the law officer, until, when he was abreast the jailhouse, he reined up, and all those hard-eyed men reined up behind him. Frank and Reg were on either side of their father. Carlos was farther back.

"Collins," said John Setter, "I want to talk to Pete Sloat."

Texas Jim stood, wide-legged. "Alone?" he asked.

Setter nodded. "Alone," he said. "We'll take up our personal business when I'm finished with Sloat."

Jim moved back, raised an arm, and flung back his jailhouse door. "Come along," he said, and waited for Setter to get down stiffly and just as stiffly cross over, pass on by, and enter the jailhouse. Collins kept a brief watch on John's sons and riders, then, when it was clear none of these men was going to dismount, Texas Jim walked on inside and halted to close the door, and lean upon it, saying: "There he is, Mister Setter, in the cell yonder."

Pete Sloat was gray-faced. He was clinging to the bars of his cell with white knuckles, staring dry-eyed at John Setter's grim and rugged face. Before Setter moved forward or spoke, Sloat said: "Mister Setter, I was within my rights, but all the same I'll pay for the critters."

Setter stood like stone, glowering over at Texas Jim's prisoner. He was wearing a gun and he looked ugly, but he didn't say a word, he just glowered.

"All right," croaked the prisoner, becoming rapidly unnerved under that grim and totally silent stare. "All right, Mister Setter, you can take your pick of six critters from my herd to replace them shot ones."

"My beef, anyway," growled Setter. "If I picked six head, they'd more'n likely be calves from my cows, Sloat."

"No, sir. I give you my word on that, Mister Setter."

"You afraid to die, Sloat?" asked old John Setter. "You're sure acting like you are."

"What do you want from me," pleaded the prisoner, beginning to quake.

"I don't want replacements, Sloat, and I don't want payment."

Sloat, thrusting around for some clue as to what Setter wanted, said in a rush of words: "All right, I'll work it out ridin' for you."

Setter quietly shook his head.

"Mister Setter . . . what is it you want?"

"Sloat," said John Setter in his reedy, menacing voice, "one time I told you that you'd live to see the day you'd be tickled pink to sell out to me. You recollect that?"

"Yes, sir, I recollect it."

"All right, Sloat. Now's the time."

"Just over six cows, Mister Setter?"

"No, more'n likely over sixty head of cows . . . or for all I know a hundred and sixty."

"I never rustled from you, Mister Setter."

"That," said the old cowman flatly, "is a damned lie, Sloat. You know it is, and I know it is. Do you want me to prove to the marshal here that it's a damned lie?"

Sloat flinched from the fierce lash of Setter's words. He shook his head, looking very troubled. "No," he husked.

"How much, Sloat, for that lousy stone patch you call a cow ranch?"

"Mister Setter, I'd rather . . ."

"How much, Sloat?"

"Ah, twelve hundred dollars, Mister Setter?"

Old John turned his back upon Sloat, facing Texas Jim. "Let him out," he ordered.

Jim looked for a long time into Setter's unwavering pale stare. "You're dropping charges?" he quietly asked.

"What charges? There never were any charges. Let him out so he can go with me right now to the abstract office and sign a deed over to me for that pile of gopher holes he's got the nerve to call a cow ranch."

"It's not worth twelve hundred dollars, Mister Setter."

Old John's cheeks turned splotchy with dark blood. "When I want advice, dammit," he roared, "I'll ask someone other than you, Marshal Collins. Now let him out of there!"

Still Texas Jim stood still and staring. The silence ran on until it became almost tangible in the office. Finally, though, Texas Jim moved; he took up his keys, crossed to Sloat's cell, opened the door, and flung it far back. "Out," he ordered Pete Sloat, and clanged the door behind his former prisoner. "Sloat, I want to know what your plans are after you get that twelve hundred dollars."

Old John's head swung around. "That's none of your cussed business," he said to Marshal Collins.

"I'm making it my business, and you keep out of it," retorted Collins, his voice also sending reverberations through the office. "Answer me, Sloat, right damned now!"

"Yes, Marshal, sure. I'm goin' to go load up my wagon an' get out of this lousy country as fast as I can. Does that suit you?"

"It suits me fine," answered Texas Jim, passing around both men to the street door and throwing that open, too. He said no more until John Setter was moving past, then, in a quiet tone, he murmured: "I'll be waiting, Mister Setter."

"And I *will* be back," flung back Setter, then passed out into the roadway, called something to his men, and went stumping along, prodding Sloat with his bony old fist, steering Sloat toward the abstract office which lay northward several doors from the jailhouse.

Frank Setter leaned down, saying to Marshal Collins: "Did Sloat sell out?"

Texas Jim nodded.

Frank straightened back in his saddle and made a wry little grin at his brother Reg.

Jim stood a moment in deep thought, then he went over beside Reg Setter's mount and said:

"I'd like to talk to Miss Christel. Will you tell her that for me?"

Reg looked a little curious, a little round-eyed, but he nodded. "I'll tell her, Marshal. I doubt if she'll come, but I'll tell her."

Texas Jim went back into his office, kicked the door partially closed, tossed aside his hat, and sat down. He was not ordinarily a smiling man; in fact, there could be found dozens of people in Buellton who would take an oath that in twenty-five years they had never once seen Jim Collins even grin. But now he sat there very close to smiling. He was still sitting like that a half hour later when the door shuddered inward and John Setter appeared in the opening.

Without any preliminaries Setter said: "Marshal, you've got a choice. Resign or fight."

"Fight what?" asked Texas Jim. "You? Hell, that wouldn't be any fight for me."

Setter reddened. He half choked over his next words. "You are an old man, Collins. You can't fight me and you ought to know that."

"You personally, or those cur dogs that ride for you? Listen, Mister Setter, I'm not a very patient man. After all these years you should know that. Now, if you want to make me fight, it won't be hard. You just turn around and call in your toughest gunman. After I down him, I'll take on the next toughest in your crew, and so on."

"You are a damned fool, Collins. You're an old

man. You can't buck me and you can't buck my whole crew. They are young men."

Texas Jim stood up; he was a half head taller than John Setter, even with the slouch his knocked-down shoulder gave him. "Get out of here," he said. "Don't come back until you've got something worthwhile to say. Go on now."

"Collins, I meant that . . . fight or resign."

"I'll fight. You said I'd be dead by this time today. Go ahead and keep your lousy word, Setter. Call in your fastest gun."

These two fierce old men stood, glaring. Outside, in brilliant roadway sunshine, Setter's big crew of riders sat on quietly. Buellton was as quiet as a tomb. Setter turned abruptly, went to the doorway, and twisted there to glare back at Texas Jim.

"I'll give you an alternative to fighting, Collins. Get that stranger out of Buellton no later than tomorrow. That's my final word."

"And if I don't . . . what then? You going to threaten to have me killed again, Mister Setter?"

Texas Jim got back no answer to this. John Setter stamped across the plank walk, struggled up into his saddle, jerked his head at the men around him, and started northward back out of town the same way he'd ridden in.

Texas Jim, standing in the jailhouse doorway, shook his head back and forth in deepest puzzlement. *John Setter,* he thought, *the toughest transplanted Texan of them all, had backed down once more. Why? Why had he let this happen?*

Hoag Balinger called from across the way: "How did it go, Marshal?"

Texas Jim squinted over at Balinger, then turned without a word and went back inside, kicked the door closed, and stared over at that empty cell. $1,200 for Pete Sloat's gravel pile; it wasn't good sense or good business, either. Sloat had been so frightened he'd have sold out for half that amount. Texas Jim gave a little start. Chris Madsen would be sitting out there, waiting for Setter riders who would never appear.

Jim re-crossed the room, passed outside, and started around to the horse shed; he'd have to go get Madsen himself.

As he was saddling and bridling, and, afterward, as he was riding through the afternoon, westward, he continued to think of the price asked, and immediately accepted, for the Sloat place. He finally said aloud to his horse: "How do you judge a man like that? He scares 'em out and he's burned 'em out . . . but always he gives 'em the price they ask. How do you say a man like that is as bad as folks believe he is . . . and really believe it yourself?"

The horse flicked his ears and went plodding along.

"But how could I ever have been blind for so long? Hell, John Setter's not tough at all. He's

248

ruthless about things he wants, but tough . . . hell, if he was any softer he'd melt in the sun and run all over the place like butter. Good Lord, for twenty-five years that man has fooled an entire county . . . and me. He's a better actor than Wilkes Booth ever thought of being. Wilkes Booth play-acted for one evening. John Setter's been play-acting for half a lifetime."

A few miles farther along, with afternoon shadows beginning to show here and there, Texas Jim Collins threw back his head and roared with laughter. Even his horse was startled now. But he wasn't half as astonished at that rumbling great sound as the people of Buellton would have been had they heard it.

Texas Jim gasped for breath; he swiped at his watering eyes with a sleeve and he eased back in the saddle to recover. Then he shot a narrowed gaze far onward toward the Pete Sloat place, and at once his mind began to pick at the riddle of Chris Madsen.

He was still wondering about Madsen when he sighted a loping rider cutting along southwest ahead of him more than a mile. This rider was leaving a standing plume of dust in his wake; the lowering, reddening sun caught this dust and made it sparkle.

Texas Jim became his usual considering, alert self at once. He gauged the distance, the course, and the speed of that unknown horseman. From these things he decided two things at once. One of them was that he could not possibly overtake the onward rider, and the second thing—and this held his attention longest—was that this stranger was heading as straight as an arrow for the Sloat place, also.

IX

In a man who had survived this rough life as long as had Texas Jim Collins caution and courage were carefully blended and balanced. As soon as he was certain that onward rider had not noticed him, he changed course so as to approach the Sloat place without being seen. This posed no great difficulty for in this area the land broke and buckled, leaving little knolls, long-spending ridges, and thickets of buckbrush.

It was more difficult, though, later on when he came down behind Pete Sloat's little bachelor shack, for here the land had been cleared in all directions as a precaution against fire. Still, Jim found a stake-and-rider fence overgrown with bushes, left his horse concealed there, and slipped along on foot until he was behind Sloat's ramshackle barn. Now he stood motionlessly in barn shadows, making a very thorough search of the surrounding yard for signs of people.

He saw a saddled horse, finally, when the beast

flicked its tail. He did not recognize this animal, yet he was sure it did not belong to Chris Madsen. For one thing there was no saddle boot; for another, although the horse was identical in color to the horse he'd looked at in Joe Karns's livery barn, this horse was easily two hundred pounds lighter and a hand shorter.

There was not a sound. For quite a while Texas Jim remained hidden. He thought that whoever owned that visible horse might be lying in wait for Madsen. This thought made him regret not fetching along his saddle gun. Then he heard the unmistakable approach of a ridden horse, and he angled around the corner of Sloat's barn in the direction of this sound.

It was Madsen. He was coming on from the south, from behind Sloat's shack. His horse was walking easy with its head low and the reins slapping. Madsen, too, was sitting up there, looking totally unconcerned. Texas Jim drew back a breath to call a warning. He took one step, planted that forward foot down hard, ready to spring around the barn—and Madsen raised his head at that exact moment, looked ahead with late afternoon sunlight fully upon his face, and sang out: "I thought you'd never get here."

Texas Jim froze. Madsen was looking toward the little honeysuckle-covered shed that housed Sloat's dug well. He was addressing someone who he had evidently known would be there.

Texas Jim sucked back around the barn wall and flattened there; he could not right then explain why he did this.

Madsen's voice came on again, light and lilting. "I didn't see you ride in, but I'm glad you got my message."

Jim strained to hear more, to hear the reply of the other person. He heard nothing at all, except the abrupt stopping of Madsen's horse, the squeak of leather as a man dismounted, and the afterward jingle of rein chains as a horse shook its head. He did not wait long enough to weigh the significance of Chris Madsen's meeting someone here; instead, he passed along the barn's north wall, got safely back across to the fence where thickets hid him, and began a careful, crouched southward moving until he was in a position to see the well house. This took time, the shadows were lengthening, and, after Jim got there, he found that Madsen's horse was the only living thing still standing there. The beast had been tied to a rank vine trunk and faintly visible over on the porch of Sloat's shack were two moving, vague figures.

Texas Jim, committed now to this pattern of stealth, never once thought of stepping into the clear and announcing himself. He began the long, circuitous creep back to the fence, along it to the rear of Sloat's house, and from there on around the shack's eastern wall to its abrupt cornering with the front porch wall. There he at last heard the distinct murmur of voices around front, and he drew gradually upright, astonished at the identifiable sound of one of those voices: Christel Setter.

It all struck Texas Jim at once: no carbine boot on the saddle, the finer-boned horse than a man would ride, the direction from which he'd earlier seen the rider hastening along. He stood in soft gloom, thinking these things, and at the same time hearing those soft, confiding tones around front, not exactly meaning to eavesdrop, but not willing, either, to let go this opportunity.

Christel was saying, in a quietly insistent way: " . . . Jasper got your message from Toby at the Golden Slipper. That's why I was so late. Anyway, Chris, it's a long ride down here, and I wasn't sure I'd dare come after what else happened. I was afraid I'd run into Carlos or Frank down here."

"No," came the calm tones of Madsen, "no one's shown up here at all. It's so late now I doubt if they will."

"They won't," Christel confirmed. "My father bought Sloat out this afternoon. It must have happened after you left town."

There was a little pause, then: "Bought him out? You mean your father went to Sloat at the jailhouse?"

"Yes, Jasper told me that. He was with my

father and brothers in town, but he left them to get a drink at the Golden Slipper . . . that's when he got your message from Toby. Then he came on home. He had to start preparing supper for the men at the cook shack. I met him at the barn when I was saddling up to go for a ride. He told me you wanted me to come down here to Sloat's."

"Why?" said Madsen. "Why would your father buy this place? Christel, it doesn't make sense. In the first place it's not worth anything. In the second place this Sloat shot . . ."

"Chris, listen to me for just a moment. I know how you feel about my father and my brothers, Carlos particularly. But you don't know my father. Honestly, Chris, he's not at all as you think him. Believe me . . . he isn't."

Madsen said slowly: "Christel, I don't know your father. I know he has my watch, though, and from that I figure he knows about . . ."

"That," interrupted Christel swiftly, just when Texas Jim was straining hardest to hear, "is why he wants you to leave the country. Don't you understand how that is, Chris?"

"Yes, I understand. But I don't agree with his reasoning. I came here deliberately. I wanted to see for myself . . ."

"You've seen, Chris. Now, please leave."

Madsen turned. Texas Jim could hear his spurred boots grind into Sloat's old porch flooring. For a second there was no further talk, then Madsen said to Christel Setter: "Walk with me. It's a beautiful night."

They moved out into the yard. Night was fast dropping now, the mystery of it pressing close and cutting off everything in Texas Jim's view but those two swaying shapes onward. Christel's pale blouse faintly shone under pewter star shine. There was a rhythm to her body; Texas Jim could imagine Madsen being very conscious of this. The pair of them halted where a sighing night breeze came vagrantly along, then passed on southward. Christel turned squarely and looked up into Madsen's face, shadowed by his hat brim: "What will it take to make you leave this country?"

Madsen's answer came back softly yet very distinctly. "You. If you will come with me, I'll leave tomorrow . . . tonight even."

"Chris, you don't mean that. Not really. We've been flint on stone, you and me. But even . . ."

"Flint and stone go together, Christel. Marshal Collins told me you were spoiled, that you'd be nothing but trouble and heartache for some man."

"He said that?"

"You've given folks the right to think that, Christel. You gave me cause to think it the first day we met."

Over by the house Texas Jim scowled blackly, turning angry, turning indignant toward his deputy.

Christel half turned. The rising moon touched down upon her beautiful face and Texas Jim could very plainly see her expression when she said: "I know I've had that coming. But, Chris, it's been such a long, long wait."

"What has?" asked Madsen with genuine puzzlement in his voice.

Christel turned swiftly without answering, without speaking a word, and swayed against Madsen. Texas Jim was rooted; he was very astonished and very shocked.

She kissed Madsen, raised up on her tiptoes, sought his lips with her mouth, put both arms up around his wide shoulders, and pressed herself into the full length of him. Texas Jim forgot for a moment even to breathe. Those two swaying, blended figures clung to one another for what seemed to Texas Jim to be an eternity. Then very slowly Christel pushed Madsen away; she was pale in that silvery moonlight; she was gazing steadily upward at Madsen.

"That," she murmured. "I meant that's been a long time coming, Chris."

Madsen stood still without speaking for a moment before he said: "I'll leave. We'll go away together."

The sudden wistfulness that swept over Christel was visible even over where Texas Jim was standing. Her shoulders slumped and her eyes dropped. "No," she murmured, "I can't go with

you. Chris, there's something you don't understand. My father depends on me entirely."

"He's got your brothers."

"No, not really. They're men now, and they
seldom go to him any more. They have their work
on our range. Men drift apart, Chris, even fathers
and sons. I suppose that's right and natural, at
least my father says that it is." She shot him an
upward look. "They don't really understand
him, anyway. They're like everyone else. They
think he's made of iron. They respect him, and I
suppose even Carlos, in his way, loves him.
But he's not a young man any more and he's
terribly lonely. Oh, I know you don't think of
John Setter as a lonely, sad man. But I'm his
daughter, Chris. I know him. We're very close."

"Then," said Madsen, "I'll stay here. It doesn't
really matter to me anyway, Christel. I have no
roots. I'm a person looking for something. I've
been that way ever since I left Nevada five years
ago. I reckon you and I are alike in that. We've
both been looking for something."

"Chris, tell me . . . do you think you're in love
with me?"

"I don't think I'm in love with you, Christel, I
know I'm in love with you. I knew it that day
you slapped me."

The beautiful girl's lips parted in a faint little
smile. "I knew it that day, too."

Madsen responded to her little smile with a

grin of his own. "You sure pack a wallop," he said.

She continued to smile a moment longer, then she gradually turned grave again, saying: "I want you to stay, Chris. I never in my whole life wanted anything so much. But . . ."

He shook his head, began shaking it before she let that last word trail off into silence. "I know why your father wants me to leave. But that's exactly why I won't leave. Don't you see, Christel?"

"I see the pain your staying will cause, Chris."

"Your father has convinced you of that."

"But it's true. The past is gone . . . it should be over and done with. Resurrecting it will only cause feelings of guilt, of agony and self-reproach."

Madsen shook his head again. "Hiding your head from life doesn't help," he said, speaking softly to her. "I'm not bitter, and, if anyone should have that right, I should."

"We aren't all the same, Chris. Some of us have more pride, more depths to our feelings than others."

"You're saying I'm not able to feel deeply. That's not true, Christel. Not true at all. But today is now, a man stands face to face with himself and what has made him as he is. Does being resentful or bitter or vengeful help any? No, of course it doesn't. Besides, what was done long ago was not a callous thing. It had its beauty, too. You can understand that. If there's anyone on this earth now who can understand that, it's you."

Christel solemnly nodded. She stood a moment just looking at Chris Madsen, then she said: "I think I'd die if you rode away." She sighed. "And if you stay . . ."

"Yes?"

"Chris, I don't know. I just don't know. I'm troubled and fearful and confused."

"Marry me," he said.

"I want to very much, Chris." She regarded him over an interval of perplexed silence, then she said: "If anyone had ever said you could hate a man one day and fall in love with him the day after, I'd have thought they were a little insane. But it's true."

She turned, took his arm, pressed it to her side, and started slowly walking toward the well house where her horse still stood. Texas Jim thought he heard her sigh. He saw her halt finally, beside her horse, turn and put a tender look upon Madsen. The moon had its soft light across her face now, showing its beauty and its strength, and showing, too, the dark, strange things lying in her eyes.

She said very quietly, very solemnly and without any trace of fire: "Chris, I love you so much. So very much."

Texas Jim felt a sharp stab of guilt, standing

there. It was a belated sensation, yet it came, and it caused him to turn away from those two yonder blending shapes near Sloat's well house. He moved along the wall to its farthest turning and halted there. He was not ordinarily a smoking man and he rarely ever carried a tobacco sack with him, but this once he wished mightily for the solace of a smoke. Something long dormant was stirred to life within him. The night, for ome inexplicable reason, smelled sharper to him. The stars seemed more diamond-bright; there appeared to be an ancient promise in the great vault of heaven. He could close his eyes and distinctly see the lovely image of Rosalia Bent; he could also see all those years between then and now telescoped into a moment. They were as ashes to him; he had let something get away from him. It could never be recalled.

He knew a depth of sadness he had never known before. He also knew a variety of poignancy that was strange to him. In that moment he felt like walking out into that yonder yard and brushing aside the exclamations of that girl and man to tell them simply to take this high promise life was holding out to them. To take it and cherish it, because life was struggle and uncertainty and a man or a woman who had no place to find solace were only half alive.

Then this strange mood passed and Texas Jim Collins, his bad leg bothering him because he had stood upon it for so long, became once more the iron legend of Anza County. Not quite the same as he'd been for a quarter century before this pale, soft night, but almost the same. The same at least in one respect—when he heard the running horses flinging on down the night, he reacted as he always had to the scent and taste of danger. He swiftly stepped into total darkness and dropped his right hand to his belt gun, gauging the strength of that approaching sound and searching for its reason in coming here this night.

He found no immediate answers to these questions, so he stood on, waiting, thinking as all fighting men think, wondering if his hidden horse would be found telling whoever these men were, that he was hereabouts. Wondering, too, what the odds were going to be, even before he had any solid reason to believe there was going to be a fight.

X

A man's high and triumphant cry shattered those layers of night hush that had until this moment filled the yard of the Sloat place.

"Here's his horse, over here!"

Texas Jim, thinking instinctively his own animal had been discovered, slipped along the back wall so as to espy whoever those men were.

Then he heard a name spoken fiercely, with hard oaths, and he halted.

"It's Madsen's animal all right, damn his lousy soul. Dismount all of you and spread out. He's close by. Don't give him a chance."

Texas Jim's breath hung up. He visualized that yonder yard at once in his mind's eye. Those men had come from the east. Madsen and Christel Setter were westward, somewhere near the well house. It wouldn't take more than a moment for those men to cross Sloat's yard. Texas Jim palmed his six-gun. He could cause a temporary diversion, enough of a diversion perhaps to let Madsen and John Setter's daughter run for it. He stepped along to the ending of that protecting back wall, peered out, saw nothing, and glided northward until, by peering out, he could see the moonlit yard.

There was a dark blur of moving animals on his right and ahead, near the entrance to Sloat's yard. Star shine shone off shiny, empty saddles. Men were moving here and there. Texas Jim could not at once distinguish their numbers but he could clearly see their raw weapons dully shining in the night. He raised his pistol, squeezed off a shot, and watched dust burst upward from the yard's center.

At once several voices bleated in quick alarm. There was a sound of scrambling men getting to cover, then several angry outcries from among the ramshackle outbuildings across from the warped old barn.

A man yelled fiercely: "Madsen, damn you, throw down that gun and step out!"

Texas Jim shot a quick look toward the well house. Madsen's horse was no longer there. He let off a relieved breath. Then it occurred to him that Christel, not Madsen, must have fled on that animal. He got down and very cautiously peered out across where Christel's horse had been. It was not there. He drew back, feeling relieved all over again. They had both gotten away. He punched out that expended casing, plugged in a fresh load from his shell belt, and rose up. He was beginning to turn away, to move back away so that he could break this off and get back to his own animal, when a lashing red-orange muzzle blast erupted from around the far-away barn, and over the echo of this shot a voice he recognized at once cried out.

"I'll step out with any one of you . . . any two of you . . . but not until the rest of you swear you'll stay out of it."

This was the voice of Chris Madsen. Texas Jim whirled. He glared over toward the barn. Madsen, apparently, had moved his horse to the barn when those men had come running out of the night. Jim whispered a savage word. He went back up to where he'd earlier fired the opening shot, and squinted over the softly lighted yard.

Someone had taken that bunch of riderless horses beyond sight and bullet range. Someone had also passed an order for those attackers to conceal themselves well.

A fiery voice yelled back to Madsen: "We're goin' to kill you, Madsen, for what you did this afternoon!"

Texas Jim knew that voice and the last vestige of patience left him. He lifted his gun, waited for a target, and meant definitely to kill Carlos Setter. The chance did not present itself. Carlos remained hidden.

Two nearly simultaneous gunshots erupted, one from the barn, the other from directly in front of it across the yard. A man loudly coughed. This was to Texas Jim a significant sound; lung-shot men coughed in that bubbly way. The gun over at the barn fired again. This time Jim saw its red-flashing muzzle blast and was thus enabled to place Chris Madsen. He began plotting a way out and around the yard so that he could join forces with his deputy. He was not concerned with Carlos Setter or the dozen or so riders with him right then, and it had not registered on Texas Jim why Carlos had said what he'd called out—something about Madsen having done something this afternoon. Right at this moment there was no time for reflection; there was time only for concentrating upon survival.

Jim left the house area, heading discreetly toward that fence with the underbrush growing up over it. He got there safely and paused. Around him the yard was as still as death. He couldn't see men moving, filtering around through the night to flank the barn, but he sensed them doing exactly this. The ways of fighting did not change; those with the strength and the initiative pressed forward. Those who were outnumbered fought with only their stubbornness and their futile courage. Jim crept along the fence until he could dimly make out a crouching man at the barn's south-western corner. He recognized Madsen by his tallness, and by something he felt but could not define.

Madsen was utilizing this silent time to reload. He had his head down as he did this and Texas Jim, running his flinty gaze onward, saw a blur of far movement northward. He fired by instinct, as a man points a finger. That distant blur sprang into the air, lit threshing in dark dust, then crawled frantically away.

A bullet hit hard into a wooden railing not three feet from Jim's face. He blinked and dropped flat. A second slug crackled through the underbrush behind him. Far across the yard there was an abrupt renewal of the onward firing. Jim pushed through underbrush below the bottom railing of that crumbling fence and looked out. Gun flashes winked. He saw Madsen turn, throw another slug in his direction, then slide beyond sight toward the barn's rear maw. Texas Jim swore. It had not occurred to him that Madsen would think he was an enemy. The forward gunfire dwindled again. It was these moments of silence that picked at a man's nerves. Carlos Setter's riders were creeping up, changing positions, getting closer, in those silent interludes.

Jim waited for a target and saw none. He looked over at that dark rear barn opening; he could reach it probably, bad leg and all, but Madsen would shoot him the second he burst inside. He sucked back a big breath. He didn't want to end this fight. He wanted one clear shot at Carlos Setter first, but the longer he lay there, the cooler became his ardor. He yelled out, his voice gritty and fierce.

"Setter! Carlos Setter! This is Marshal Collins. Order those men with you to put down their guns and walk out into the yard!"

All the gunfire ceased at once and the silence came down again to fill Sloat's yard, to drown it and run on for a long period of time before Carlos's shout came on, shattering it again.

"You know what Madsen did, Marshal? He took my sister. He's got her with him. She's his prisoner."

"You damned idiot!" yelled Texas Jim. "Your sister came here by herself of her own free will!"

"That's a lie, Marshal!"

A gunshot exploded, then another one. Texas Jim pressed his chin into musty earth as two slugs ripped close in, slicing underbrush. He swore in a muffled way and spat dust. Then he moved swiftly away from this place where he'd revealed himself and fury nearly choked him. When he could, he rose up the slightest bit and glared outward. It was completely silent again; onward in Sloat's yard moon glow lay softly, serenely puddling. Someone opened on the barn with a Winchester carbine; this weapon made a sharper, flatter sound than did those booming six-guns. Texas Jim rolled northward, kept on rolling until he thought he would be safely shielded by the barn's rear wall, and tentatively looked outward again. He could no longer see the yard at all. The barn's black opening was dead ahead.

He hissed loudly: "Madsen? It's me. Jim Collins. You hear me, Madsen?"

After a painful silence Madsen's answer came back. "I hear you, Marshal. Wait a minute. I'll get by the back door. All right, now run for it."

Texas Jim shoved up off the ground into a low crouch. His stiff knee was giving him hell from all this exertion. He squinted over the fence, estimated the distance to be covered, then felt for a good handhold preparatory to springing over the fence. There would probably be Setter ranch gun hands around in this rearward area by now; he would not be able to make this dash without peril. He gripped the railing, flexed his bad leg, took a deep breath, and hurled himself up and over the old fence, heard it splinter under his weight as he struck the forward ground, then he ran as swiftly as he could. At once a gun blasted at his dodging figure. Then, southward, another lash of red flame sprouted. Texas Jim heard the breath of that last bullet as it passed within inches of his head.

He threw himself forward and downward as he crossed the barn's threshold, struck ground, and grunted as he frantically rolled sideways. No other shots came.

A tall silhouette moved in, gun hand dully glistening. Madsen was hatless; his face, even in the ghostly light, shone with perspiration. He bent over as Texas Jim rose up and beat at his front to send off gusts of dust. He put out a hand when Jim's bad leg almost gave way under him. Jim struck this hand irritably away. He said: "How long you think it'll be before they think to toss a firebrand in here, burn this damned thing down, and shoot us by firelight?"

Madsen straightened up, looking steadily at the marshal, saying nothing.

"We got to get out of here," snapped Texas Jim. "Where is your horse?"

Madsen gestured toward a nervously dancing dark blur.

"Mine's behind the damned fence. We'll have to ride double. They'll have found my critter by now." Texas Jim looked around, suddenly recalling something. "Where is Christel?" he demanded.

"Gone," said Madsen quietly. "She left a couple of minutes before those Comanches out there came busting in here like a cyclone." Madsen began slowly to scowl at Texas Jim. "How did you know she was here?" he asked.

"That," growled Jim, "isn't important right now. What is important is getting clear of this damned place, and keeping alive while we're doing it. Have you any idea how many men are out there with that blockheaded Carlos Setter?"

"Ten or twelve. I counted their horses when they first hit."

"And I suppose by now," rumbled Texas Jim, "half of 'em are around this lousy old barn."

Jim motioned toward the rear doorway with his gun, then started onward, limping badly now, toward the barn's front opening. He gave no order, nor did he have to. Deputy Madsen understood; he went dutifully back through deep gloom to keep watch at the barn's rear. The silence was down again, more ominous than ever.

Jim could discern nothing out in the yard, but he had not actually expected to. What he wished now to ascertain was where their attackers had cached their saddle horses; two large men, riding double on one horse, could not hope to escape a dozen pursuers. It was in Texas Jim's mind to find those onward animals and scatter them. It was not something that appealed to him, particularly since his bad leg was throbbing now with steady pain and getting stiffer by the minute, but it was some-thing he knew had to be done, and soon, before Carlos thought of firing Sloat's barn.

Madsen hissed from the rearward darkness: "They're doing it, Marshal. I just saw the spark where they're making torches over by the house."

Texas Jim turned. "Come up here," he ordered, and waited until Madsen was near him in the darkness before raising an arm, pointing north-ward and slightly eastward. "That's where their horses were. They probably took them back out of range in the same direction." He dropped his arm. "We've got to find them, got to scatter them, and, if we're lucky, steal two of them." He looked into the younger man's dark-shadowed face. "You game?"

Madsen said: "Do we have a choice?"

Texas Jim checked his six-gun. When he turned, Madsen had gone back where his horse was tied, freed the animal, then returned. "Any time," he said quietly. "I'm ready any time you are, Marshal."

XI

Texas Jim Collins led out. He was limping badly by this time. When Chris Madsen mentioned this, Jim said: "You watch for those damned horses and never mind about me. I was in pickles like this before you were born and I'm still going strong."

One thing was in favor of the two law officers. Carlos Setter had taken most of his riders over by the house, there to make their switches, build their little fire, and light those firebrands. Apparently these busily occupied men were for this little time absorbed in their work, for Jim and Chris Madsen got well away from the barn without discovery.

It was darkest where Sloat's tumble-down outbuildings were, and beside these sheds the escaping men lingered longest. Madsen reached out to touch Jim Collins and say: "Stay here. I'll scout northward, then come back."

Jim offered no argument to this. He simply nodded, looking stonily back toward the house. After Madsen faded out in the night, Jim leaned back against the shed behind him, closed his eyes briefly, then sprang them wide open again. He was tired, he was in pain, and he was more disgusted than indignant. He didn't really want to shoot Carlos Setter. A thought occurred to him and he looked off in the direction Madsen had taken. He wanted to take Carlos over his knee— his good knee—and whale the wadding out of him. For some reason this tickled Jim, this unique thought; he dwelt upon it a little longer. He'd like to ride up John Setter's hill, line his children up one behind the other, and spank hell out of each

271

one of them. He almost smiled at this notion. By golly, Madsen hadn't been out of line at all. In fact, he'd done the exact thing that should have been done. Instead of fighting fiery Carlos, he should have spanked him, too.

Texas Jim's musings were interrupted by a gliding tall figure materializing dead ahead. It was Madsen. He said: "Come on, Marshal, I found them."

"Is there a guard with 'em?"

"Well, yes, but he's asleep."

"Asleep?" said Jim incredulously, not at once comprehending Chris Madsen's meaning.

"I knocked him over the head."

"Oh," said Texas Jim, and pushed clear of the shed he'd been resting against.

They went onward together, had progressed some hundred yards when a moving flicker of white light arrested their attention rearward. Texas Jim turned; he watched Setter's men slipping along behind that overgrown fence with their torches, and he said bleakly: "The fools. If we were still in that barn, we could pick them off like shooting fish in a rain barrel."

Madsen grunted and both of them resumed their forward advance, moving a little faster now, but very stealthily. It would not be long before Carlos discovered they were no longer in the barn.

There rose up ahead of them some spindly little

oak trees growing in a clump. Madsen headed for this spot, got into the darkness there, and halted. He raised an arm, pointing eastward. Texas Jim saw the horses. They were standing with heads hung, drowsily indifferent to everything around them. As he watched, one animal tossed its head and made a little chuckling sound, then relaxed again.

Madsen lowered his arm, pointing toward a vague dark lump on the ground. "The guard," he said softly. Then he looked over at Texas Jim. "I'll go get us a couple of them."

Jim, beginning to rankle under this solicitous consideration, said shortly: "We'll both go."

They left the trees, passed over the intervening few yards, and came to another halt so as not to spook the unaware animals, then they quietly talked their way in among them. The horses did not snort or even shy away. Jim caught the reins of a raw-boned, ugly-headed bay horse, checked the *cincha*, and mounted this beast. Madsen, taking a chunky little sorrel horse, was rising up over leather when Jim said: "We'll take the lot of them with us. If we just run them off, their riders may be able to whistle them back." He was passing along, scooping up lead reins before Chris also started doing this. They were nearly finished catching the Setter horses when a shout of quick alarm broke the hush from back by Sloat's barn. This cry was taken up by other men.

"They've made their discovery," said Jim. "Come on."

But Carlos Setter was quick-witted; he at once divined the purpose and route of the escaping lawmen and sent his riders on foot in a quick spring to get between Sloat's buildings and the escape route eastward, back toward town.

Texas Jim, swearing at the horses he was leading because they hung back, putting a strain upon his free arm, tried to maneuver those animals into a lope. Behind him Chris called out: "Let them go! It's too late."

Jim stubbornly hung on, cursing fiercely.

A red lash of gun flame jumped at them from off to the left. Madsen flung away his lead reins, palmed his six-gun, and fired back at that muzzle blast. Instantly other guns winked redly ahead of them. Now Texas Jim abandoned his lead horses, too, and joined this fresh fight.

Setter's riders, motivated by desperation, were running hard to get across in front of Collins and Madsen. They peppered the night with bullets while they were doing this, and, although this fire was not at all accurate, it certainly was disconcerting to both the mounted men.

Jim spun his horse to race back westward. A Winchester cracked behind Madsen and Texas Jim's hat went flinging away like a terrified and awkward bird. Chris yelled at Jim: "Hit the dirt!"

They piled off, still hanging onto their reins,

and dropped to their knees. A sharp pain from this made Jim grunt. He caught a gun flash in his sights and fired fully at it a fraction of a second after it had flamed at him. A man jumped up, cried out that he was hit, and went careening drunkenly away from the fight.

That steel ring, though, was closing around them. Jim twisted for a rearward look. Behind them was a man with a saddle gun, and another man with a six-shooter. These appeared to be their only enemies rearward. Jim leaned over toward Chris, saying brusquely: "Use the horse as a shield. Follow me."

Madsen covered Jim until he was upright and pushing his saddle horse toward those rearward men, then Chris also made his attempt at escape back to shelter in this fashion. A bullet came out of the east, stung Chris's animal across the rump, and this beast gave a wild snort, a fierce lunge, and tore free. He went racing straight for the barn.

Chris recovered his balance, ran up, and joined Texas Jim behind their only remaining animal. They saw a man with a Winchester in his hand jump up off the ground and go legging it out of the path of Madsen's blind-running animal. Texas Jim, guessing the location of the remaining gun-man, snapped off three rapid shots, in this manner keeping the handgun man too busy to make an attempt at intercepting them.

The last hundred feet to the barn was covered

with comparative safety. Red flashes far back sliced through darkness but visibility even under that serene pewter moon was inhibited by distance. Both men got back into Sloat's barn. Texas Jim let go his horse and staggered with clenched teeth to an upended nail keg. There, he eased down and pushed his bad leg stiffly out in front of him.

Madsen went on past, leaving Jim to watch the front yard. He dropped low, risked a look out back, saw where those guttering torches had been abandoned when their initial escape had been discovered, found none of Setter's men back there, then got upright, and returned to where Texas Jim was sitting, his face tight-locked against pain.

"We made a good try," said Chris, standing loosely.

"We'll still make it," snarled Texas Jim. He jerked his head rearward. "How many of those damned Setter horses ran in here when the shooting started?"

Chris twisted to plumb the surrounding darkness. He could make out a tightly milling clutch of saddled horses, but not how many of them were back there in the total blackness. It looked like there were at least six of them. That's the figure he gave to Marshal Collins.

Texas Jim did not relax his forward vigil for a second when he said: "Catch four of 'em. Lead 'em up here."

Chris nodded. "You figure to stampede them over Setter?" he asked.

Jim made a deriding snort. "Hell, no. What'd be the sense of that? The horses would be gone, Setter's men would recover, and we'd still be in here afoot."

"No, there would still be two horses left."

"Uhn-uh," said Jim, wagging his head. "Look out there. Not a sound. Those fellers are getting into position to snipe at us, Chris. Only an idiot would ride out of here sitting atop a horse making as nice a target as they could ask for. No man living could zigzag enough to run that damned gauntlet. Especially not with moonlight behind and above him." Texas Jim swung his head away from the doorway for just a moment. "Get four of those damned horses like I told you. Move, dammit. They'll fire up those torches again in a minute or two."

Chris moved. He was mystified, but he went back, caught four of the saddled animals, and led them, softly snorting and hanging back in their bridles, up to where Texas Jim was rising stiffly, painfully, up from his nail-keg seat.

Jim took the reins, critically examined the horses, and, while he was doing this, he said to Chris: "Find some rope." But he then bent to squint at those saddles. "Never mind, we got a couple of lariats. They'll do." He felt for the coiled ropes, took them down, hung them both over one arm, then swiftly off-saddled two of those nervous animals. "Do as I do," he ordered Chris, "and be fast about it."

Chris yanked two saddles loose, flung them aside, and bent far forward to be able to see what Texas Jim was doing in the nearly total blackness inside Sloat's barn.

"Like this," grunted Jim, cutting holes in two saddle blankets with a pocket knife. "Now then, weave the lariat through, tying those two blankets together." Jim held up the joined blankets briefly for Chris to scrutinize, then he tossed this double-length, tough-weave pair of joined Navajo blankets over the backs of both the horses, which were standing on each side of him. Madsen began to comprehend; he worked fast duplicating everything Texas Jim had done.

"Use the second lariat to go beneath both horses," directed Jim, "like a *cincha*, cut a couple more holes so the rope won't slip off, then lash both ends of the lariat together." Jim finished and straightened up to peer onward. At this moment Carlos Setter yelled for the pair of them to come out of Sloat's barn empty-handed or he would burn the building around them. Neither besieged man heeded this threat at all. They worked franti-cally finishing their bizarre slings, and afterward straightened up to exchange a look.

Texas Jim shrugged. "The trick is," he explained, "not to lose control of your two horses. You sit on that blanket where it sags down between them, keep your dog-goned head low, and chances are about fifty-fifty that in the darkness yonder Setter's men won't think right off that those horses aren't turned loose and runnin' free. Of course they'll right soon notice that the animals aren't just runnin' side-by-side, that somehow someone is reining them. But with luck, by that time, you should be a hundred yards beyond pistol range."

Chris tested the nearest sagging, improvised sling, and wagged his head a little skeptically. "I reckon there's another trick, too," he said dryly, "staying on that damned thing."

Texas Jim nodded. "Check your gun," he ordered, and at once set Chris an example by reloading his own weapon. A wavering white light began to flicker out back. One horse back in the barn's gloom faintly snorted at this. Texas Jim put a steady look upon Chris: "You ready?" he asked.

"As ready as I'll ever be," answered Madsen, looking rueful.

"Whatever happens," Jim said as he eased up onto the blanket slung between the foremost pair of horses, "keep one horse. If we get clear of them . . . then wind up on foot . . . we won't have helped ourselves a whole hell of a lot."

Chris holstered his weapon, watched Texas Jim ease his entire weight onto his blanket sling, take both sets of reins in his hand, and turn.

"Get on the damned thing, Chris."

Madsen got onto his sling, too. He reached up to yank his hat brim, then he nodded, saying to Marshal Collins: "Let 'er go!"

Texas Jim eased off on the two pairs of reins he was holding; his pair of horses fidgeted, bewildered and nervous. He clucked at them as a dirt farmer might do; they inched toward the moonlit yard. When they were nearing the yonder opening, Jim lashed them both with the reins. The horses, already near to panic, plunged with a bound out of the barn and kept running. Jim clung to his improvised seat with grim determination and one hand. With the other hand he fought to hold the heads of those joined horses in the same direction. He had no time to look back, but, pounding furiously behind, he heard Madsen's tandem hook-up charging furiously after him.

One solitary gunshot came. After that someone's loud shout ordered the Setter riders to hold their fire. This voice boomed out that Madsen and Texas Jim were trying to stampede loose horses over the men on foot.

Texas Jim passed completely out of the ranch yard. Chris Madsen's wild-eyed animals swept up, then passed the marshal. Jim had one very brief glimpse of those animals; he saw only a flash of Madsen's head between their backs, then he had to fight his own animals in order to keep them from swinging out from each other.

XII

It worked better than Jim Collins had dared hope it might. He was a half mile out and fighting his horses down to a halt when ahead a hundred yards Chris got his animals stopped, climbed off the sling, cut one horse loose with several quick slashes of a pocket knife, and led this beast back to where Jim was also working at freeing one of his animals.

"That's the damnedest thing I ever saw," panted Madsen. "They didn't even shoot at us."

"Didn't see us!" exclaimed Jim, freeing one of his animals and holding tightly to the reins of the other one.

From far back came the distance-softened popping of guns. Texas Jim turned to gaze back, then he limped back around, saying: "Here, give me a leg up. I'm not so good at mounting bareback horses any more."

Chris moved in at once, bent his right leg at the knee forming a step, and in this manner Marshal Collins got astride his animal. He put a final long look backward as Madsen also got astride, then he led out for Buellton in a slow lope.

They went down the starlit night for close to a mile before Jim reined down to a walk. He looked wordlessly and ruefully over at Chris, shaking his head.

"You've got to have a cast iron behind for this kind of riding," he muttered. "It may be fine for Indians, but it sure isn't for white men."

That's all either of them said until they were nearing town. Then Chris threw up a hand and halted. Texas Jim reined up at once. Out in the northward night a large party of hard-riding men were passing overland in a furious rush.

Texas Jim said grimly: "The rest of Setter's crew." He eased out again, walking his horse. "I'm going up to old Setter's hill as soon as I can get a saddle under me and we'll settle this thing once and for all."

Chris remained silent until they got to the livery barn, got down, and handed the Setter horses over to the night hawk with instructions to put them into the public corral. Under the pop-eyed stare of this man, Chris said: "Marshal, let me go up there first, alone."

Jim squinted. He hobbled over to a wall and leaned upon it, placing his bad leg straight out, the boot heel resting lightly upon hard-packed earth. "Why?" he asked. "You think Christel ought to be prepared before I jail the lot of 'em?"

"No," answered Chris, shaking his head. "I think she might be able to get her father to make Carlos give up without a killing."

Texas Jim saw the hostler standing close by,

listening. He growled at him—"Get on about your damned business."—and waited until the night hawk hurried away to continue. "No," he said, flatly and solidly. "No more appeasing that old devil up there. I've looked the other way for the last time. I won't have those pups of his running loose like a wolf pack any longer. Chris, I've put up with them since they were kids. Now, no more." Texas Jim gingerly flexed his leg, eased his weight carefully on to it, swore, then said: "I'm convinced that whelp of a Carlos meant to kill us both. I don't give a damn about his reasons or his feelings. He's got a blind hate for you because you whipped him to a fare-thee-well before all of Buellton. He's mad at me because I called him a punk . . . and worse. Well, he wants a fight and now, by God, he's going to get one."

Jim turned, bawled for the night hawk, and ordered two fresh horses saddled and brought up. Madsen stood looking at him. He said: "Marshal, give them a chance."

"Yeah, like they gave us. I'll give 'em hell, that's what I'll give 'em. Hostler, confound it, hurry up with those horses!"

Texas Jim looked at Madsen for a thoughtful moment. He seemed near to speaking, then he didn't until the hostler brought two fresh horses. Chris was taking the reins to one of these animals; he was frowning downward when the marshal spoke again.

"You can stay in town if you like, Chris. But I'm going up there as soon as I can get me a posse."

"No," murmured Madsen, "I'll go along."

"Why?" snapped Texas Jim. "To keep me from committing some kind of an atrocity?"

Chris put his steady dark stare upon Collins, watched the lawman get laboriously into the saddle, then said: "To keep you from caving in. You've had about all you can handle for one night."

Texas Jim flared out angrily. "Listen, damn you, I've ridden ten men as good as you are into the ground in one lousy night, and I can do it again if I have to."

Chris mounted up. He nodded, saying: "Sure, Marshal. Let's go get our posse."

Texas Jim never had any trouble getting posse men. He had so very rarely called upon Buellton's male citizens for this service, and his personal fame was so colorfully established, that townsmen were ready to ride at his first call. That's how it happened when he and Chris Madsen rode across to the Golden Slipper and Texas Jim fired his handgun into the air, then bawled out for volunteer riders. Men came bursting from the saloon in a rush. They whooped, then dashed for their mounts. In fifteen minutes Texas Jim had close to fifty armed, mounted men ringing around him and Chris Madsen. Several of these riders swayed in their saddles, making boisterous catcalls. The marshal ordered them to dismount and stay in town. Several near arguments ensued, but in the end Texas Jim's frayed patience and savage rejection of these men cowed them entirely. He then passed at a slow walk among the remaining men, looking to see that these riders were sober, adequately armed, and suitably mounted. When he got back beside Chris Madsen, he said: "Come on. Mister Setter'll be up there with maybe only Jasper Jones, the ranch cook, and a wrangler or two. It'll be best this way." He considered Madsen's expression, then said quietly: "I don't want to shoot any of them. I only want to arrest them." He turned, lifted his rein hand, and loped northward up Main Street. Around him the posse men clattered along, too, appearing to Chris Madsen like a guerilla band.

At the ending of Buellton, Texas Jim swung easterly toward Setter's hill. Moonlight dappled the land here, bisected by rolling country and swales; the posse alternately passed into and out of light and dark places. Marshal Collins held the lead, riding straight in the saddle. Chris Madsen, watching him, knowing he was in anguish from his bad leg, could find no trace of expression outwardly to show this pain to the men riding with him. It was not difficult for Madsen to understand, through these rigorous moments, how the legend of iron-man Jim Collins persisted.

There was something in the constitution of Marshal Collins that was totally unbending, something rare that few other men ever had.

As though in some way conscious of Madsen's stare and his thoughts, Texas Jim swung his head, looked over, and exchanged a long look with the younger man. Then he faced forward as the posse struck up over the approach to Setter's hill, and swept forward, holding his lead position.

At the top out overhead twin carriage lanterns burned, one on either side of the great doorway to John Setter's home. Toward these orange beacons that hurrying party made its upward way until, with the ground turning level underfoot, Marshal Collins slowed to a walk, paced along to a tie rack, and there, before dismounting, looked over at the house. Chris Madsen was beside him, also looking. Jim eased forward, preparatory to dismounting, he said—"Quiet as a tomb."—then swung down, caught his full weight on his good leg, and carefully distributed this load until the bad leg was also carrying part of it.

Posse men made saddle horses fast along the tie rack, then to the trees nearby until that horse area had the appearance of a cavalry company's bivouac. The men crowded up close to Texas Jim. For most of them this was their first trip to the lair of the most powerful man in Anza County, and the exuberance they'd had down in

Buellton had steadily diminished the higher they'd ridden up John Setter's hill until now, silent and solemn, they stood with Marshal Collins, saying nothing at all.

Texas Jim looked at Madsen, then beyond him to another familiar face. He said to this other man: "Take twenty men and go around back. If there are any men at the barn, the cook shack, or the bunkhouse, disarm them and herd them around here. Leave 'em guarded, then surround the house. Get under cover. There may be no trouble, but we won't assume that." Texas Jim looked at Chris again. His expression was sardonic. "You come with me," he said, then paused as though expecting Chris to speak. When he did not, the marshal nodded to the balance of his posse men. "Spread out. If anyone comes up the hill, disarm them. If Carlos, Reg, or Frank show up . . . arrest them in my name and hold them. Now remember this. No shooting unless you're fired at first."

Jim started limpingly forward. "Come along," he growled as he passed Madsen. The two of them went along as far as the porch steps. Here, Jim had trouble, but his quick and challenging look at Madsen prevented the younger man from saying a word. When they were before the door, Jim drew his six-gun, reversed it, and struck that gleaming white panel a strong blow. Reverberations sounded beyond the door and a deep indentation was made in the wood.

The silence lingered. Madsen twisted to look back where the posse men were moving out. Marshal Collins struck the door again, hard. That time it swung inward. Christel Setter stood there, looking pale and big-eyed. When she saw Chris Madsen, her lips turned loose and a quiet breath ran past them.

"You're all right," she said, making a statement of it.

"He's all right," said Marshal Collins, biting the words off short. "I want to see your father."

"He's not here, Marshal."

"What?"

"No, I'm the only one here. As soon as I told my father what was happening out at the Sloat place, he called our riders and led them out there."

Texas Jim shot a look at Chris. "Those riders we heard," he murmured. Then faced Christel again. "What was he up to?"

"Marshal, I was at the Sloat place this evening. I'd just left when . . ."

"I know all that," Texas Jim snapped impatiently. "I was out there, too. I saw you. In fact, I watched you and Madsen here, was still there when Carlos and your father's gun hands came charging up."

Christel was staring at Texas Jim. "You were out there . . . ?"

Jim guessed this beautiful girl's thoughts. He

brushed this dawning embarrassment on her part aside, saying: "What was your paw up to, taking the rest of his men to the Sloat place?"

"I told him what was happening down there. He went to stop it."

"Or to join Carlos in finishing it," Collins said.

Madsen's quick, hard tone broke in here: "Easy, Marshal, don't call her a liar."

Texas Jim swung a savage look at Madsen. The younger man braced into this glare, giving as hard as he got. Christel returned the attention of both men to her by saying: "Marshal, I saw our riders heading for the Sloat place when I wasn't more than a quarter mile from there. I didn't see who was leading them, but . . ."

"It was your brother Carlos."

"Yes, I thought it probably was. That's what I told my father." Christel looked at Madsen; she hesitated over her next words. "Carlos told our father that he'd heard from a rider who'd been in the Golden Slipper that Mister Madsen was going to abduct me." Chris's eyes widened. "It was a misunderstanding," said Christel, rushing on. "I told my father that. Maybe that rider heard Mister Madsen mention my name to Toby Hostetter. I don't know. But somehow the story got completely twisted, and, when Carlos heard it he . . . went wild."

Marshal Collins put out a hand and leaned upon the door casing, easing the weight from his bad leg. "Were Frank and Reg with him at the Sloat place, Christel?"

"I didn't see them, but my father said he thought they'd all gone down there together . . . along with half our cowboys."

"That," pronounced Texas Jim, "is what I want to be sure of. I'm going to arrest your three brothers and your father."

Christel said in a voice so low it scarcely carried: "Marshal, no. Please don't do that. Give them a chance to explain."

"I gave Carlos a chance at the Sloat place, Miss Christel. I told him who I was and told him to stop fighting. Instead, he opened up on me with everything he had." Marshal Collins's scarcely contained wrath burned with a steady fire in the depths of his eyes. He continued to look straight at Christel. The lovely girl seemed to wilt, to sag. It was apparent that the adamant expression of Texas Jim, the iron-like set of his jaw and lips, discouraged her from pleading further with him.

Chris Madsen stepped over, put an arm around Christel's waist, and turned with her, walking deeper into the house. Texas Jim looked backward. His posse men were out there and somewhere beyond sight he could hear the shrill protests of Setter riders being driven behind the guns of his deputies. There was nothing to do now but wait; old John and his three sons, along with their coterie of riders, would be coming soon.

Jim crossed into the house, limped to the parlor entrance, saw Christel and Chris Madsen standing close there in the middle of the room, her head against his shoulder, and here he paused. Then he went back to a chair in the hallway and dropped down there, tired and exhausted and covered with perspiration and dirt, thinking his savage thoughts. Here he would await the arrival of John Setter.

XIII

It was an unexpectedly long wait, and, after an hour had passed and Jim's town riders were becoming restless, the marshal acceded to a suggestion from Christel Setter that Jasper Jones be permitted to go to his cook shack and make coffee for everyone.

After that the posse men settled down. They strolled around John Setter's big white house, talking together while maintaining their surround. At the entrance to the big yard, down where a covered gate stood, a lounging detachment of sentinels alternately listened for oncoming riders and idled the time away in speculative conversation.

Texas Jim's bad leg continued to ache, but the sharp and plaguing pain diminished, so that he took a stroll, also, to pass away this fretful wait. In this manner he passed around back, and, although the moon was down now, he could distinguish Chris Madsen and Christel Setter, standing close near the west end of a long verandah. Madsen had washed; he was hatless and silent, listening to what Christel was saying. Texas Jim paused out in the shadowy night, watching those two. The girl's red-gold hair looked nearly black now. It was caught up at the nape of her neck by a tiny green ribbon. She had on a fresh white blouse and a long, rusty-colored riding skirt.

"I would tell him in an instant," she was saying to Madsen. "Except that my father explicitly told me not to."

Madsen inclined his head. If he'd turned a little, he might have seen Texas Jim standing out there, although that was problematical because of the moonless gloom. "I could tell him, I suppose," Madsen said to Christel, sounding reluctant.

"But, Chris, don't you think it might be better the way my father wants it to be?"

"To leave?" replied Madsen. "No, I don't think so, darling. First off, I've my personal reasons for wanting to stay on. I mean, aside from you."

"I understand."

"Secondly . . . well . . ."

"I understand that, too, Chris."

Texas Jim saw Madsen's teeth show white in a

little grin at the beautiful girl. "You're reading my mind," Chris said.

Christel stood a moment longer as she was, then she half turned away from Madsen. When she spoke again, her tone was tired-sounding and near to sadness. "I suppose he'll find out, Chris. He's a proud man and in most ways a distant one. It will hurt him. I'm sure of that."

Chris put his hands out to turn her back toward him. "Part of the responsibility of a person's actions are the things which follow them," he said, holding her at the waist, looking steadily down into her face. "I'm not saying he should have thought of that, Christel. What I am saying is that I doubt very much if it would have always been kept from him. Life has a way of revealing a person's failings sometime, somewhere."

She put both hands up to his chest, ran them higher, and held his shoulders. She stood up, leaning into him. "Chris, I love you so, and yet all this . . . this trouble makes me sad about that."

Texas Jim began walking along; she would kiss him, and Jim didn't want to see that again. Not that he felt anything personal in this, but in the back part of Marshal Collins's mind was that faint although persevering memory of another beautiful woman and another time, long ago.

He made his rounds, saw that the posse men were in place, more or less, then he went along to the chair upon John Setter's front porch, next to the wrought-iron table, which was old John's favorite seat. There, he eased down, pushed out his aching leg to its full length, and turned loose all over, thinking that whatever Madsen and Christel had been discussing had something to do with old John. They had mentioned a proud man, that he would be hurt by some revelation. It never once occurred to him in his present tired and sluggish mood that it might not have been old John at all he'd heard discussed. What did occur to Texas Jim was the reaction that would follow his arrest of prominent, wealthy, and powerful John Setter and his three sons.

Jim had watched John Setter's influence grow; he knew how strong politically Setter was in the state. He also knew old John wouldn't be in his jail overnight. He'd roar for attorneys, get free, then throw himself violently into this battle with Anza County's famous iron legend. A man of Texas Jim Collin's beliefs could wonder which was most valued in this life, the moral righteousness of dedicated lawmen, or the wealth and power of rich cattlemen. He wanted very hard to believe moral righteousness was superior, because, if it wasn't, then he himself had spent a lifetime believing in the wrong things, making him a fool. There was no place for foolish old men. Those who had admired him the most for a quarter century, such as Hoag Balinger, would see him then in a fresh new light. They would pity him. They would shake their heads over his mistaken ideals, and, of all the things a proud man could stomach the least, pity was foremost.

Chris Madsen stepped up onto the porch, passed over, and eased down in a chair near Marshal Collins. He was smoking a cigarette. "I guess they'll be along directly," he said, studying Texas Jim's face.

"They're overdue," murmured the marshal. "He's a tough old cuss to figure sometimes, is John Setter. I've known him a long time."

"What do you think of him, Jim?"

Collins's eyes drifted to Madsen's face. This was the first time the younger man had called him by his first name. Normally proud Jim Collins discouraged familiarity of any kind. Right now, though, sitting on Setter's porch with his melancholy thoughts, he didn't mind; in fact he rather liked it, at least coming from the proven-tough and capable man beside him now.

"Oh," he muttered, speaking very slowly, "when you've lived with a man like John Setter for as long as I have, Chris, you sort of fit him into a mold. But actually, until yesterday, I never really sat down and went back over the things he's done, in an objective way."

"And . . . ?"

"Well, it's never easy to admit you've been wrong. Maybe I'm worse that way than most folks."

"But you think you've been wrong now, Jim?"

"I think so, yes. Right a lot of the time, but mostly wrong." Texas Jim continued looking at Madsen. His expression was sardonic. "I imagine you're thinking that a man who's known John Setter as long as I have, and who has mostly misjudged him all these years, must be an idiot. It's possible you're right on that, Chris."

"But you're still hell-bent on arresting him tonight?"

Marshal Collins nodded his head. Then he sighed. "You know," he stated quietly, "I'm tired, Chris. Tired to the damned marrow of my bones. Not just a tiredness of the body, but a tiredness of the spirit. Just before you came along a few minutes ago, I was thinking it's possible for a man to spend his whole lousy life believing in the wrong things."

Madsen lowered his head. He killed his cigarette and continued to look down at it. Texas Jim went on speaking.

"I don't think any man willingly and knowingly does the wrong thing."

Chris shot an upward look at Texas Jim. "Not even Carlos?" he said.

"No, not even that young hot-head. He really believed he was trying to save his sister out there tonight. He thought I was on your side, somehow. He felt he was doing right."

"Jim," said Madsen gently, "you're making

excuses for the men you're up here to arrest."

"Not exactly, Chris. I'm seeing two sides of the same coin. Sure, I'm going to jail the Setters, but you remember this, boy. It's something I learned a long time ago. When a man knows only his own side of a dispute, he really doesn't know anything. Carlos, and maybe even his brothers and his paw, think they are right. I operate by the legal writ, and the legal writ says definitely they were wrong. So, I try to understand their side at the same time I believe in the right which is on my side." Texas Jim paused, put a querying stare forward, and concluded with: "Does any of that make sense to you, Chris?"

"Yes, it makes sense. But, Jim, something else makes sense to me, too. I don't want to see you arrest them."

"Why not?"

"You just said it . . . because they thought they were doing right."

"That doesn't change anything. They tried to kill you tonight."

"Carlos misunderstood about Christel and me, Jim."

"He still tried to kill you."

"I'm not going to sign any complaint, Jim."

The marshal's gray, slack, and tired countenance began to firm up; his stare hardened against Madsen. "You won't have to," he declared. "I'll issue the warrant. They tried to kill me, too."

"Don't do it."

"I'm going to do it!"

Madsen sat on, returning Texas Jim's glare. He said, after a quiet moment: "I'm sorry. I'm really sorry you won't give them a chance, Jim. Because I'll be on their side if you force this thing."

"Against the law, Madsen?"

"Against you, Jim."

Marshal Collins, detecting something quite indefinable in the younger man's voice, sat for a long time simply studying Madsen. Then he reacted in his lifelong way. "That'll be all right with me," he said coldly, then checked himself as the thought of Christel Setter's imploring face crossed his mind. He looked away, let his gaze drift on over the broad yard while a totally foreign kind of anguish bowed down his spirit. In his trade, which was the hard trade of triumph, there had never been a place for sentiment. There was nothing, actually, in his vocation that fostered or supported or nurtured friendship, either. Sooner or later everyone with whom he'd come into contact officially walked away from him.

He could not rid himself of that haunting look of John Setter's girl. After a time he could not be certain that those pleading dark and liquid eyes actually belonged to Christel Setter at all. They could have been another set of imploring eyes from back down the years in his own heart, in his own memory.

"I don't want to fight you," he said roughly to Chris Madsen. He had never before in his life said this to another man. "I'm asking you not to force me to it, Chris."

Madsen was gravely thoughtful. "I reckon that goes for me, too, Jim. Is it asking too much for them to be given a chance to straighten this mess out before you arrest them? That's all I want."

Texas Jim wavered over this, but the way of an uncompromising man, after half a lifetime, could not crumble so easily. "After I arrest them," he said.

Madsen abruptly stood up to his full tall height. He looked down at Texas Jim and said quietly: "I'm sorry, Jim. Nothing is changed." He walked westerly to the porch's far ending, stepping down, and Texas Jim heard the solid crunch of his boot steps coursing on around toward the rear of the house. For the second time this night Jim Collins wished mightily for a smoke.

A shadow swayed forward over the Setter yard; it struck the porch steps, coming on. It materialized out of darkness to become one of the Buellton posse men. "Marshal, there's a bunch of riders comin' from the direction of town. Some o' us figure it's old John Setter an' his riders. There's sure as hell a mob of 'em."

Texas Jim placed both hands firmly upon the

arms of his chair and pushed. No sharp pain came spiraling upward but his bad leg was as stiff as a ramrod. "Go pass the word," he ordered, not wishing to move at all until the posse man's observing eyes were gone. "Tell every man to keep a sharp watch. Repeat what I said earlier, too . . . no shooting unless we're fired upon."

The posse man turned away.

Texas Jim pushed his tiredness away. He hobbled down off the porch, stood briefly working the stiff leg until it could be bent a little, then he went limping along toward the covered entrance to John Setter's yard. Here would take place the initial meeting between these two iron-like old men, if it took place at all.

XIV

Chris Madsen was with John Setter's daughter when he heard the first fluting cry of alarm down by the covered gate. He left her at once and sprinted onward through darkness. Ahead of him, distinguishable by his limp, was Marshal Collins. They arrived near the gate simultaneously.

Texas Jim's posse men were standing unnaturally erect and watchful. After one of them had let off that one outcry there was not another sound. Plainly audible beyond sight in the night was the steady pacing and rein-chain sound of many horsemen passing around the lower roadway that passed upward.

Marshal Collins harkened to this sound, assessing it for strength of numbers. Then he turned and barked to a posse man standing by: "Go tell every man up here to watch sharp! If they go back down this hill, it's probable they'll try slipping up on us from around back, or along the hillsides. Hurry up now."

When the marshal swung forward again to listen, his gaze fell upon the grave countenance of Chris Madsen. For a split second these two exchanged a chilly look, then Texas Jim went onward to the gate, and leaned there.

Posse men thinned out; some took careful positions back where shelter stood, while others knelt, Winchesters and handguns up and ready, in a rough semicircle behind Texas Jim and beyond that gate, which was now closed.

Jim turned from the waist to consider the stances of the men nearby. He was making this careful assessment with that sound of many horsemen growing faintly louder as John Setter led his riders on up his hill, when a posse man said: "Hey, what the hell?"

Texas Jim found this man, looked at his puzzled, frowning face, then turned back around following out this man's gaze to where Chris Madsen had been, and now was not.

Fading out in a hurrying way down the twisting

roadway, Madsen's silhouette became blended with the night even as Marshal Collins watched. He parted his lips to call out; no words came. Instead, a heaviness touched his heart and he watched the shadows where Madsen had disappeared, saying nothing at all.

"Where'n hell he think he's going?" someone behind Texas Jim plaintively demanded. "He'll walk right into them."

No one answered this and evidently the speaker expected no reply because he fell silent.

For a moment longer Marshal Collins heard those riders continuing their advance around the hill beyond sight. Then they halted. There was only the sound of rustling leather, spur rowels, and horses near to home impatiently pawing upon hardened earth. Madsen, Texas Jim knew, was with the Setters now; he was without any doubt warning old John what lay ahead, awaiting his arrival atop Setter's hill. Anger stirred deep down in Marshal Collins, anger and fierce resentment, and also disappointment. He could not understand how any man could go to the people who had only hours ago sought so hard to kill him. It seemed to Texas Jim to be a weakness for a man to do such a thing.

"One horse," said a posse man in nearly a whisper at Marshal Collin's elbow, "is comin' on. Probably old John himself."

Texas Jim did not think so and he was correct.

When that lone rider came around the last curve and stopped, back some fifty feet from the gate, it was Chris Madsen mounted on someone else's animal. Texas Jim leaned there, dark in the face, waiting.

"Jim," said Madsen, "they are all here. Back down the road. Mister Setter will go back to town with you as your prisoner. He passed me his word on that."

"And his three boys," said Jim, his voice as hard as steel.

"No, Jim. He won't allow that. But he said to tell you he'd give his word they'll stay here at the house until everything's settled."

Marshal Collins uttered a fighting word, then he said: "Your meddling has spoiled everything, Madsen. My way, they would've ridden up here, been surrounded, and taken. Your way . . ."

"My way, Marshal, is fairest."

Texas Jim's wrath turned hot, turned unreasoning. "There's a name for traitors like you, Madsen."

"I can live with that, Marshal. What I couldn't live with is unnecessary killing."

Marshal Collins glared out. He probably wasn't going to say any more, but now he didn't get the chance. From the west rim of Setter's hill a furious exchange of thunderous gunfire erupted. At once men cried out, some running along the slope from the top of the hill, searching for John

Setter's riders who were obviously attempting to climb upward undetected and surprise the posse men.

Texas Jim bawled an order: "Get them! Give it to them!" Then he whirled toward where Chris Madsen had been, but there was no longer any horse and rider there. He swore savagely over this, drew his handgun, and moved clear of the gate, bawling out to the men positioned there: "Make those bullets count! Keep your places! Capture 'em or kill 'em, but see that they don't get in among you." He limped rapidly to the house area. From here he saw the fight fan out completely around Setter's hill. Somewhere down the hill and beyond sight two men were stoutly yelling indistinguishable orders to Setter's riders. Jim was starting forward when Christel appeared, white from throat to eyes.

"You did it!" she screamed at Marshal Collins. "You wouldn't be satisfied, would you? Men have to die before you . . . !"

"Be quiet," snapped Jim, reaching to catch the girl by her shoulders and shake her roughly. "Some of your father's men started this. They crept uphill and opened on my posse men."

Christel wrenched free and cried over the smash of gunfire: "You don't care who you hurt, do you? You never have. You and your ridiculous pride. Who really cares that you're the fastest gun in Anza County? No one. Only you, Marshal

Collins . . . and now you're an old man. Is that why you've let this happen? Because you're an old man who can't grow old, who has to go on and on proving something?"

A man came running. Texas Jim limped swiftly out to him. The man said: "Marshal, there's a lot of 'em around back, tryin' to get into the stable from the downhill side. There's only four o' us back there, an' we got to have help."

As Jim left with this panting posse man, a bullet struck glass somewhere behind him. He turned at this tinkling, discordant sound, saw Christel Setter standing exposed back there, her white blouse a perfect target, and he said angrily to the man with him: "Go take her inside the house. Make her stay in there. Lock her in some damned room if you have to."

Texas Jim went on alone to the stable area. Here, very obviously, John Setter's riders were making their fiercest effort to storm on up the hill. Gunfire was deafening and men's excited yells punctuated it. Jim was driven to cover almost at once by blindly flying lead. He forgot at once his aching leg, his troubling thoughts, and concentrated wholly upon the raging fight around him. A posse man limped past, saw Texas Jim, and said: "We may outnumber 'em, Marshal, but damned if we're outfightin' 'em."

When Marshal Collins got into position to see safely downhill he understood why this strongest effort was being made behind the barn. There was a dense chaparral thicket down there. Muzzle blasts could be seen when John Setter's men fired, but the darkness and that sheltering undergrowth prevented the posse men from sighting any human targets, while at the same time the posse men, with a white-painted horse barn at their backs, were visible at once when they rose up to fire.

A perspiring man crept over to Texas Jim to say: "They're comin' up through that brush, Marshal, an' we got no way to hold 'em off."

Texas Jim took this man back with him to the barn's interior. "We'll stop them all right," he swore. "Hunt up some kerosene lanterns." He did not wait to see whether the posse man obeyed this order, but went himself through the barn to Jasper Jones's cook shack, and there found and seized two gallon jugs of lamp oil. He hastened back to the barn with the jugs, found the posse man there, waiting with three partially full kerosene lamps, and, as he put his jugs down, he said: "Take the pole off that phæton and be quick about it."

The posse man obeyed, after casting only a slightly puzzled look at Marshal Collins. He went to Christel Setter's imported buggy, removed the kingpin, dropped the shaft, seized both connecting singletrees, and dragged the pole aside.

"Wheel it over here!" yelled Texas Jim, busy

with rags and horse blankets in the middle of the barn runway. When the phæton was pushed close, Jim piled oil-soaked rags into it. He then seized a front wheel, motioned for his companion to take the other, and between them they steered the buggy to the rear, open doorway of John Setter's horse barn.

"Now hold the damned thing," commanded Texas Jim, panting from exertion. When he was sure the posse man would not let it roll on down the steep hillside prematurely, he drew upright, released his grip on the wheel, struck a match, and tossed it into the heaped pile of oil-soaked rags. A roar of fierce flame exploded at once. Jim grasped a wheel and yelled: "Push!"

Christel Setter's handsome little phæton went over the lip of ground at the horse barn's rear, tilted up drunkenly, and went careening downhill, wrapped in a sheet of high-twisting flames, straight toward the chaparral thicket.

The gunfire abruptly ceased in this area and men's cries took the place of the fierce thunder, some crying out exultantly as they saw other men go leaping out of the path of that fiery buggy, some roaring warnings to others in the thicket to run for it.

The phæton had sufficient momentum by the time it crashed into the first tier of wiry old chaparral to rip deeply into that oily, thorny growth. Then it snagged on a particularly stubborn old bush, raised high into the air, and upended, scattering fiercely burning débris for several hundred feet in all directions. From the posse men atop John Setter's hill a great shout went up, and afterward all that roaring gunfire dwindled down to an occasional shot while the attackers in other areas sought clarification of what was progressing around back.

The night became alive with hot and writhing flames; the phæton was gone but that ragged old oily chaparral thicket blazed on with fierce heat and a furious crackling, sending flames nearly a hundred feet straight up. John Setter's great white house stood out eerily; from miles off, down in Buellton where the raging gunfire had been faintly heard, people stood along the byways, staring up at that powerfully illumined house in total awe.

Texas Jim was standing, shielded by the horse barn's rear siding, when two men came through to him from the southward night. One of these men was armed while the other man, walking stolidly, was not. This second man was holding a soggy red neckerchief to one cheek. Until he was close and that quivering firelight shone strongly upon him, Texas Jim did not recognize who this second man was.

Jim squinted at this unarmed man, then he made a profane exclamation. "Reg," he said, and paused long enough to look at Reg Setter's captor. "How'd you get him?"

"We was tradin' shots. I didn't know who he was. He'd rise up an' shoot, then I'd rise up an' shoot." The posse man made a little shrug. "The last time I shot, he flopped out into plain sight. I figured I'd killed him sure 'cause I'd aimed at his danged head. I went down to see." Another little shrug. "I'd creased his cheek bone and knocked him about half silly, so I fetched him along. You said you wanted 'em taken prisoner if possible, Marshal."

Texas Jim nodded, returning his attention to the prisoner. "I want you for attempted murder," he snarled at Reg Setter.

"What attempted murder?"

"Down at the Sloat place. Don't deny you were there, either."

Reg Setter mopped blood from his cheek, looked at the soggy cloth in his fist, and said very calmly: "Marshal, Frank an' I rode down there to stop a murder, not cause one. We were returnin' from town when we met a ranch hand. He told us where Carlos was leadin' about half our crew. We went bustin' after him to prevent him from killing that Madsen feller."

"You were there," said Marshal Collins stubbornly. "You heard me call out who I was when I ordered those men of your father's to stop shooting."

"Sure I was there. So was Frank. We did everything but fight Carlos ourselves to make him stop. He wouldn't listen. We tried to tell him Madsen hadn't abducted Christel at all." Reg wagged his head and sighed loudly. "That fight was too hot, too exciting. We couldn't reach Carlos at all. We couldn't reach any of them, Marshal. Did you ever try to reason with a man whilst he's bein' shot at?" Reg did not await an answer, he once more wagged his head.

Texas Jim said: "Who started this thing up here? Carlos?"

"I don't know who started it. No, not Carlos."

"How do you know he didn't?"

"Because," said Reg Setter firmly, "when my father came up, back at the Sloat place, he struck Carlos in the face and took his guns away. I've never seen him as upset as he was back there. Carlos had no guns, Marshal. I think it was possibly one of our riders. They were all pretty guyed up when that Madsen feller halted us part way up the hill, warnin' us not to keep on going, tellin' us that you were up here with a big posse." Reg Setter shrugged again, looking straight at Marshal Collins. "How can you ever determine who fires the first shot in a battle, Marshal?"

Texas Jim jerked his head. "Take him over to the house," he ordered the impassive posse man, who still had his cocked six-gun against young Setter's back. "Put him in the same room with his sister and stand guard there over 'em."

Before he started away, Reg Setter spoke one last time. "Marshal," he said, speaking still in that same calm tone, "you'd better stop this. It's all up to you now. Madsen tried hard to stop it, but he's gone on to town. My father tried to stop it, too."

"Why couldn't he?"

"He's lying down the roadway part way between here and flat country. He overexerted himself, Marshal, making that wild ride to the Sloat place. When the firin' started up here, he let out a cry an' fell down. He's lyin' down there now, unconscious, with his head pillowed on a saddle. He had a stroke, Marshal Collins. Madsen's gone for the doctor at Buellton. Unless you stop it, there's no one else left now who can."

Reg waited, looking into Texas Jim's gray, slack face, then, when Collins said nothing, he turned and started toward the house with his captor.

XV

The versatility of each individual man is seemingly endless, and yet, under the duress of instinctive, primitive reaction to violence, no man is entirely rational or even wholly sane in the civilized sense. Texas Jim Collins, lifelong gunfighter, stood there, watching Reg Setter walk across the fire-lighted yard, thinking the

311

same bleak and relentless thoughts he'd been concerned with since that first shot had been fired in this fight. In the rearmost part of his brain the information of old John Setter's sudden collapse from strain registered well enough, and what young Reg had said also registered. But Texas Jim Collins, the lifelong man of violence, knew only that he was in the middle of the bitterest battle of his existence, and he could, right then, react only in the instinctive way.

While those writhing flames still brightly burned, Texas Jim limped around his battle line, seeking places where John Setter's cowboys might break through. He encountered two casualties, neither serious, and he found many men who had been mildly intoxicated in Buellton who were now stone sober and as pale as death.

The fighting went on stubbornly, neither the posse men nor the Setter ranch men willing yet to concede anything. A lanky and raw-boned posse man, seeing Texas Jim going by, stepped back from his shielding oak tree at the hilltop's farthest edge, and walked over to say: "Marshal, how's all this going to end? Why not quit firin' an' let them fellers come up here. They want to mighty bad, seems to me, and, if we let 'em, you'll have your prisoners."

Texas Jim flared at this suggestion: "Get back to your place! You're here to fight, damn you, and that's all you're here for!"

As the marshal went on, that tall, raw-boned man leaned for a moment upon his carbine, staring after him. Then he spat, lifted his Winchester, and turned to stride back where he'd been. There, he got down upon one knee again and resumed fighting. He was like most of the other posse men atop John Setter's hill—and the men below it, too, for that matter—he was doing what he'd been ordered to do, not because he thought it was right but simply because he lacked sufficient individuality to stop doing it because it was wrong.

The man who Jim had sent to the house with Reg Setter approached Texas Jim from in front of the house. He jerked his head, saying: "They want to see you in there, Mister Collins."

"Who does?"

"Miss Christel an' her brother."

"To hell with them," growled Texas Jim, and started down toward the covered gate.

"But, Marshal," protested the guard, "Miss Christel says it's plumb important that she talk to you."

Jim stopped, looked over at the house, then went stumping forward toward it without looking again at the posse man.

Christel was in John Setter's large parlor. She had bandaged her brother's cheek and he sat now, loose and sprawled, in a chair, staring ahead at nothing. Texas Jim shot Reg Setter only one darting glance, then Christel came toward him, her pained and anguished face gone pale.

"I want your permission to go to my father," she said, stopping a foot from Marshal Collins. "Reg told me of his condition. Surely, Marshal, you wouldn't make me stay here while he's possibly dying . . . ?"

Texas Jim could see the lovely girl's tightly clasped hands, white from straining; he could see the distinct look of agony in her gold-flecked eyes. He said to her: "Christel, I don't believe you can make it, but I'll go with you to see if your father's men will hold their fire." He looked uncertainly over at Reg, then back again. "Christel, if you get down where Frank and Carlos are, I want you to do something for me. I want you to find Chris Madsen. I want you to tell him to get behind your brothers and throw down on them, disarm them, and make them order your ranch riders to put down their guns."

Christel stared. "Are these the terms?" she asked. "Is that what I must promise before you'll let me go, Marshal Collins? I didn't think you were that . . ."

"No. No, Christel, I'm putting no terms on your leaving. I'm also asking this of you so we can end this fighting."

They stood, looking at one another. From over where he sat, Reg Setter called to his sister: "That's fair enough, Sis. Do it. Promise him you'll do it. Don't worry. Madsen won't shoot Carlos or Frank."

Texas Jim stood waiting, his expression turning gentle, turning tender, toward this handsome girl.

"All right, Marshal Collins. You have my word. If Chris is down there, I'll ask him to do what you wish."

Texas Jim started to reach out, then checked himself, let his arm drop back to his side, and said: "Just one more thing, Christel. I told you it was possible for you to be a finer person than you've been thus far in your lifetime."

"Yes, I remember, Marshal."

"Christel, I think sometimes maturity comes all at once for people. Sometimes it never comes at all, but with you I think it's come these last two days. You're wondering why I'm saying this to you at this time. I'll tell you. I may not have another chance to say it to you. But that's not the main reason at all. The main reason is because I know how you feel about Madsen. I saw you two out at the Sloat place. Well, girl, this is what I'm trying to say. You hold Chris Madsen's happiness in the palm of your hand, now and for all time. Don't ever stop cherishing his happiness. Don't ever stop caring for it, Christel."

"Marshal . . ."

"Let me finish. A long time ago I had the same chance you now have. I didn't take it. That's why

I'm saying this to you now. You've been spoiled and headstrong and arrogant. I hope to God this late maturing will have changed that in you, girl." Texas Jim stopped speaking; he swallowed and felt Reg Setter's eyes widely upon him, but he did not turn. "All right," he said, "come along, young lady. You're going down that hill to your paw . . . and Chris Madsen. Come along."

Reg Setter started up from his chair, saying: "Marshal?"

"Sit back down!" thundered Texas Jim, reverting in a twinkling to the man he'd been for fifty years. "And you stay here. If you try leaving this house, you'll likely get more grief than that little scratch you've already got."

Reg Setter sank back into his chair. He said— "Yes, sir."—and watched Texas Jim and his sister step out of the parlor.

The yonder gunfire was still loud and sporadically furious, but the initial fury had long since gone out of it. Marshal Jim Collins's stubborn posse men had clung to their hilltop. John Setter's perspiring cowboys were no closer to storming these heights than they had been a half hour earlier.

It was late now, well after midnight, and a little chill was in the air. When Texas Jim preceded Christel to the onward edge of Setter's hill, he took a jacket from a posse man for her, and told its owner to pass along the word for all firing to cease.

Then he stood there beside Christel, grim-looking and weary, his face lined with the deep etchings of physical exhaustion, listening to that gradually diminishing shooting. Finally there came a silence in some ways more disconcerting than the gunfire had been, and somewhere, beyond sight down the hill, a reedy voice called out garrulously, saying: "What the hell, them fellers up there givin' up?"

Texas Jim stepped craggily forward into plain sight of the attackers. He put his bold and scornful gaze upon those men who were uneasily peering upward. "Listen to me," he said. "Miss Christel is coming down to be with her paw. We captured young Reg and he told us about Mister Setter. Now you whelps hold your fire until she's safe, you hear?"

A rasping voice called back. "Sure we hear, Marshal! She can come. And, Marshal, you ready to quit up there?"

Texas Jim glared toward the sound of that voice, but, instead of replying, he turned, beckoned Christel forward, and gave her a hand part way down the hillside. After that one of the Setter cowhands stepped recklessly into clear view of the overhead watchers, holstered his gun, and went up to meet Christel and escort her the balance of her downward way. Then, when the girl was farther down near the road, this cowboy twisted to squint upward and say: "All right, you trespassers, if you're smart, you'll get off Setter's hill before we . . ."

A gunshot drowned out this man's last words. A great gout of dust burst into mushrooming life six inches in front of the cowboy, and he gave a tremendous leap to land beyond sight in a dense brush patch. As the gunfire began to swell again, this man's thin and vibrant profanity could be plainly heard overhead. A number of loud cries and taunts erupted along the top out and several men laughed.

Texas Jim stepped back to safety and waited for a lull to call for a second cease-fire; it had occurred to him that without Reg and old John, perhaps those men down there might be of a mind to stop fighting. He knew he was ready to stop and he could tell by their faces that the men from Buellton, on this hill with him, had also had all the fighting their spirits had earlier craved. But no such opportunity came; the gunfire swelled anew and became louder than it had been up to this time. Jim stood in the lee of a bullet-pocked oak and methodically shucked out spent casings from his handgun and plugged in fresh shells from his cartridge belt.

A moment later the firing began to dwindle again and men's voices could be heard murmuring back and forth on Texas Jim's right. He finished reloading, left the oak tree, and went out to see what was happening.

Part way down the slope two of what appeared to be Setter's cowboys were stalking one another. It was impossible in the night gloom to identify either of these men and, except when they threw a shot, it was difficult to be sure exactly where they were. One would creep forward, fire at the other, then spring away from the spot he'd fired from. In this manner those two men passed along the side hill beneath the Buellton posse men. Texas Jim, like the men around him, was intrigued by this fight within a fight. Gradually all gunfire stopped, and except for an occasional yell of encouragement to one or the other of those battlers down there, total silence ensued.

A posse man stood up to peer downward, then he moved over by Marshal Collins to say: "One of them fellers must've stung the other one with a slug. Which one you bettin' on, Mister Collins?"

Texas Jim did not answer for a while, not until he caught a fleeting glimpse of the gunman farthest south who was forcing this fight. Then he said—"I'll take the tall one."—and afterward closed his mouth tightly, watching that drama between the lines of his posse men and the lower Setter ranch men.

Now a light breaking of voice sounds drifted up to Texas Jim from the men below Setter's hill. It sounded as though the gunmen down there were arguing among themselves about whether or not they should take sides in that bizarre fight.

Jim listened to this talk a moment, then called out: "Leave 'em alone! We're not going to interfere and don't you interfere, either, down there."

Someone catcalled up at Texas Jim, but no one broke cover to take sides in the duel. As the moments passed, all talk atrophied as every man put his full attention upon that strange fight. The man who was whipping from cover to cover northeasterly around Setter's hill seemed unwilling to stand his ground and shoot it out. He would fire, duck away, fire again, and retreat again. His opponent kept pressing him. He was seeking to close the distance between them and at times was almost reckless the way he did this. It was nearly impossible to glimpse the retreating man, but his adversary from time to time sprang into full view, then ran on again, fading out where shadows or boulders or brush hid him. He handled his six-gun well. Texas Jim noticed that he never appeared to fire dry, which no experienced gunman ever did; it meant simply that the taller of these two men was reloading as he went along in order that he would always have bullets ready.

Texas Jim shifted his glance, ran it on around the side hill's northeastern curving, and saw what he'd expected, a petering-out of underbrush between the horse barn and where that retreating gunman now was. Texas Jim knew the end of this unique fight was very close. Jim also noticed some-thing else; the burning chaparral downhill from the horse barn was behind the retreating man. He had made what in Texas Jim's view was an inexcusable error—he had put light at his back when he should have sought deeper darkness farther downhill. Texas Jim began to feel con-tempt for that retreating man.

A full sixty seconds passed during which the stalking man glided ever closer without firing, and his retreating adversary, uncertain where his enemy was, began again to whip from brush patch to brush patch—until he suddenly found himself as far as he could go without stepping out into cleared ground. After that long, furious battle, the silence that engulfed Setter's hill was now so totally without sound that it was possible for men to hear the breathing of other men.

At Texas Jim's side several posse men stood, peering. One of them said in nearly a whisper: "He ain't goin' no farther now." He meant the retreating gunman. Another man said tartly: "He didn't work that right. He should've dropped farther downhill. He's either awful green or a fool."

"A fool," muttered Texas Jim, suspecting who that retreating gunman was. "A fool in more ways than one."

The hush deepened. Most observers could see the stalking man now. He was moving again, pressing onward a foot at a time. He was using both hands quietly to push aside brush as he advanced. He had holstered his six-gun.

Jim leaned forward, attempting to locate the second man; he could not see any trace of him and thought he was crouched low somewhere, waiting. He could do that, or he could jump backward and spring erect in the clearing, making a final attempt at getting his enemy before he was shot himself.

Jim straightened away; the hidden man would not take that last alternative. Jim was sure of his identity now. He was certain that this man would prefer ending it from hiding.

"Yonder he goes!" exclaimed a posse man, pointing out where the stalking gunman passed as a blur across a little opening and disappeared at once in underbrush again. A posse man who had been startled by this sudden exclamation growled: "Shut up an' just watch."

They were less than a hundred feet apart now. In Texas Jim as in all the other spectators to this grim fight, tension grew and increased, turning them all wire-tight and nearly breathless. Then the stalking man, evidently considering himself close enough now, spoke out. His voice and words carried in all directions, bell-clear and solid-sounding: "Carlos, come out of there. Come out shooting or come out unarmed . . . but come out."

"Come in after me, Madsen," came back the

immediate sharp answer. "I'm waiting. Come along."

A man at Texas Jim's elbow breathed: "Mexican stand-off."

Jim said shortly: "Don't you believe it." He was watching the chaparral where the tall man had last been visible. "There's more'n one way to skin that kind of a cat. Keep quiet and watch."

Madsen spoke again, his voice sounding bleak now and threatening: "Carlos, use your head. I can sluice fire from here. Give it up."

"Make me, Madsen."

"You damned fool," said Madsen, his tone crackling with sudden impatience. "You want to get killed? Listen, so far there've been no dead men. Don't be the first one."

"It won't be me, Madsen. It'll be you."

There came back no reply to this and Texas Jim faintly nodded. He would have ended the conversation there, too. If the hot-headed whelp wanted to wind it up fighting, then that's how it should be ended.

Time passed; the silence ran on. It drew out to its very limits. Men around Texas Jim fidgeted and whispered among themselves. They knew something was impending but the waiting was deadly. Finally Jim turned an irritable scowl upon them, commanding silence. He got it.

Several simultaneous things occurred, and after so long a wait no one, with the possible exception of Texas Jim whose attention was riveted downward, saw them in proper sequence. What looked for all the world in that pale star shine to be the hurtling form of a man, arms up and whipping forward, sailed over the topmost branches of chaparral and fell into the last tier of brush where Carlos Setter crouched. Somewhere southward around the hillside where the Setter ranch men were watching, a man let off a wild scream of warning.

Carlos Setter appeared, whirling upright off the ground to meet the charge of that hurtling man shape. He fired twice. Both flaming bursts of gunfire pierced the night with red-flashing tongues of fierce flame and that hurtling shape quivered, struck twice, then it fell against Carlos and the oldest of John Setter's sons dropped his gun to strike out against the limp and engulfing arms.

Among the men standing with Texas Jim there rose up a loud and anguished moan when those two bullets tore into Carlos's hurtling adversary. Only Texas Jim remained unmoved, his eyes still bright and interested.

Finally the last event of this split-second sequence occurred as Carlos was staggering back with both arms pumping blows. A tall shape materialized up out of the chaparral, bare to the waist and glistening with star shine. This silhouette hesitated for a fraction of a second, then it sprang onward, struck Carlos with a low-held shoulder, and that struggling, swaying blend of bodies crashed down from sight into the wildly threshing brush.

From among John Setter's riders a man cried out: "Come on! Carlos needs help against 'em!" This man leaped out, with two or three other men responding to his cry, when Texas Jim stepped forward, clear of his surrounding posse men, halted upon the rim of Setter's hill, and fired one shot five feet in front of those moving men. They jerked back instantly.

"Leave 'em be," warned Jim. "Let 'em fight it out."

"Sure!" roared the cowboy, glaring upward. "You'd like them odds, wouldn't you?"

"There are no odds down there. That's Chris Madsen and Carlos Setter. There is no one else down there with either of 'em."

"Like hell. We seen that other . . ."

"You saw," snapped Texas Jim, "a man's shirt stuffed with chaparral. That's what went sailing over that brush for Carlos to fire into."

The cowboys looked from Texas Jim to one another; they seemed disbelieving at first, then sheepish. Without looking up where Texas Jim still stood, six-gun cocked and ready, they turned and shuffled back among their companions. Someone down there laughed; this was taken up by several other Setter riders. Texas Jim went back among his own men and waited for the furious fight to end.

It was impossible to see how that battle was going. Between night shadows and dense underbrush, the only thing that could be determined was that a savage fight was certainly in progress. Chaparral limbs waved wildly, cascading their little leaves earthward. Dark dust lifted from the springtime soil, and for perhaps a full three minutes the progress of those straining men was progressively downhill.

"Hey, Marshal," a Setter rider cried out, "you care to place a little bet?"

Texas Jim answered without moving his glance from the course of that unseen fight. "Is that you, Dave?"

"Yeah it's me. Twenty bucks on Carlos. You game?"

"Naw," responded Texas Jim scornfully. "That's not fair to you, Dave. I'll take your twenty bucks and give you four-to-one on Madsen. My hundred dollars against your twenty."

"Done!" shouted Dave Wesson exuberantly. "Hey! Anyone else up there want those odds?"

Voices erupted at once, shouting names and wagers back and forth. This went on until Texas Jim, booming his own shout over all those others, said: "Betting's over, boys! The brush has quit threshing. Directly now somebody's going to stand up down there."

Once again that endless silence settled. Every man was watching. No one spoke as a distant figure began slowly and painfully to rise up out of the chaparral. Men began edging forward to determine which of the battlers this was, and a little sigh of soft sound came from all those throats.

It was Chris Madsen.

XVI

Texas Jim seized the initiative now. He turned, calling to his posse men to rally around him. They came, trooping from all around the house, trailing their saddle guns and holding fisted six-guns. Jim led them forward out and over the rim of John Setter's hill, telling them under no circum-stances to fire.

He went awkwardly down that side hill, planting his good leg down, then dragging after it his stiff leg. On both sides of him, but keeping slightly to the rear, came the Buellton posse men. Below, watching this mass of men descending, their faces tilted upward with star shine making them glisteningly pale, stood the silent cowboys who several minutes earlier had been fighting these same posse men. Dave Wesson, standing slightly apart with Frank Setter, said quietly: "Easy, boys, let 'em come. Put up your guns." Frank Setter, looking grim and bitter, did not countermand this order. In fact Frank was the first to holster his handgun. He turned from watching the descent of Marshal Collins only when bare-chested Chris Madsen came forward, pushing groggy and badly beaten Carlos Setter ahead of him. Madsen had his six-gun leathered and Carlos's holster was empty.

Carlos had an eye that was rapidly swelling closed, and a broken mouth from which blood steadily dripped. He sank down upon a large rock without looking at his brother or the other Setter men, put his face in his hands, and leaned loosely forward. One of the cowboys removed his jacket and held it mutely toward Madsen. Chris took it in silence, put it on, and tried without luck to button it across his corded chest.

Texas Jim made the last fifty feet off the side hill, got onto the roadway, and stood, hip-shot, with nearly all his weight upon his good leg. He looked over at Dave Wesson wordlessly, and held out one hand palm upward. Wesson dug down into a pocket, brought forth some bills that were soiled and crumpled, counted out twenty dollars, and put the money into Texas Jim's hand. No one said anything until this act was completed, then Marshal Collins, looking steadily at Frank Setter, said: "Every man here who works for John Setter is under arrest. Put down your guns."

There was a spontaneous move among the Setter

ranch riders to comply with this order. Texas Jim was looking straight at Frank Setter and Dave Wesson. Both men tossed aside their weapons. Then Texas Jim shot a brief glance at Chris before saying to his posse men: "Round them up, send someone up the hill for our horses, then wait for me here." He beckoned to Madsen and limped on around the roadway's gradual curve.

Madsen caught up with Texas Jim a hundred feet beyond those milling men behind them. He paced along for a little distance, gauging his steps to the movements of the marshal.

"You thought you could stop it," said Jim dourly. "I could've told you differently."

"Then why didn't you?" asked Madsen. "Why didn't you at least try?"

Texas Jim limped along a ways before he said: "That's something you'll learn if you live long enough. When men are fired up to fight . . . they'll fight . . . and, if you act the fool and walk in between them, you'll wind up in a bed or a pine box." Jim looked around. "Any of Setter's men hurt?" he asked.

Chris shrugged. "One got a thumb shot off. Another got hit in the hams."

Texas Jim went limping along, looking onward. "You could've been the third casualty," he said, "walking away from us like you did."

"I had good reasons."

Jim kept walking. The road began to rise, to hug

its lifting way around Setter's hill, and Texas Jim slowed a little, inconvenienced by his bad leg. "Did you get the doctor?" he finally asked.

"Yes. I brought him back. How did you know about that?"

"We captured Reg. He told us about old John. How bad off is he?"

"Bad enough from the looks of him. I left right after I got back with the doctor, went after Frank and Carlos. Went after Reg, too, but couldn't find him."

"We saw you fight Carlos. How did you handle Frank?"

"I didn't have to handle him. He was all for stopping the fighting by the time I returned. He was too worried about his father."

"Carlos . . . ?"

Chris shuffled along. "No, he wouldn't listen to me. He kept prodding the cowboys to fight harder. I tried every way I knew to make him listen to reason."

"Then you went after him alone. We saw it. Pretty good fight, Chris."

Madsen lifted his head, gazed onward where a pale little lamp was glowing, and said: "Up ahead." That was all he offered but Texas Jim understood; he saw the kneeling medical man. He also saw Christel Setter standing, loose and forward, looking downward.

The two of them came up and halted. Christel

saw Madsen; she put her liquid-dark eyes upon him, then moved over to stand there at his side.

Texas Jim put a hand upon the kneeling doctor's shoulder to steady himself as he knelt. His jaw rippled from clenched teeth as his bad leg refused to bend sufficiently until he forced it to. Then, seeing the doctor's unfriendly gaze upon him, Jim said: "How is he?"

"How would you expect him to be?" answered the doctor gruffly. "He's had a bad heart for years. He had no business doing what he did tonight."

Jim's eyes hardened against the doctor. "Don't look at me like I made him do it," he snapped.

"Well, didn't you? I mean . . . you came charging up here tonight like . . ."

"You don't know what you're talking about," snarled Texas Jim. "This thing happened long before tonight." He jutted his chin at the pale, still, and wasted man lying there in the road, his head upon a saddle seat. "*That's* your department. Get on with it." Jim fought awkwardly back upright again. He was breathing hard. "Just one more thing," he said sharply. "I've had all the idealism I can stand for one night. You keep your damned thoughts to yourself, Doctor."

The medical man began to arise. Chris Madsen stepped out. "Easy," he said, looking down into that angry, white face. Then he switched the conversation, saying: "Can we take him on up to his house?" And bent to look closely at John

Setter, thrusting his body between the doctor and wrathful Marshal Collins.

For a moment longer the tension lingered, then the doctor returned to considering his patient. He mumbled in a sulky voice: "We'll have to take him somewhere. We can't leave him here."

Madsen faced Marshal Collins. "You're going on back to town," he stated, making no question of this, "with your posse men and your prisoners. I'll stay here and help move Mister Setter."

Texas Jim continued to regard the ailing man. His expression was flinty. Finally he nodded and without another word turned and started back the way he had come.

It was along toward dawn with stars winking out one and two at a time by the time Texas Jim had his posse and his captives astride, heading downcountry from Setter's hill. He rode with rancor like a solid core within him. He was worn out and in pain; these things colored his thinking as he passed overland, leading that large body of mounted men. When he was spoken to, he made no attempt to reply, and after a while there was no talk at all among the riders behind him.

No one spoke until they came down Main Street in Buellton and shadowy figures came forth from the pale predawn to stand and gape and ask awed questions. Then Marshal Collins said to his posse men: "Leave your horses here, herd these prisoners down to my jailhouse . . . then go on home. I'll put in with the town council for your pay . . . and thanks."

He walked southward alone toward his office, not once looking back. Men, and a few women, too, turned to watch him pass by. No one, after seeing the darkly stormy expression on his face, spoke to him at all.

At the jailhouse Texas Jim flung off his hat, went to the office stove, poked up a little fire, and slammed his graniteware coffee pot over a hot plate. Afterward he went to the washstand, filled a commode bowl with water, and vigorously scrubbed his face. This made a little difference in how he felt. He went to his desk, rummaged there until he found a tobacco sack, and scowlingly twisted up a smoke, lit it, and exhaled a great bluish cloud. This familiar building, its quiet, and its welcoming comforts, plus the cigarette, made a difference. He went to his desk chair and sank down there, settled his bad leg gingerly upon a nearby stool, and looked at that limb as though it were a physical enemy.

For the better part of ten minutes he was entirely alone, then the posse men came trudging in from the roadway with their dour-looking prisoners. Texas Jim didn't stir; he caught up the key chain off his desk, tossed it to one of the posse men, and jerked a thumb toward the reinforced oaken door in the west wall, beyond which were his cells. "Lock 'em up," he ordered, and smoked on as this was done, the keys brought back to him, and the posse men began filtering back out into the night again. To the last man he said: "You boys handled yourself right well. I'm grateful."

The posse man looked around, his expression full of round-eyed surprise. Then he broadly smiled and rushed on to tell his companions what Marshal Collins had said. It wasn't much, but coming from Anza County's iron legend, it was more than enough for those townsmen. Their dourness dropped away at once. They struck out for the inviting lights of the Golden Slipper, there to recount all that had happened atop old John Setter's hill this night.

Texas Jim sat on. This night was not yet over. There would be other callers. While he waited, the nagging weight of his shell belt and gun bothered him. He took these things off, threw them upon his desk. Then, after a long moment of contemplation, he pulled out the gun, examined its cylinder, raised and lowered it several times, then let it lie with his hand around it in his lap.

He was sitting like this, cigarette dead between his lips, when he heard the rattle of an oncoming buggy in the empty roadway, and around it several riders. He got up, buckled the belt around his middle again, pushed that loaded six-gun into its holster, and went to the door. There, with soft lamplight limning him, he looked out.

Christel Setter was dismounting before the doctor's office. Madsen was helping Reg Setter lift the blanket-shrouded figure of old John from the buggy. None of those people looked down where Marshal Collins stood in plain sight, watching. They went along behind the hurrying medical man, paused before a locked door, then passed beyond sight, leaving the roadway devoid of human beings again.

Texas Jim threw down his dead cigarette. He put a slow glance up and down the length of Main Street, then reversed himself, crossed the office, and shoved on through that reinforced doorway to the strap-steel cells beyond. He stood in the dimly lighted narrow corridor, seeing all those solemn faces peering out at him. No one spoke. Jim limped over where Frank and Carlos stood against their bars, looking out. He said: "How do you feel now?"

Carlos dropped his one good eye from the marshal's face. He also dropped his arms from the bars and slowly turned away. Frank, though, stood on, returning Texas Jim's stare.

"It wouldn't do any good to answer that," he said.

"You could try."

Frank shook his head. "I wouldn't know the right words, Marshal. I never was any good at puttin' feelings into words. Right this minute I wouldn't even attempt it."

"That's a pretty good start," said Collins, shifting his weight. "Maybe I could help you. How about some words like damned fool and ingrate, like spoiled pups and overgrown punk kids? Would those do for a starter, Frank?"

"Yes," murmured Frank Setter in a very low tone of voice. "They'd do for a starter, Marshal. How's our paw?"

"I don't know. I'm going over to Doc's place now. They just brought him in." Jim shifted his glance. "Carlos?" he said. The fair-haired eldest son of John Setter shuffled back around. "You pretty proud of yourself, Carlos?"

"No."

"You ought to be, though," went on Texas Jim, rubbing salt in Carlos's raw wounds. "Hell, boy, you ought to be. Today and tonight you damned near got your brothers and your sister killed. You came within an ace of getting me killed, not to mention Chris Madsen and half a dozen others. That's quite a record, Carlos. A feller like you ought to be proud as a peacock about that."

Frank said, in a softly protesting way: "Marshal . . ."

Texas Jim looked around. He put out a hand to steady himself upon the wall and let his smoky glance rove over the other men in his strap-steel cells. Most of those men looked away from him. Then he said to Frank: "Sure, you're right, Frank, enough is enough. Anyway, the sight of the lot of you makes me sick to my stomach." He paused, holding Frank with his unwavering look. "Tell me why it all happened, Frank?"

"There were some misunderstandings, I reckon, Marshal."

Texas Jim nodded, still wearing that bitter-hard look. "Some misunderstandings. Two men got shot at the Sloat place. Two more men got shot up on your paw's damned hill. All because there were some misunderstandings. Frank? It ought to be something grander than that, something bigger and more heroic than just some misunderstandings, hadn't it? Suppose old John dies tonight. What a lousy thing to die over . . . some misunderstandings."

Texas Jim turned, limped out of the cell room, and slammed the door.

XVII

Dawn was not far off now. As Marshal Collins limped along toward the doctor's place, he could see a faint pinkness off in the hazy east. There was that good smell in the crisp air, too, and somewhere beyond town a rooster crowed. He slowed and halted outside the medical man's little building, looked far out and upward where old John Setter's white mansion stood atop its aloof hill. A solitary golden flash from over the horizon struck down over that house, giving it warmth and beauty and strong perspective. Then Texas Jim pushed on inside, heard murmuring voices in the back room, and went there.

He halted in the doorway, seeing those faces lift, turn toward him, and remain expressionlessly watchful. He ignored them and went ahead to stand over the still, lifeless figure under a white counterpane. Christel Setter was on Texas Jim's right; Chris Madsen was on his left. Across from him the doctor pointedly ignored and Reg Setter, looking a little lost, a little bewildered, scarcely noticed the marshal at all.

Old John Setter's eyelids fluttered from time to time, but beyond that he was absolutely still under that white coverlet. Texas Jim considered John's face for a long time, then he brushed his fingers over the doctor's arm, saying in a scarcely audible voice: "Well . . . ?"

The doctor raised his eyes. He regarded Texas Jim steadily without speaking, then he looked down again. He made no effort to answer Jim's little question.

Chris Madsen bent low, saying to Collins— "Step away with me."—and left the small group around Setter's bed. He and Marshal Collins went over to the doorway, and there Madsen said: "He's regained consciousness. I reckon that's why the doctor didn't want to say anything. He would have heard it."

"He might have told me that," growled Texas Jim. "He's been looking for trouble with me for a long time. Tonight he just might get it."

"Never mind him," said Chris. "He's got a right to think whatever he wishes to. About Mister Setter . . ."

"Yes?"

"Doc said a few minutes ago he'd come around."

"He'll be all right again?"

"No," murmured Chris, "not all right. He's paralyzed in one leg and his left arm isn't responding as it should."

Texas Jim twisted to look over at John Setter. "Crippled," he muttered. "I could tell him it's better'n being dead, Chris. His leg, you say? I'll be damned." Jim continued to stare at John Setter as Chris spoke again.

"He asked for you the first words he said, Marshal. I don't know whether the doctor'll let you speak with him or not, but don't go away. He wants to see you."

Texas Jim said very dryly—"I can imagine."—then he limped back over to the bed, took a position beside it, and felt Christel lean far over toward him. He half turned; the beautiful girl put a hand upon Texas Jim's arm and gently squeezed. Then she whispered into his ear: "I'm going to take Chris and Reg out of here, Marshal. He wants to talk to you . . . alone."

Collins screwed up his eyes at the girl, looking perplexed, looking at a loss. He said nothing, though, and she made a little gesture to her brother on across the bed. Reg looked briefly into Marshal Collins's eyes, then he stepped back, turned, and went around the bed toward the door. Christel swayed a moment close to Texas Jim. She smiled at him out of misty eyes, then she went over to Chris, and the three of them tiptoed out and closed the door.

Jim gazed wonderingly from the doctor to old John's bluish lips. A little more color was in Setter's cheeks than Texas Jim had noticed in his face up at the battleground. He was considering this when the doctor leaned over and said: "Marshal, he wants to speak to you privately. He said that the first thing he came around."

"I know," growled Texas Jim, not forgetting this man's former hostility.

"Marshal, don't say anything . . . just listen. Don't say anything or it might upset him. If he has a second seizure right now, it'll kill him. Promise me you'll listen and say nothing?"

"Promise you nothing," growled Texas Jim, flaring a hostile look over the bed.

The doctor had evidently expected this, for he now inclined his head, saying: "Not for my sake . . . for his sake. Leave our personal feelings for one another entirely out of this. Please give me your word, Marshal. Then I'll leave you two alone."

Texas Jim looked at John Setter's gray face, his closed eyes, and faint breathing. He wasn't at all sure he wanted the medical man to leave him here alone.

"Your word, Marshal . . . ?"

"All right. I'll keep quiet. But, Doctor, don't go very far." Texas Jim rolled his brows inward in an uneasy frown. "He can't talk, can he? Look at him. He doesn't look . . ."

"He can talk. He's resting now. Those were my orders. He's a great deal better than he was, believe me."

"He'll make it, Doctor?"

"Yes. But he won't be taking any horseback rides for a long, long time, Marshal."

The doctor moved back. He put a final look upon John Setter. He seemed hesitant, but he turned eventually and went on across the room, out the door, and closed it after himself.

Texas Jim stood there, his weight entirely upon his good leg. Perspiration dappled his upper lip and forehead. He'd seen many men die in his lifetime, but never before had he stood beside a bed like this.

Without opening his eyes John Setter said quite distinctly: "You son-of-a-bitch." He called Texas Jim Collins that first, and then second opened his eyes. Jim was as astonished by the strength of Setter's voice as he was by the piercing, wholly rational gaze that followed it. "That suits you," said Setter. "I always wanted to call you that . . . but until now I never got the chance. What have you done with my boys?"

"All but Reg are locked in my jailhouse," said Texas Jim, forgetting he was not supposed to speak, only to listen. "Reg is here with Christel."

"I know that," said John Setter testily. "I'm not as near dyin' as everyone thinks I am. But I got my reasons for letting them think I am. Collins, you damned overbearing relic you, how are my children taking this?"

"Hard, Mister Setter."

"Carlos . . . ?"

"Maybe the hardest. I didn't let him forget the blockheaded things he's caused."

Old John's eyes softened. He stared at Texas Jim for a moment, then he said: "You know why we were never friends, Collins? I mean aside from the rivalry over Rosalia. I'll tell you. Because you're too damned dumb to figure it out for yourself. Because we're too much alike, that's why."

Texas Jim stood there, looking into those hard, pale eyes, saying nothing.

"I wanted something and you wanted something. You got it and I never did."

"What are you talking about. You own this

town. You've got most of the land and half of all the cattle in Anza . . ."

"You fool," interrupted old John Setter. "Sure, I got those things. But they weren't what I've been struggling for all these lousy years. I wanted respect. I wanted folks to nod when I rode by."

"They do."

"No. Not like they nod when you ride by, Collins. You're Anza County's iron legend. I've heard about you for a quarter damned century until I could throw up at mention of your name. I got so's I hated the sight of you. I had the wealth, but, by God, you had the respect." Setter paused, hoarded his breath, then went on speaking. "Even now . . . who's still standing upright and who's flat on his god-damned back."

"Listen, Mister Setter . . ."

"That's another thing. That 'Mister Setter.' Stop that, Collins. Don't you ever call me 'Mister Setter' again as long as you live. You hear me?"

Texas Jim glowered. "It's a good thing you're sick," he rumbled. "Talking to me like this."

Setter's indomitable gaze turned sly, turned ironically amused. "Collins, you're an old man. So am I. When I said for you to resign as marshal, I meant it. Not as a threat, but as sound advice."

"Not as a threat?" growled Texas Jim. "You dog-goned old reprobate, you threatened to have me killed. If that wasn't a threat, what was it?"

"A warning, you damned old fool. And I meant

343

it, too. I meant to bring in a couple of fast guns to make a fool out of you in front of the whole town . . . but not to kill you. Collins, give it up."

"You go to hell, John Setter."

Setter made a wicked little grin. "Don't get me excited," he said. "Remember what that sawbones said. Collins . . . ?"

"What?"

"I've got a reason for askin' you to resign as lawman."

"You've got reasons for everything. You always have had, you damned old son- . . ."

"Collins, there's a gold watch in my coat pocket." Setter paused, watching the odd transformation these words caused in Texas Jim's face. When he spoke again, old John's voice was entirely altered to a low, gentle softness. "I didn't mean for you ever to see that watch. I've done everything one mortal man could do, trying to keep you from seeing it."

Now Texas Jim Collins was wholly still, wholly silent. Something had passed into him from John Setter, something that suddenly made it hard for him to breathe. He looked unblinkingly downward, feeling the icy touch of premonition.

"I've done everything humanly possible to keep this secret, Jim, but now I can't keep it any longer. Do you know why?"

"Why?"

"Because that boy out there is going to marry

my daughter. That's why. He'll never leave Anza County now, so the secret can't be kept any longer. Jim . . . ?"

"Yes."

"Reach into my right-hand coat pocket and hand me that gold watch from there. Just hand it to me, never mind opening it."

Texas Jim rummaged under the counterpane, found John's right-hand pocket, rummaged in it until he felt the smooth, cold roundness of the golden watch, and drew it forth. As Jim stood there, looking at the watch, John Setter said a swear word and sank back.

"Can't make my damned left arm work," he said. Then he looked up at Texas Jim. Old John's eyes were large and very round and much darker than they normally were. "Jim . . . ," he said, "listen to me for a second before you open the back of that thing. There's an inscription in there. Listen to me now. . . ."

"I'm listening, John."

"The greatest mistake a proud man can make is to refuse to admit he ever made a mistake. Now, open that watch and read aloud that inscription in there. Aloud, Jim, aloud."

Texas Jim opened the watch. He read and his face very slowly crumpled, turned loose and flaccid and old-seeming.

"Aloud, Jim."

"It says . . . it says . . . 'For Christopher Madsen

from his godfather, John Setter. Never forget, son, that the iron legend of Anza County is your father. Grow up trying to be as brave, as fair, and as honest as he is.' "

Setter licked his lips; he blinked his eyes rapidly, and finally rolled his head so that he did not have to look at the expression on Jim Collins's face. He said very softly: "Rosalia told me before she left, Jim. She said she couldn't ever tell you, because otherwise you'd feel honor-bound to marry her."

"John, you kept in touch with her?"

"Yes. When Chris was born, she married a rich sheepman over in Nevada named Madsen. She and Madsen were both killed in a train wreck, Jim, and after that I lost track of your son."

Texas Jim closed the watch gently and dropped his arm down to his side. "Is that why you . . . ?"

"That's exactly why, Jim. I didn't want him to stay here. I tried every way I knew to get him to leave Anza County. What good could it do . . . you finding out after all these years?"

"But, John, that boy's my son."

"Yes. And he'll soon be my son-in-law." Setter rolled his head back; he looked upward, and these two hard old men looked very solemnly at one another. "Well," said John in a fading tone, "it's all done now. It's all over. I tried my damnedest and I failed. In one way I'm sorry. In another way I'm glad."

"He knew, John. Chris knew all the time."

"Of course he knew. That's why he came to Buellton, to see just exactly what kind of a man his father was . . . the iron legend of Anza County."

"He didn't say a thing, though."

Setter kept staring up at Texas Jim. "No. Maybe he hadn't made up his mind about you, Jim. Maybe he meant to ride on out just like he rode in. I don't know. I do know he won't leave now."

"If he'd ridden on, I'd never have known. John . . . I feel kind of sick."

"What's past is past, Jim. You couldn't help your boy to grow up, but you can help your grandsons grow up."

Texas Jim went to a chair and sat down. He was still gripping that gold watch.

John Setter watched him for a while, then he said: "That was my reason for asking you to resign, Jim. You've established a legend your grandchildren and great-grandchildren will always be proud of. But you're like me now. You're not a young man. Don't keep on wearing that gun until some punk shoots you down in the roadway of Buellton. Hang it up, and help me raise a brood of grandchildren . . . Jim? Are you listening to me?"

"I'm listening."

"How about it?"

"I'll quit, John . . . My God, I never felt like this

before in my life. I . . . I don't feel good, John."

Setter faintly smiled in a tender way. "I know. I felt the same way when I found that gold watch on Leffingwell. I thought I'd be sick to my stomach. Jim?"

"Yes?"

"About my sons . . . You can understand something about how a father feels now, can't you?"

"Yes."

"What're you going to do about them?"

Texas Jim lifted his head with an effort. He looked steadily over at John Setter. "Why should I do anything with them?" he asked. "No one's signed a complaint against them. But, John . . . I think my son can help you keep them in line from now on."

Setter said: "Come over here."

Texas Jim got up, limped over beside the bed, and stopped.

"Help me hold up this damned arm." Jim helped him. "Shake?" said Setter.

"Shake," said Texas Jim Collins, the iron legend of Anza County.

About the Author

Lauran Paine who, under his own name and various pseudonyms has written over a thousand books, was born in Duluth, Minnesota. His family moved to California when he was at a young age and his apprenticeship as a Western writer came about through the years he spent in the livestock trade, rodeos, and even motion pictures where he served as an extra because of his expert horsemanship in several films starring movie cowboy Johnny Mack Brown. In the late 1930s, Paine trapped wild horses in northern Arizona and even, for a time, worked as a professional farrier. Paine came to know the Old West through the eyes of many who had been born in the previous century, and he learned that Western life had been very different from the way it was portrayed on the screen. "I knew men who had killed other men," he later recalled. "But they were the exceptions. Prior to and during the Depression, people were just too busy eking out an existence to indulge in Saturday-night brawls." He served in the U.S. Navy in the Second World War and began writing for Western pulp magazines following his discharge. It is interesting to note that all of his earliest novels (written under his own name and the pseudonym Mark Carrel) were published in the British market and he soon had as strong a following in that country as in the United States. Paine's Western fiction is characterized by strong plots, authenticity, an apparently effortless ability to construct situation and character, and a preference for building his stories upon a solid foundation of historical fact. *Adobe Empire* (1956), one of his best novels, is a fictionalized account of the last twenty years in the life of trader William Bent and, in an off-trail way, has a melancholy, bittersweet texture that is not easily forgotten. In later novels like *Cache Cañon* and *Halfmoon Ranch*, he showed that the special magic and power of his stories and characters had only matured along with his basic themes of changing times, changing attitudes, learning from experience, respecting Nature, and the yearning for a simpler, more moderate way of life.

Center Point Large Print
600 Brooks Road / PO Box 1
Thorndike, ME 04986-0001 USA

(207) 568-3717

US & Canada:
1 800 929-9108
www.centerpointlargeprint.com